The Old Masters

The Old Masters

THOMAS BAIRD

New York
Harcourt, Brace & World, Inc.

Oh! Que ce monde-ci seroit une bonne comédie,
si l'on n'y faisoit pas un rôle.
—Diderot, Letter to Sophie Volland
July 25, 1762

Contents

PART ONE

A Monday in

February

One

While he waited for the first of the morning's customers, Edward Maule, dealer in paintings and objects of art, reflected upon his profession. He was frankly excited, for he had arrived at a point in his career as momentous as any he had ever faced. Much was at stake, including a large amount of money. Almost more significant to him than that, however, was the melancholy realization that it might be the last of such points, given the virtual disappearance from the art market of that most desirable of commodities, the important old-master painting.

Stiff-legged—his crusty-old-colonel walk—Maule paced from the outer reception room to his own office and back, and, feeling the need of a confidant, he so favored his receptionist, a handsome Negro youth of about twenty-four, who sat behind a small Sheraton writing table.

"Yes. Yes, indeed," Maule said. "Its quality is established, Thackeray. One has rarely seen anything whose quality is so uncontroversial. It is simply a masterpiece, quite simply that." Thackeray had unavoidably been admitted to the secret the preceding Friday when the crate came from storage; for the handyman was sick and the receptionist had had to open it, Maule's health being too delicate for him to do so. "One catches in it all the fragrances . . ." Maule jutted his chin forward. "All the perfumes of the gardens of Saint-Cloud, as somebody wrote—of another picture. Anybody would want it, don't you know." He disappeared into the inner office.

"Yes, sir," Thackeray called.

Maule came back. "The money's the same, Thackeray. Same currency, same amount." He caught himself. "I don't have to say that this is all confidential. If you haven't learned that in these months, you may as well leave." He moved off into generalizations again. "No, I don't have to worry about my price, but dealing in the higher spheres involves far more than mere prices. Psychology. Sociology. And a conscience."

"Money is only a small part of it, I know," Thackeray offered.

"Umm. There is, for example, the crucial question: who is the right buyer? I have my treasure. I'm sure of my price. But to whom shall I trade the one for the other, Thackeray? The right person—who is he?"

Maule disappeared again, but looked back through the doorway. "Of course, an error could cost me a part of the price, too, you know. A refusal gets around. I dare say that a blunderer, given the *Mona Lisa* to sell, could cut her value by a third within an hour."

"What would the *Mona Lisa* bring?" the colored youth asked.

"What? How much? Nonsense, man. Keep your feet on the ground. Who's that?"

The elevator doors in the hallway slid open, there was a shuffling of feet, and then a low buzz signaled a caller at the outer door.

"Let me get settled inside, then open it," Maule ordered, and hurried from the reception room, a colonel in full retreat.

He composed himself to receive clients. That is to say, he sat in the enormous leather chair behind the massive leather-topped desk and poured himself an ounce or two of water from a carafe that sat upon a silver tray. He sipped it

—it was stale, for Thackeray had been late that morning and hadn't had time to change it, which was, on principle, a significant demerit—then scrubbed his mustaches with one knuckle, a gesture he had acquired on his way up, as he had most of his personal style, in those vernal days of his career when he was still engaged in selling hunting prints and an occasional Stubbs Thoroughbred to those who were anything but.

He waited for the ring of the interoffice telephone, but nothing happened. "Damn that darkie." Maule regretted his recent confidences, imagining whispers and conspiracy in the reception room.

There was a soft knock on the door, and after Maule's reply, Thackeray came in holding some letters. "It was only the mail," he said, and placed them just at that point to the right of the blotter where Maule exacted that his mail be placed.

Maule coughed. "I didn't think he would be early."

The receptionist sensed somehow that he had nearly been in trouble, and he tried to smooth it out. "Even as a newcomer, just beginning," he said, "I can see how complicated a day like this is for you."

Maule might have jumped either way, but all in all, it *was* too important a day to begin it by snubbing Thackeray. "It is, it is. I'm glad you have been able to see that. These are the moments when one really feels justified." He stood up and paced the floor, legs once more stiff, hands once more clasped at his back. Then he stopped and looked at his employee, who stood waiting and whose high cheekbones and thin arched nose made Maule wonder suddenly where such stock had originated. The upper Nile? Nubia, or Abyssinia, perhaps. "Thackeray, you are a little on my conscience. I've broken you in to routine here, but I haven't taught you as much as the master ought to teach the serious apprentice." He began to pace again, suddenly amused. "Let me tell you some of the principles of good art dealing. Commit them to memory."

He threw up a finger. "Firstly, on the simplest level, the tone is all important. Every dealer should have his own manner. The gentleman dealer. The scholar. The eccentric. The daredevil. The connoisseur. One of those, or a great many others. For you the choice might be a little limited, but you can find a good manner for yourself—why not the enthusiast, for instance. You should be thinking about it." He added, "Don't overdress, in any case.

"Secondly, under no circumstances must the faintest whiff of penny-consciousness ever blow through a dealer's showrooms. Never."

"Keep everything expensive," Thackeray said.

"That idea, though your word is a bit vulgar. One does not, after all, deal in bargains. One permits a client to think he has won a hand of poker now and then. That is all."

"And everything should be like your offices here, shouldn't it, Mr. Maule? Richly furnished. Everything very nice, I mean."

"Absolutely. Everything tasteful. And if you're in moderns, then only the best handmade Scandinavian furniture, or whatever. Now for the third point—I ascend in the ethical scale, Thackeray: you must stand absolutely behind the authenticity of everything you sell." Maule brought his palm down smartly on his desk top. "There it is, man. There is the ethic of the first-rate dealer. No questions asked. If a client so much as breathes a doubt, even should one hundred thousand dollars be involved, one says, 'Bring it back; here is my check.'" Maule paused. "Fourthly, and this can sometimes be a problem, always

6

know the provenance of everything you sell, so you won't get caught up in any kind of . . . let us say, any embarrassments. That's a way of putting it. Sometimes you can't quite help yourself. Sometimes one can't help but take something on faith, gamble, guess, hope." His train of thought led him, for the first time, into a real indiscretion. "That is the only little flaw in the circumstances of my new masterpiece."

Thackeray perked up. "Really, sir? You mean you don't know where it comes from?"

Maule scrubbed his mustaches and stared coldly at the youth. "Another law of the good art dealer. The good art dealer, Thackeray, is never merely curious," he said, colonel once more.

"Yes, sir. Excuse me, Mr. Maule."

"I repeat. These matters are confidential."

"That goes without saying."

"Nothing gets you blacklisted in the profession faster than talking out of school, Thackeray."

"I don't wonder."

"Yes. Now, where were we? Ah, yes. Well, let me just add one general consideration to what I have said, which is this: the art dealer is not a merchant, Thackeray, far from it. He is a strategist. He is a diplomat. He is advocate and solicitor, rolled into one. He is also *gros joueur*, in the grand ducal manner. Perhaps most important, he must have an ideal. He serves civilization and culture, for without him the art market would resemble an arena of wild animals snarling and snapping over the *disjecta membra* of the past. Our great museums, young fellow, have been formed more . . . no, not more, but at least as much by the wisdom and will of those who have purveyed them their objects as by the fortunes of their benefactors or the ambitions of their

7

directors. Without the honest dealer, there would be no art," he concluded emphatically.

"No art," Thackeray echoed. "Yes, sir."

Suddenly Maule's elation fizzled out. Here he was, indulging in grandiose fantasies, expanding the importance of his function, boasting, just in order to reassure himself and incidentally to impress this little chit of an inquisitive blackamoor.

His tone of voice changed entirely. "Looked at from another point of view," he said, "one is engaged in a transaction no more dignified, no more complex, no more basically elegant, than selling someone a pair of gloves that fit. An opulent atmosphere in an office need not reflect any comparable richness of inner life, Thackeray. It is easy to worship false gods. Note that well." The doorbell rang and he shook himself to his senses. "On the other hand, what is important is to function successfully in the particular world in which you find yourself. My world, our world, if you continue in it, is surely no stranger, no worse or better, only more chromatic, really, than the Army, Law, the Stock Exchange, or even circles of State."

Thackeray was on his way out now. "We mustn't push our self-examination too far, eh Thackeray?" The door closed. "No," Maule said into the air, "we are never obligated to ask too many questions."

Two

The offices of Edward Maule and Company were of course in New York City, on the main and second floors of a once-private house just off Madison Avenue above Sixtieth

Street. The whole place had been done over, after Maule bought it, by a fashionable architect who was famous for his abilities to stretch space and exceed estimates; and, in fact, the conversion was so recent that the basement floor, whose hallway served as an entrance to the entire building, had not as yet been rented out. Maule himself had an apartment on the top floor with a stairway leading to a penthouse study and roof garden. The apartment was small, but then he was a bachelor and planned to retire before too long and thereafter would probably travel a great deal to both warmer and cooler places.

The business rooms consisted, on the main floor, of the reception room, Maule's own office, and a kind of back office occasionally used by a researcher and a part-time secretary, where the confidential files were kept under heavy security. From a little hallway at the rear of this floor a separate elevator carried up to the second floor, half of which consisted of storage and work area—which could be reached by the main elevator and by stairs via a steel door—and the other half, in back, of a large windowless room hung with *aubergine* velvet so saturated with color as to be almost black.

The furnishings throughout were reasonably sumptuous, as Thackeray had observed. The reception room had its delicate little table—it was not actually period—where Thackeray sat erect and protected the polish of his shoes and the crease of his trousers. It also had three windows with heavy silk draperies at the front end of the house, and along the lateral wall opposite the entrance, a row of deep mahogany cabinets upon which rested a little exhibition of Renaissance majolica, a piece or two of Meissen, and in the center, held in a bracket, one dazzling plate of Rhodian ware. Thackeray, when he typed, used a light European portable, but it was always concealed when a client was expected so as not to mar the effect, and his telephone was as hard to find. On the walls of the room were hung a few minor Dutch paintings that nobody would ever want, and whose ranks Maule raided, from December to December, for a gift to a little museum somewhere, to get a tax deduction.

The private office, on the other hand, contained more important works of art: a small Italian bronze, which sat on Maule's desk, attributed, so said the label on its black marble base, to Jacopo Sansovino; a large Magnasco oil, *The Deluge*; and a pair of Rosalba portraits. Behind the desk hung a rather mechanical Romney of some flaxen-haired English girl. It would probably never sell either, unless fashion changed, but it looked well, and it went with Maule's general Anglicized manner.

As for the room upstairs, hung in somber velvet, there nothing showed—nothing, that is, until with a snap of his fingers Maule summoned a lackey in white gloves, and a priceless work of art was placed upon an easel, or set upon a pedestal, or, depending on its size, put on a block of polished wood or laid on cut velvet and set out on a table. There, in the showroom, on the February Monday in question, a dual possibility was prepared. The table stood in a corner with several chairs around it, but there were also chairs placed in such a way as to face the empty easel put against one of the velvet walls. One could have guessed the arrangement was set up for several different visitors. So it was; and when the first collector of the morning was brought in to his office, Maule had still not quite decided how much he would show him, how much reserve for later appointments.

Three

"Jesus, Edward, what profits you must have been taking to afford all this."

Maule got up and walked toward the great man whose figure filled the doorway to the reception room, and behind whom he could see the willowy form of Thackeray staggering beneath the weight of a fur-lined overcoat nearly six feet in length, the whites of his eyes showing above the massive karakul collar.

Maule thought, almost simultaneously: I am over-mortgaged; Thackeray must learn to take a coat less awkwardly; this man is really a terror—he will see that tiny mend immediately and will probably know another version of *it*, too, if I show it to him; I wish he hadn't come today.

Maule said, "Arthur van Zandt. What a great pleasure. Welcome to the new quarters of Maule and Company. They're actually smaller than my old ones, you know. All laid out so that I can stop working from them as conveniently as possible, which won't be long now. You dwarf them, I must say. The paltry New York town house of this modest scale was not designed to contain Zeus Olympius. Please do sit down."

The giant looked around. He stood at least six feet five, had close-cropped gray hair, and heavy black brows with dark eyes. His cheeks were ruddy with cold, his pupils sparkled. He stamped his feet and rubbed his hands.

Maule continued: "Or a Rubens personification—Winter."

Van Zandt still gazed about distractedly, curious, roving, noting and evaluating. "You old spider, Maule," he said, "I'm seeing how you've baited your web today." They knew each other quite well, within the ceremonial limits placed upon their relationship.

"But remember, you called me," Maule replied, probing now to find out if there could have been any leak of his secret. "I assumed you had something in mind."

"No, no. A routine call. Just checking up on you. Have you got anything in my line?"

"Perhaps." Maule knew it would never do to rush too precipitately into business. "Your wife? Your son?" he asked.

"Henrietta? Oh, I suppose she's shining up a tea service, as usual." He laughed harshly. "Literally, you understand. She does it herself, just so I won't be one up on her, since I try to take care of my own stuff. And as for Artie, who knows? With the allowance she gives him, he may be on his way to buy the Taj Mahal."

"A fortunate youth."

"Some would say it's ruined him, but I rather think he was ruined to begin with."

Van Zandt lumbered over, an old bull elephant, to look at the two pastel portraits. "I detest this woman," he said, drawing a magnifying glass out of his pocket and flicking it open, all in the same movement. "I've got a better one, done when she was in Paris. Looks like the Regent himself, but her likenesses are so flimsy you can't be sure. These are later, I should think," he said, moving to the companion piece.

"Done in Vienna. 1730."

He looked closely. "As usual, lots of losses. Nothing to be done about it, though. Can't stop the pigment from falling off. Look at the bee-stung lip—pure Mignard, one would say, and very stupid; but it's really just the idiot simper of the nineteenth century, struggling to be born prematurely. That's what I can't stand."

"Poor Rosalba," said Maule. "You are hardly chivalrous to her. By the way, I hear that Mrs. van Zandt has just added a superb epergne to her collection."

The big man snorted and headed back for a chair. "She did. A famous one. Paul Lamerie, done by him in 1740 for some German princeling. Real state piece. Eight waiters plus four candle brackets, casters, and so on, and a unique centerpiece representing unlucky old Actaeon—a story that makes Henrietta's mouth water. She bought it just to irritate me, though, I think. She knows how I hate her English silver, and besides, now she can say we're too low on money next time I want to buy something. It's been a bad year for us, for some reason. God knows everyone else seems rich enough. Keep that in mind when you set your prices, Edward. I'm a poor man."

Maule guessed, for such information spread around, that his client was not entirely exaggerating. The van Zandts were not ostentatious, considering their general position, but something more than their customary conservatism was going on—that much the art world had heard. Perhaps an unduly careful broker, it had been suggested, a falsely predicted tumble in the market, an ill-advised retrenchment into low-return bonds. Still rich, it was possible that they were not outlandishly rich any more, and particularly not Arthur van Zandt, who had married more money by far than he had ever inherited or made. Maule balanced out what he knew—putting aside for the time the temptation to speculate about the rather succulent possibility that one or both of the van Zandts might be forced to sell off parts of their collections—and came to a conclusion. If his giant could not afford to buy, then there really could be no tactical error in showing him the new painting, no restrictions later on the dealer's freedom of action. Van Zandt was the most knowledgeable collector of older French art in the country, and his opinion was worth having, if favorable; if not, it could be laid to sour grapes.

Maule returned to his desk and sat down, sipping his stale water. "Well, if you want a bargain, perhaps you'd like the Rosalba Carriera pastels after all. I could let you have them both for—oh, let's say for forty thousand dollars. Perhaps in your magnificent library the unborn simpers would turn to smiles of sheer delight."

"I wouldn't have them at half the price." Van Zandt settled farther down into his chair. "You live in this house, too, I hear. All fixed up yet?"

"Not entirely. I'll give a party. Perhaps you and your wife will come."

"I will. She won't. She'll have friends from Baltimore or Philadelphia or Boston visiting her. They'll all be eating sweetmeats off her f——g epergne and talking about boxwood mazes—the only subject about which such women can make sense." He leaned forward suddenly toward the Renaissance bronze. "Anyway, she'd never go to a party given by a dealer."

Maule took the remark without flinching.

Van Zandt glanced up. "As you know, Maule, there are only two kinds of people involved with art for whom I have any respect: dealers and collectors. They put their money behind their opinions. I exclude museum types, who use other people's money and are therefore mostly interested in playing it safe, that and publicity, and scholars who haven't any money and therefore can be and are as frivolous with their opinions as they wish to be—the irresponsibility of indigence. The only good artists, of course, are already dead." He returned to the bronze. "What about this?" he asked.

"Jacopo Sansovino. After the Bacchus in the Bargello. Reduced." Maule smiled. "In scale."

"Something wrong about the patination, isn't there? Of course, it's out of my field."

"Umm," Maule said, in a way to throw doubt on the doubt, but he knew the observation to be true, and the bronze not a sixteenth-century casting.

The big man leaned back in his chair, dropped his magnifying glass into his pocket, and glowered at Maule. "Well, come on, now. You can't expect me to look seriously at your Romney. So . . . ?" This time he meant it. The preliminaries were over.

"Would you like to step upstairs to another room with me? I do have one or two things to show you, and we can see them better there."

"Of course." With rough energy, van Zandt hauled himself out of his chair and went toward the inner door, there to await the more dignified Maule, who came forward once more the colonel, stiff-legged from years of service. He passed in front of his client and led the way to the second elevator. "If you please," he said, standing clear.

The door closed behind them.

A quarter of an hour later a buzzer rang and Thackeray, after a brief telephone conversation, hastened from his territory into the inner office to an unlocked cabinet, took out a folder full of photographs, then went upstairs. A moment later he returned and sat at his desk. He had just got himself settled and had dialed an outside number on his telephone when the buzzer sounded again. This time he went to his employer's desk, and from a drawer took a humidor with an ivory panel set into the lid. He opened it, sniffed the contents, shook his head and wrinkled his nose with displeasure but drew the label from a cigar and put it in his pocket anyway, so that he would know what to buy if ever he needed to buy any, then took the box upstairs. He came back down again, but once more his effort to make an outside call was interrupted. "No, Mr. Maule, he's not here. He called in to say he was still sick. Yes, I'll be right up to help." Thackeray disappeared for the third time.

A half hour later he was back in the reception room, wiping his hands on his handkerchief.

A few moments after that the back door to Maule's office opened and he and his client entered. Automatically, the dealer went first to the forward door and closed it. He himself seemed a little tense, but his companion was considerably more changed, no longer so self-possessed, less gruff—a worried and preoccupied man who bit at a fingernail.

"The Clodion's very, very good. Fine quality, I'll admit. Charming the way the little faun children clamber over their father's legs."

"I think it's a good piece," Maule said, handing an ash tray to take the now nearly consumed cigar. "In fact, if I may say so, I think it's a first-rate Clodion. None of the usual atelier feeling about it."

"Derived from the *Nile* in the Vatican, I should think," said van Zandt, letting his hand drop to his side. He stood square in the middle of the office, looking down at the floor. "I think most Clodion terra cottas have quality. They're rarely atelier work, in the worse sense."

"One rarely stands out, though. I mean, Clodions, as opposed to a fine Clodion, turn up in every auction."

"Too bad about the chip."

"What chip?"

"The one that's mended—on the foot of the Marseilles *soupière*. It's sad that such a good thing should be, nevertheless, imperfect. Almost edible-looking, that lobster on the lid. I've got a better one anyway, but you might have sold it to someone like Cariatis. Not with a mend. He hasn't got eye enough to see beyond that to the fact that after my tureen, it's probably the best anyone could buy. Better than anything from the Veuve Perrin factory in the Victoria and Albert, I'd say offhand."

"You mean mine or yours?"

"They go in for that sort of thing," van Zandt replied noncommittally, still very preoccupied.

Then he suddenly lifted his head and turned on Maule, his dark eyes and black brows ferocious. "I don't know where to start—about your painting. It's superb. Marvelous. Desirable, by God."

"I thought you might like it."

"Like it. *Like* it! Don't play any of your games with an old hand like me, Edward. Of course I like it. More than that, I *would* like it. Like to own it. Like to choose the very place on one of my walls where it would look best. Like to gloat over it and like to show it off, too, and boast about it, and have other collectors envy me, and have a dozen museum directors whimper for it in my will. Like it? I'd say I like it. I've never seen anything I ever wanted more."

"That is very gratifying."

Van Zandt doubled his hands into two huge fists and threatened the air. "God damn the high cost of things nowadays," he bellowed. Then he became sharp. "You haven't told me the price yet."

"You didn't ask me," Maule said.

"How much?"

"He's so difficult," the dealer demurred, easing himself behind his desk and fiddling with the folder of photographs that he had carried back downstairs. "Damned if he isn't." He allowed himself a slight shrug of the shoulders and an opening of hands, gestures associated more with the market place than with the Army, Law, or circles of State. "I know he wants the right price, but he seems to have other considerations, too."

"And you won't tell me who this 'he' is. I suppose I ought to be able to guess."

"You will never guess."

Van Zandt imagined the painting he had been looking at. "That little dancer on the right. Can't get her out of my mind. The way her head turns. She's related to a drawing somewhere, isn't she?"

"You need certainly never apologize for your knowledge of the period in any of its media, Arthur. The drawing is in Rotterdam. The Boymans."

"Of course. I saw it two summers ago. I've got to have your picture, you understand that, Edward."

Maule repeated his earlier gesture.

"It's so unquestionably . . . illustrious. It's what I need. Am I the first to see it?"

Maule hesitated. He wanted nothing firm to happen, not yet. "You are the first to see it, but I have promised others that chance, too. And if I may be frank? I don't know how serious you were when you spoke earlier of money, but the price will be very, very high."

"I don't care. I'll raise it. Just remember, when this mysterious owner sets his price, I want to know it."

"But surely there are other pictures that would do as well."

"That's for me to say, not you, Maule," van Zandt said. "I have his drawings, of course, two genuine ones, one by a pupil. But a collection of the importance of mine always has a couple of major holes, and you can't plug them with just any piece of canvas. When you have what I already have, then the whole point, well, in life, very truthfully, is to bring your collection as near to perfection as you can. I've got to have that painting."

Maule glanced at his wrist watch. "I'm afraid . . ." he murmured.

Glad for the chance to act violently, van Zandt threw open the door. "Get me my coat, young man," he shouted into the reception room, and when Thackeray held it aloft, he thrust his arms into the sleeves and hunched into the shoulders. "When a man like you, Edward, looks at his watch, that means business is really over."

Maule followed him out. "I was only considering you. You told me over the telephone that you had another appointment for eleven o'clock, and it's after that now."

"Good God. It's with my G.U. specialist. Had a little trouble last year, and it's important to keep the drains open." Van Zandt noticed the ceramics on the cabinets. "Still showing that stuff, are you? I once started to collect Urbino and Faenza pottery. A false start, before I discovered where my heart really lay. I'm off. Don't forget me," he cried, and as he reached the door and pulled on the handle Thackeray touched a spot on the floor to release the latch. The elevator had already been on its way up with a passenger, for when it opened, van Zandt spoke to someone. "You here, Cariatis? Don't put out your eye on the doorknob."

Maule ran for his office. "Hold him," he whispered to

Thackeray. His door swung shut behind him and the hall buzzer sounded, both at the same time.

Four

Theodore Cariatis was not tall, although he was scarcely so short that his eyes were endangered by doorknobs, if that was what van Zandt meant. He was a sleek, rounded man, with a neat little comma over each lip—like Maule's mustaches, these made a point about their owner. His dark hair was worn long, and was groomed tight to the head with a coarse comb. It was almost certainly dyed around the fringes. He wore a large diamond ring on the little finger of his right hand.

He was not alone.

Thackeray stumbled over her name when he called in to announce them. "Mr. Cariatis is here to see you, Mr. Maule, with Mademoiselle Angélique de la . . . Angélique de la Cou . . . Cou . . ."

Maule heard a noise, then the voice of Cariatis, its exoticism lying more in its nasality than in any strong accent, saying, "Tell him that I am here with a lady. I will introduce her."

Thackeray duly repeated this message, and was told to bring the pair into the private office.

Maule varied his manner a trifle from that used in dealing with van Zandt, for now he was dealing with a man largely exempt from income taxes. He managed both to be less man-to-man, more distant—Cariatis was a foreigner and probably a crook—and faintly obsequious, so as not to grate upon any Ionic sensibilities.

"Mr. Cariatis. How delightful. What a pleasure to see you again, although why you have left your warm Aegean for these arctic Atlantic shores I cannot imagine. Still, we must be thankful that you have."

Mr. Cariatis displayed his teeth, with their many fillings, which reminded Maule that he had once heard that the little man was nicknamed "Croesus" Cariatis in his native land. "My Archipelago is not all that warm just yet, Mr. Maule, and won't be for a month or two. May I present Edward Maule, Angélique? Mr. Maule, may I present Mademoiselle de la Couronne d'Epines?"

Maule bowed, considered kissing, but then did not kiss her hand. While not seeming to take undue note of her, he nevertheless opened up a mental file with her name on it, for today's newcomer, in his business, might be tomorrow's mainstay. She was a stunning woman, whom he dated somewhere in her middle thirties, perhaps five inches taller than her escort. Her hair was auburn, what passes for blond in sub-Latin regions, her eyes the bright blue of those of some shaggy Germanic ancestor. Her lashes were too long to be quite real, one would have said, but then, reconsidering, one would not quite have dared to put money on it. Her cheekbones were broad and heavy, her body large and splendid. She was as full blown and handsome as a prize-winning rose, but seen perhaps a day or two after the competition. She wore the latest fashion, purple wool, with a matching cloth coat, and sables. Her hat, trimmed with two or three dabs of fur plucked from the same favored animal, was circled with veils, which descended below, but did not hide, her eyes.

"So you are the famous Mr. Maule," she said.

"Hardly that, my dear lady," Maule said, bowing again and scrubbing his mustaches.

"No?" She turned to Cariatis. "Is he not famous, Theodore?"

"He is being modest. Aren't you, Mr. Maule?"

"You place me in a dilemma, Mr. Cariatis, with your question."

"Just so, just so," the little man said, satisfied with the answer. He looked around, rubbing his delicate hands together. He noticed the pastels and strolled over to look at them. "Charming, charming." He turned. "Do you fancy them, Angélique?"

She had to incline her head slightly to see them. "Perhaps. What are they?"

Maule told her.

"They are not French," she said with finality.

"Rosalba worked for a time in Paris. She was à la mode there."

"They are sweet," Mademoiselle de la Couronne d'Epines admitted. "And were these done then?"

"Alas, I am afraid she was also called to Vienna. By the emperor. These are Austrians—"

"That explains it," the lady said, drawing back.

"—like Marie-Antoinette."

"We are here to find something for Angélique," Cariatis explained, casting a libidinous look in her direction. "Some little present. She has a birthday coming up."

"Delighted to help," said Maule. He turned to her. "Have you any ideas?"

"Many," Angélique replied. "I am going to be very *exigeante*, you know. I want a special kind of thing. I want a souvenir of my country, to help me feel at home in this city. Roots, Mr. Maule, stretching back through a millennium cannot safely be ignored, do you understand?"

Cariatis said, "Since the tenth century her family has lived always in the same part of France, Mr. Maule, always, it might be said, with the same view through their machicolations, always either marrying their neighbors or fighting with them, or sometimes both. I want to buy her something to remind her of all that." He touched her shoulder.

She laughed and batted her eyes through her veil. "*Je suis vieille France*," she cried.

"I fear I am quite out of Gothic armor," Maule said. "Were this last year, I could at least offer you an evangelist portrait from a manuscript done in the scriptorium of Saint-Denis, dear lady, but I have nothing of the sort now."

"Just so long as it predates the *débâcle*, that is all I care. I refer to the Revolution."

"I understood," Maule replied.

He glanced about his office. "I see nothing here that will fit the requirement. Perhaps you will be kind enough to come upstairs with me, and we will have a look there." He buzzed Thackeray and told him to stand by in case he needed him, which kept the latter off the telephone during this, the second visit of the working day.

When, a half hour or so later, Maule, Cariatis, and Angélique de la Couronne d'Epines emerged again into Maule's office—Thackeray had not been summoned after all—Maule and Cariatis had reached an understanding over her head, or under her nose. Cariatis wanted to pay neither too much nor too little, and it was toward such a sum that Maule had directed his salesmanship. Under his management, she had decided that she did not really want a painting. Rather, something in the decorative arts was more to her taste, preferably some precious bit of eighteenth-century elegance. Maule had at first steered her toward the Clodion terra cotta, but then, so delicately that she had been unaware of pressure on the rudder, had aimed her toward a little Sèvres chocolate service (dated 1777—not of the best period), which cost a good bit less than the sculpture. Somehow, Maule had implied, it more became her. One could so easily imagine her offering a cup to some witty pet *abbé*, or Diderot, or even rustic old Ben Franklin. Maule was pleased with himself. He had performed at his best. He was still, even at his age and with his bad heart, one of the most adroit in a business filled with cunning people.

Then, almost to his own surprise, he heard himself violate one of the cardinal principles of good procedure. He got himself involved in doing two things at once. He introduced, in a conversation following a visit made for the purchase of one kind of thing, the subject of another.

"By the way, Mr. Cariatis, I have a little painting upstairs that you might like to see sometime. Quite important, I believe. I am offering it for someone."

"I have more time," little Cariatis said. "I would like to see it."

Mademoiselle had an appointment with her *couturier* at noon, and it was almost that, but she asked, "Is it French?"

Maule nodded.

"And not too new?"

Maule shook his head.

"Then I, too, will look at it. I will give it a peek."

Maule buzzed the outer office. "Thackeray," he said, "please put the new painting on the easel again." Once more he led the way upstairs.

Later, after they were gone, Maule sat at his desk and worried, thrown into what he called one of his "black moments." Why had he done such a thing? What had led him to it? Pride? Damn the impulse to show off. And the impulse to get another millionaire eager. He didn't use to do things so ill-considered, so unwise. Now there were more and more of them, and more and more areas where his life wasn't neat. The wrong side popped up more and more. A black, black moment, this. Disaster, one was ringed with it.

Cariatis had not been much interested, or at least had pretended not to be; but Mademoiselle de la Couronne d'Epines had been captivated. Just such a fete, she said, had often been given at her family's château. There were records, account books. It reminded her of that beloved place. No mention was made of price, naturally. It was not even said directly that she wanted the picture. It was all abstract, as if taking place before a painting in a museum; but all three of them knew precisely where it was taking place: at a dealer's. Angélique had fluttered her eyelids at Cariatis, then lifted her veils so that he could see her better. Cariatis had touched his lips with his tongue (sad, so sad, thought Maule—an aging lecher at a burlesque show), but when he turned to look at Maule, the look was cold and suspicious. Yes, it was a disaster. She had made up her mind. Her little bauble was going to be the painting, or her name wasn't De la Couronne d'Epines. That was how Maule read it. But the price! She must have known. A really mad multiple of that of the chocolate service. She was out to sting little Cariatis properly, thought Maule, and he himself was being made party to the nasty business.

He twisted his hands together and felt his brow growing damp with sweat, even as he realized that his present state of nerves was all out of proportion to the magnitude of the crisis—at least so far. But what would he do? Whatever would he do? He took a pill and washed it down with stale water.

Finally he began to pace the floor, then opened the door so that he could talk to Thackeray. The latter put away his telephone, once again interrupted before he could complete his call.

"I'm worried, Thackeray," Maule said, always moving. "I'm quite worried. This business is getting complicated."

Without the slightest idea what Maule was talking about, Thackeray, revolving behind his desk, answered, "Mercy, Mr. Maule, you'll have me worried, too, in a minute."

"I think I am too old."

"Now, don't think that, Mr. Maule."

"Where should it go? Where *should* my painting go?" Maule knew he was talking too much, but he didn't care. He put the tips of his fingers to his eyebrows and pressed. Sometimes, like the jiggling of a kaleidoscope, this pressure, nowadays, rearranged the thoughts in his head into an orderly pattern. "Where? Where?"

Thackeray sat back and crossed one leg over the other. "You *could* sell it to the first person who brought in enough money."

Maule held summary court. "You did not understand much of what I said this morning," he snapped, angered by the youth's joking about so serious a matter, and by his familiarity. "It is not funny, Thackeray. Your attitudes are immature. I am lunching with Mr. Dane today. What will I tell him about you now?"

"Tell him I'm trying."

Maule turned quickly back toward his office. "Perhaps we won't even discuss you."

Thackeray grinned at his back and formed an almost un-sounded sentence with his lips. "And perhaps you will."

But Maule heard. He about-faced. "Thackeray!" he ex-claimed.

"Excuse me, Mr. Maule. It was just a joke."

They confronted one another, each wondering, until they were interrupted by still another visitor at the door, which forced Maule to retire once more. And then, a mo-ment later, Thackeray announced, "Mr. McCaffrey and Mr. Kant to see you, sir."

Five

"Edward."

"Matt."

The two men exchanged handshakes and claps on the shoulders, although one was a museum director, the other a dealer—natural enemies.

"You're looking great, just great." "Welcome to New York." "Good luck to get in to see you on such short no-tice." "Always in for you, Matt. What kind of a fall did you have?" "Busy as a bird dog. One thing after another. And you?" "Well, moving into this house, you know . . ."

"Edward, I want to introduce you to Barney Kant. Bar-ney, this is Edward Maule. He's sold us a lot of things, all of them, so far as I know, genuine, including the Lawrence *Marshall von Ellrich* and that frieze of Hittite feet—I've always wondered where he sold the upper half. Edward, this is our new president of trustees. He's in New York with me to get an idea of how this funny world of art works."

"A great pleasure," said Maule. "The name Kant is well known to anyone who sees the *Wall Street Journal*."

Kant was a bright-eyed (blue) and lively old man, but to Maule, himself aging so quickly, almost distastefully scrawny—the Old Year. "Glad to meet you, Edward Maule," he said. "Edward Maule," he repeated, as if he memorized names aurally. "They do like me down at the *Journal*. So does *Time*. It's all because when I was a boy I had to count my pennies."

Maule smiled and scuffed a mustache. "I'm a self-made man myself," he confessed. "I had only one year at college, which made some difference, even in those days. But I've come along all right, I guess. Not that my career is comparable to yours, Mr. Kant."

"I've never thought there was anything so darned wonderful about being self-made," Kant replied. "It's overrated. Maybe it does give a man one advantage: he isn't so afraid of losing his money as the people are who've always had it."

"A subtle observation, sir, and probably a true one."

McCaffrey had been looking around the room. "Very, very nice," he said, "but you don't have as much space as you did in your old place, do you?"

Maule explained how much more convenient it was, also that he lived on the top floor and had a study and garden built onto the roof, also that he didn't expect to remain in business too long and the offices could then be easily rented.

"I'm glad you're not planning to retire to Europe somewhere, where we'd never see you again." McCaffrey went and stood beside Maule, looking, by contrast with the rather formal older man in London-made clothes, even more like the college graduate twenty years later, the sort who has but does not display a Phi Beta Kappa key, and whose frank and open manner and still remarkable good looks are taken to reflect comparable qualities of character. "Anyway," he went on, "an old war horse like you, Edward, won't ever give up. You'll always have a couple of things sitting in a cupboard that any museum would gladly trade its Women's Committee for."

Maule sent Thackeray up to his apartment to get ice and some glasses so that the three of them could have a drink, it being by then twelve thirty; and while they waited there was a silence, almost awkward, which Maule allowed to continue. Finally McCaffrey said, "We have a little problem to talk over with you, Edward."

Barney Kant waved a thumb at the objects on exhibition in Maule's office. "Any of these do, Matt," he asked, "speaking of our problem?"

"I don't even have to look at them," McCaffrey answered. "No!"

"I didn't know. I guessed probably not."

"No harm in asking, Barney. One of the funny things about the art business—you don't ever put your best foot forward. Maule would never stick the kind of thing we want out in the open, like just any picture you might have hanging on any wall."

Thackeray came back downstairs with the required ice and glasses, and Maule took bottles from a desk drawer and made the drinks, adding a splash of stale water to each of them. As he worked he said, "It's not really polite of you, Matt, to talk about me as if I weren't here at all. Particularly not when you're describing my professional tricks. There, now." He handed the glasses out. "Cheers." He drank. "Let's sit down."

When they were settled, McCaffrey said, "Let me tell you our problem, Edward. Okay, Barney?"

"Shoot, Matt."

"You know about our big expansion program, don't you?"

Maule nodded. "I've seen the plans you published in your bulletin," he said.

"Well, the new 'wing,' as we call it—it almost doubles our space, by the way, so it's hardly a wing at all—is almost finished. The most important new plant in the region. Chicago is going to look pretty sick next to us, and Cleveland'll expire."

"Most efficient way ever devised to get a crated picture from truck to platform to carpenters to registrar to photographer to storage to galleries and back again," Kant said. "Smooth as a Detroit assembly line."

"Fabulous architecture," said McCaffrey. "Fabulous, Edward. The last word. Done by Munakata and Hamilton, and they both admit privately that it's their masterpiece. All the fittings specially designed for us by Claude Mitchell."

"A new auditorium seating eight hundred, and with all fittings there you could want, too," said Kant.

"The conception of the lighting is absolutely new, and if I may say so—I had a hand in it—radically creative."

"All costing us more than five million," Kant remarked.

"And there, Edward, is the trouble. You see, old Gloag, when he died a couple of years ago, left us a big fat bequest for the new wing, but costs keep going up, and when we got down to building it, it seemed like a good idea to put in a lot of refinements—you know, so that the darn place wouldn't go out of date in five years—and, well, it wound up costing a whole lot more than we expected. We've spent Gloag's fund and everything else we could get our hands on."

"This was all decided before my time," Kant said.

"Maybe we were too extravagant or optimistic. Still, an art museum is no place to cut corners. It ought to be a work of art itself. Its architecture ought to set a standard for the community. Even you admit that, Barney."

"I'm only president of the board," Barney answered, grinning. "There's the treasurer. He's got to have his say, too."

"Well anyway, what's done is done, and I'm glad for it," McCaffrey said. "Now we've got this great new wing, beautiful in form and beautiful in function. But there's one trouble, Edward."

"Which is?"

"We don't have anything to put in it."

Scrubbing his mustaches, Maule said, "I see."

"The big opening is in September, and it's now February, so you see, it's a problem that's got to be faced."

"That's been my argument. He's giving you the argument I've been making ever since I was made president, Ed," said Barney. "They've all been so busy with the showy part, the building, that they haven't had time to worry about the opening date and what they were going to do about it."

"Now, Barney, we've worried a little," McCaffrey said, winking at Maule.

"I can see it's a good thing they made you president of the museum, Barney," said Maule.

"Wasn't it!" McCaffrey agreed, with considerable emphasis. "Because Barney has come to our rescue."

"I wouldn't put it that strong," said Barney.

"I'll explain to Edward. You know that old saying, Nature abhors a vacuum. Well, we figure our empty rooms will begin to fill up as soon as it's known we have space to show things, and show them well. And no one-week-a-year business, either. There are still a lot of good collections around, and a lot of collectors don't want to leave their things to an older museum where they just get lost and aren't appreciated anyway. For the opening we plan a loan show borrowed from other museums and private collections and also dealers."

"I see."

"And we'll have a show of local artists, and also we'll drag out every old print and shred of canvas and potsherd we've got. Somehow we'll fill the rooms. We're going to ask you for something."

"Anything you want," Maule said, an offer all three of them took at its proper value.

"It's going to be a real bang-up function, Edward. Parties and distinguished international guests brought over at our expense. There'll be a dedication ceremony with the Governor and a half a dozen Senators and Members of Congress. We even hope to have the Soviet Ambassador. The loan show I mentioned, it's going to be the biggest thing of its kind ever held west of Chevy Chase. Contrary to what Barney says, I've been working on it, and so has Pretorius. I think the Louvre is going to send a Meissonier and we'll get things from Amsterdam, too, and maybe the British Museum, and even the Uffizi may lend us a couple of drawings."

"Wonderful," Maule said carefully. McCaffrey, while considered one of the most likable men in his profession, was also considered a very slippery operator, a man to watch, for all the guilelessness of his friendly enthusiasm. "How is Pretorius?"

"What? Oh, he's all right. Let me finish. We feel that all this won't be quite enough. We feel the museum ought to have one very important new acquisition to show, a major work of its own, never seen before. It will get featured. Headlines. 'Magnificent new X, never before on public exhibition, highlights the blah blah blah.' We'll do everything on the publicity side we can—and that is going to be a lot. Barney has offered to pay for the best press agent we can get. *Fortune* might do something. *Life* certainly will, with a color spread of the new picture, if it's suitable at all. Barney has also offered to get us that one great, big, major work of art we need to highlight our opening."

Silence. Then, as if mesmerized, Maule slowly repeated his last words. "That major work of art you need to highlight your opening."

"That's right. Isn't that right, Barney?"

"That's right, Matt. And I'll spend some money for it, too, Ed."

"To get what you need will be costly in today's market," said Maule, as if he were in no way involved.

"We've looked, Edward. We know. And there's so little on the market. The good old days are gone forever. You aren't the first dealer we've been to, and you won't be the last, but it's very, very hard to find anything. Those national patrimony laws, just to begin with. Also, we've set our sights high. It's got to be the right kind of thing. It can't, for instance, be sculpture, unless it's by someone as famous as Michelangelo. It's almost got to be a painting, and we've ruled out the English school and the German school. Nobody cares about the first any more, not since the disappearance of big dining rooms, and nobody's heard about the second—in spite of Pretorius's arguments. Also, I don't want a portrait, if I can help it."

"I won't pay for any Catholic picture," put in Kant.

"Landscape is always popular, and a really great one

might do, but your average landscape doesn't have enough ping," said McCaffrey.

"I don't want a lot of fat women. If it's of naked women, they've got to be women I'd take to bed with me," said Kant.

"Still life is out. The last thing we bought was that beat-up Kalf."

"I call it our Martini picture, because of the bottle and the glass and the lemon rind," said Kant.

"The Impressionists and Post-Impressionists, in spite of their astronomical prices, have become so commonplace that, frankly, to highlight our opening with a Seurat or a Cézanne . . ."

"Whoever they are," interjected Barney.

"One can't know everybody," murmured Maule.

". . . would be a little infra dig," finished McCaffrey. Maule nodded his agreement. "Banal," he said.

"Exactly."

The dealer reached across his desk for the buzzer, but hesitated. This was a major move to make. His new picture was precisely what they needed and wanted, and from his point of view, it could not possibly be better placed. What a triumph! Color spreads in large circulation magazines, publicity from New York to San Francisco and around the world. Only two little difficulties: he had already shown it, and Barney Kant would need a bit of handling. He knew the type well from his old days in hunting prints. They didn't know much, but they were not fools to be parted easily from their money. Problems. And so he hesitated, but then his finger went down on the button. It was unavoidable, logical, desirable. If McCaffrey and his museum would buy the painting, then to them it must go.

* *

"There it is, gentlemen. The only thing I can show you of the importance you need. The most important Watteau to come on the market in our century. Comparable in quality and significance to the *Embarkation* in Paris or the *Gersaint Signboard* in Berlin."

The exhibition room was dark except for the precious burden upon the easel, which was illuminated by spotlights mounted in the cornice of the opposite wall. Maule turned a rheostat, and other lights came up slightly, but their force seemed to be soaked up by the heavy purple velvet of the walls. Nothing impinged upon the dramatic primacy of the canvas.

Maule let them look a few minutes. "It needs a bit of cleaning, as you can see. As a matter of fact, Tait is supposed to be stopping by to see it just about now. Maybe it will need a tiny touch here and there, but otherwise it's in mint condition." He stopped talking and let them look some more.

He spoke up again. "I know how hollow it sounds when a dealer mentions difficulties in connection with a sale," he said. "But I should tell you that you are not the first to see this painting. Nobody else has precisely taken an option on it, but on the other hand, I could not offer it to you, either, without notifying one or two other parties. Also, the sale must . . ." He stopped himself, deciding suddenly not to put in this complicating factor, but both men turned their heads with curiosity when he interrupted himself. It seemed to him wiser to go on. "The sale must be approved by the owner, whose agent I am."

Again he let them look at the picture in silence, then he remarked, as he went to the same knob and increased the general lighting in the room even more, "Frankly, it is the most important painting I have had in twenty years. There.

Now we can see each other, too." He walked back to stand beside them. "May I be blunt, Matt?" he asked. "I think it is worth the whole of your present collection put together."

"Say, wait a minute now," said Barney Kant, but neither of the other men paid any attention to him.

"I know how you mean that," McCaffrey said. He stood back from the painting as far as he could get, visualizing it in other, more festive circumstances. "It's so damn big for a Watteau, that's what's so terrific about it," he said.

Kant grinned. "The men sure look sissy to me," he said. Then he asked, "What's the name of that building?"

"What's the provenance?" McCaffrey asked at the same time.

"Probably imaginary," Maule said.

"What?" said McCaffrey sharply.

"I mean the building, of course. The history has a few holes in it, Matt. It belonged to Jean de Jullienne, who was almost surely the first owner, then later to the Duc de Choiseul. It disappears about the time of the Revolution, and then reappears in the mid-nineteenth century belonging to the Comte de Chambord, no less. It later entered the collection of Achille Proust—a distant relative of the novelist—and was seen and described by the Goncourt brothers. I have the reference if you want to see it later. Then it disappears, and turns up in the hands of its present owner."

"Who'd you say he was?" Kant asked.

"I didn't say. Confidential," Maule replied.

"Huh." Barney walked over to the picture. "How much?" he asked.

Maule thought a moment. "I don't know precisely."

"How can we talk business if we don't know how much it is?" Barney demanded.

"Do you think you might be interested?"

"I should say so," said McCaffrey.

"And I should say that that depends on how much it is," said Kant.

"I *could* telephone," Maule said uncertainly. "He happens to be in New York right now. I could explain your problem to him."

"Then do. Let's get our cards on the table." Barney's remark.

"In that case, let us go back to my office," Maule said.

When they were there once more, he wrote a telephone number on a slip of paper and summoned Thackeray. "Get this for me, please, and when the call comes through, switch it directly over without announcing me or mentioning any names whatsoever," he said. Presently a button flashed on his telephone base. He picked up the receiver quickly, cleared his throat, announced who he was and described his business, and told of the need for a rough price on the new Watteau. Then he stopped. "Umm," he said. "Umm . . . yes . . . yes." He jotted a figure down on his note pad. When he had replaced the receiver, he rose and went to where Barney and McCaffrey were standing at a tactful distance, pretending to look at the Magnasco. He held the paper with the notation on it out in front of them. "This is what he said."

Barney craned around McCaffrey's shoulder. "Jee-sus!"

Maule tucked the paper in his pocket, then clasped his hands together behind his back and teetered forward on the soles of his feet. He smiled and looked down.

"Don't say anything yet, Barney," interrupted McCaffrey. "We'd better think this over. It's expensive, but on the other hand, that picture is ten times as important as any other we've seen."

"For that price, it ought to be," said Mr. Kant. "What the hell does he mean by 'well in excess' anyway?"

Maule shrugged. "Hard to say."

"Huh. When I buy something I like to know the price," Kant said angrily, his head wobbling from side to side like an irritable old turtle's. "This is a hell of a way to do business, Ed."

Maule looked regretful. "Perhaps, then . . ." he began.

Once more McCaffrey interrupted. "Perhaps what we had better do is to go off to lunch without discussing it any more right now."

"Suits me," Barney said. "There isn't anything to discuss as far as I can see."

"Well, we'll see, Barney."

McCaffrey hurried him out into the reception room, where Thackeray helped them with their coats. While he was doing so, McCaffrey noticed the slip of paper with the telephone number of the owner on it, but was unable to get near enough to the desk to read it. Thackeray must have noticed his interest, for when he had finished helping with the coats, he stepped pointedly over, wadded the paper up, and dropped it into a tiny leather wastebasket.

Going down in the elevator, McCaffrey said to Kant, "So now you've met old Maule, Barney. One of the best in the business."

"Smart fellow," Kant said dryly.

"You know, Barney, if everything about that picture is okay, it's a priceless masterpiece. Maybe it's too much money for you . . ."

"What do you mean, 'if everything about the picture is okay'? What's 'everything'?"

"Condition. History. Expert opinions."

"Who was this artist?"

McCaffrey explained. "Very important. Very rare," he concluded.

"It's a lot of money."

They hailed a taxi, which took them to the restaurant where they were meeting another dealer for lunch. Barney let McCaffrey pay the fare—that is, he let the museum pay it—then he said, "That guy Maule. There's something phony about him."

"About Edward? No, Barney, you're wrong. You're put off maybe by his manner. That's all."

"I didn't get where I am by being wrong about people."

"He's a new species to you, though, Barney. You shouldn't bring preconceptions into play. He's a man with a golden reputation."

"Maybe. But remember, Matt, it's my money still, and I am going to see to it we aren't taken to the cleaners."

As they checked their hats and coats McCaffrey thought: too bad the old bastard had taken a dislike to the only man who had what they wanted. And Barney thought: it was too slick. It happened too neatly. Was McCaffrey getting some kind of kickback? He watched the well-shaped head, the broad, still-athletic shoulders of his companion, who preceded him toward the table. McCaffrey's chief asset was that he was so obviously a regular guy, who could talk golf just as well as he could talk art. Wife with money. Could go to houses Barney couldn't get into. Would he risk that for money? No, not likely, Barney thought; but, as a matter of fact, I'd like him a hell of a lot more myself if he would. The trouble with McCaffrey is, he wouldn't really risk anything for anything.

Six

Maule was in a hurry. He was going to be late. Why did the man have to be so damned deliberate?

Pearson Tait, unaware, was leaning forward to examine the picture by the light of a strong hand beam that was connected by an extension cord to a hidden wall plug. The resulting reflections and glare made it impossible to read his eyes through his glasses.

A cold fish, Maule thought. But everybody wants his word on a painting today. I'll be glad when the fashion changes.

Methodically, never varying the pace, Tait ran the light across and back over the surface of the Watteau.

What repellent hands, thought Maule. Fat, fingers too fat, then too pointed. Saurian. Prehistoric.

Tait finished, snapped off the light, stood up, and hooked the cord over the back of the chair. He was of medium height, very broad-shouldered, but strangely put together, having unusually long arms and no perceptible neck.

Gross and obscene, thought Maule irritably. If one can't be handsome, one should at least be trim. What have I ever heard about his private life?

Nothing. Nothing at all.

Aloud he said, "Well, Dr. Tait, what do you think of my picture? It's a great Watteau all right, don't you agree?"

"I beg your pardon?"

"I mean, you think it's genuine, don't you?"

A horrible little smile lifted Tait's upper lip. "Mr. Maule, that is not for me to say. I leave that kind of thing to other people. I know only what my instruments tell me, my X rays, my infrared light, what my ultraviolet lamp, my microscope, and my chemical laboratory tell me. I do not go in for soothsaying."

"Sorry. No offense."

"None taken, Mr. Maule. I was only stating my point of view."

"Quite right."

"Then we understand one another. I believe, from what the unaided eye can see, that there is not much damage to the painting. It needs to have the old varnish removed, as you already know. We can see then what comes off with it. If you wish me to continue my examination, you will have to send the picture to my office."

"Naturally. I didn't expect you to work here."

"It wouldn't matter if you did, Mr. Maule."

Maule considered his problem. Should he have the painting worked on immediately, or should he wait so that he could show it to other possible buyers? He decided that he had already started quite enough balls rolling. The word would get around, too, and it might, in fact, be quite convenient to have the thing out of the way for a while.

"I will send it over as soon as possible," he said. "I may want to bring a customer by to see it later on, though."

Dr. Tait nodded. "As you wish. You already know that my fees are in part based on the time I spend on a painting. I will insist on being present if you show the picture in my studio; but if you want to use my time in that way, it is entirely up to you."

"I understand."

"Then I will wish you good day."

The two men descended to the main floor and walked to

the reception room. "I'm going in your direction for lunch. Can I drop you off?" Maule asked.

Tait shook his head. "It is part of my regimen to walk at least three miles every day, Mr. Maule. I prefer to go by foot."

"Too bad," Maule said cheerfully, pushing open the door, so intent on getting the restorer out of his office that he did not notice that the man was trembling when they shook hands.

Trembling, too, were Maule's own knees by the time he had his own outer coat on, for now he had to face the fact of his difficult lunch partner—would he be nice or nasty? —and that inevitably brought on the shaking.

"I won't be back until after three o'clock, Thackeray," he said.

"Say hello to Mr. Dane for me," Thackeray replied.

Maule hesitated. The back of his neck turned red. He could feel it, hot inside the collar. Several things to say came to his mind; he chose the most cowardly. "Take a long lunch yourself," and he went out.

As soon as it was safe Thackeray dialed a number. He waited a long time before a voice answered.

"Momma," he said, "hello, Momma. How's the foot to-day?" He listened, presumably to clinical details, then said, "Well, you just take care of it. Don't go to work tomorrow, either. You'd better stay at home all week, Momma." Another listening period. "Well, it's been an eventful morning, Momma, that's why I couldn't get you before." He recounted everything that had happened. It took him fifteen minutes.

When he had finished, his mother spoke to him again. "But somebody had to get it, Momma. People can't drink without ice and glasses. . . . I know that, too, but the handyman didn't come in this morning, and Mr. Maule is too old to handle the painting by himself. . . . But that's only polite, Momma." More objections. "Well, I still say you can't have people struggling with their own coats. I'm the receptionist, Momma, so it's like I was in my own home. . . . No, Momma, I'm not forgetting, but it takes time. I'm still an apprentice here, Momma. I'm still learning how to do things the right way, and it *does* take a lot of time. Things will change, don't you worry, and maybe it won't be too long. I'm studying the situation, don't you worry, Momma. Now remember, keep off that foot. Good-by, Momma."

He went to one of the cabinets and took out a small parcel, which proved to contain two sandwiches he had brought with him that morning. He decided he wanted some milk with them, so he put on his coat, went out to a delicatessen, bought a pint, and returned to the office. Then he sat at his desk and ate his sandwiches, stopping now and then to lift a crumb with the tip of a moistened finger. He was thinking. Principally he was thinking that he had met more multimillionaires in that one morning than most people get the chance to meet in a whole lifetime.

Seven

It was a little Chinese restaurant, not too far from Times Square, called The Celestial Chopstick. Famous people sometimes went to it because they were never supposed to see anybody there. At a back table, whose bamboo and paper lantern they had switched off to achieve maximum privacy, sat a young man and a girl, each in the early twenties.

"How did you get away today?" the girl asked, turning around to scan the other furtive lunchers, for she had been seated, by her own request, with her back to the room. She was striking-looking, with very black hair and eyes, and white teeth, evenly set and large.

"I didn't say anything at all. I've run out of reasons. I just won't turn up. If I'd said I wouldn't be there and didn't say why, I would have had to submit to cross-examination. She would have broken me down. I would have told her, and then she'd have kept me at home somehow." The tall, seriously underweight young man uttered a forced little laugh that trailed off into something like terror. "How about you?"

"He's got a new lady friend. I told you. I'm forgotten."

"Have you seen her? Is she young?"

"Old enough to have launched the *Normandie*, I should think. Isn't that . . . ? No, I'm mistaken, it isn't. Don't you think it's simply disgusting that we have to dodge around to a place like this to see each other?"

"I wonder if we really do. I'm getting tired of it."

The waiter brought menus, and the girl looked at hers. "Not that it matters what we choose," she remarked, "since everything here tastes just like everything else."

"Drink?"

"Daiquiri."

He ordered two daiquiris. "It's all right for me to have one today, since my appointment is in the morning on Mondays."

She showed a purely reflex interest. "Is it? Mine's always the same time—three o'clock. I don't care if I've had a drink, though. It makes me talk more—unless I fall asleep."

"That old business, am I or am I not legitimate? It came up again this morning."

"Has your unconscious decided which parent it wants to be real?"

He shook his head. "Sometimes I favor one, sometimes the other. Logistically, it's easier if it's the mother. Sometimes I think the best solution is that there was a switch-around in the obstetrical ward and I don't belong to either."

"At least your accidentals turned out to be respectable. And they've only tried to seduce your will."

"So that's still bothering you."

"I'm pretty well convinced that it didn't happen. Not quite."

The waiter brought their drinks and took their order. When he had gone off, the young man said, "Let's get married, Ursula."

She fiddled with the stem of her glass. "We can't talk about marriage over won ton soup."

"Will it be any easier over moo goo gai pan?"

"Don't press me, Artie. You know I'm not ready for all that yet."

"But we could rescue each other. I need rescuing. Even if it didn't last, just to be rescued for a year would be something. Mine says that to achieve any kind of human relationship is something to be proud of."

"I've told you, I just can't love anybody, not yet, much less make love. I need time. Don't make me decide anything now. Anyway, there's the little problem of our parents."

"I have enough in my own name for us to get by on."

"I doubt it. Don't forget, I'm used to lots of clothes and Florida, at the very least, in winter. And five sessions a week when I'm in town."

"Would your father mind so much?"

"Yes, I think so. He hates your father, and he'd also mind that your mother would mind so much. Anyway, I don't think I want him to support my husband, when I get one."

"Mother would mind a lot."

"Don't you agree that there's just too much against it right now? Neither of us is strong enough yet. Isn't it simply disgusting? You want to be rescued, really, not loved. I'd rather be safe than anything. It's boring, because people feel sorry for us."

"Who knows enough about us to feel sorry?"

"I mean they *would*, Artie, if they did know. It's the same thing. But thirty years ago we would have run away from home, moved down to the Village . . ."

He giggled. "Done the Charleston."

"Yes, and lived in sin and flouted both our families and written articles on free love. And everybody would have thought it was simply marvelous and chic, and maybe it would have worked out and maybe not, but at least we could have had a good try at it. Now people just feel sorry for us. We're all weighted down by our own reservations, too. Don't you feel all of them?" She raised both her hands above the table top and let them fall heavily down on either side of her plate. "Like that."

"Not, I guess, as many as you do."

"Well, we have them, whether you know it or not. You'll get the insight eventually. Anyway, nowadays people are supposed to fall in love and get married and have lots of children somewhere fifty miles from town. It's the pattern; I can't do it. Yet when I complain about it, mine says there's nothing wrong with going with the herd when the herd is going in the right direction. Don't you see, from the point of view of everybody now, we're missing out. We're emotional mules. Who wants to be pitied?"

"You mean you'd rather be censured than pitied?" He giggled again.

"Oh, Artie, you can be so impossible."

"Sorry, Ursula. You see, I want to get married and leave home—no theories behind it at all. I see it as simply as this: that with you pulling one arm at the big scene, and Mother the other, I'd probably go in your direction because you're younger and stronger than she is."

The girl imagined it, and soon smiled, parting her lips to show her fine white teeth. Then she said, "But what you haven't counted on is that, just as I was winning, I'd let go."

Suddenly the young man stiffened. "God damn," he said. "There's old Maule coming in the door. What luck! I'd never have expected to see him in a place like this. Move over to the center of your seat and hide me."

"Who's he?"

"An art dealer. A friend of my father. Yours must know him, too. The man with him looks sort of familiar."

The girl turned around. "It's Philip Dane. Not the most reputable person to be having lunch with."

"How do you know him? I mean, who is he?"

"The actor. He's opening in *Green Leaf, Yellow Leaf* in a few days. You've probably seen him in something."

"What's the matter with him?"

"The usual. And flaming."

"Oh." The young man thought this over. "That's funny. Maule must have some kind of business with him."

"I can imagine."

They ate quickly and left rather early so that Ursula could get across and uptown in time to be markedly in advance of her three o'clock appointment, and as they had to pass close to Maule's table, there seemed to be no way to avoid greeting him. Artie went up and said hello.

47

Maule had not, in fact, seen him until that moment, and had no idea whatsoever who the girl with him might be. It took Maule some seconds to place the gawky young man, seconds during which he suffered from considerable embarrassment, until Artie reminded him of his name, Artie van Zandt.

"Of course. Oh, of course—how stupid. How have you been, Artie? How is your father?" Maule flushed. "What a silly question. I just saw him an hour ago. I forgot. Well, anyway . . ." Somehow, he did not manage to introduce his luncheon partner before Artie backed awkwardly away. His nervous, yapping laugh sounded from the door as he and the foreign-looking girl he was with went out.

Philip Dane, brushing back his hair, which off-stage seemed excessively long, said, "That was pretty cute, Edward."

Maule blinked. "Artie?" he asked, astonished.

"You know exactly what I mean. You actually had the effrontery to be ashamed, ashamed of *me*, Edward. If I weren't simply starving, I'd leave this table right now."

"Philip, please. Let us not argue. I wasn't ashamed of you," Maule said, realizing that he had been. "I hardly know the lad. His father's a client of mine."

"You know him well enough for him to have gone to the trouble of coming up to say hello."

"Oh, who knows why people do that? I wish sometimes they'd leave a man alone."

"You mean times such as this, when you're lunching with your less *fashionable* friends. Or less *what* kind of friends, Edward?" He paused, then said viciously, "When you're caught. That's what you mean."

"It isn't what I mean at all, Philip. Please."

Dane eyed Maule with distaste. "Fake British mustaches.

48

A fake accent. Clothes too correct for words. I know it all. My dear Edward, what you don't seem to realize is that you don't look like a respectable old-bachelor art dealer at all. You look like an aged fairy glove salesman."

Maule winced. How typical of Philip—and how revealing of the terribly sympathetic harmonics of their souls, that he should have read Maule's own worst misgiving of the morning about himself, even down to the particular line of haberdashery.

"I've had such a strenuous morning, Philip," he said. "Let me tell you about it."

"I should be too bored," the other man said, turning a haughty profile in another direction.

They sat thus for several minutes, while Maule cursed Artie and the excessive sensibility of his friend. Then, too tired, too old to hold out, he crawled up to nudge a hand for attention.

"Thackeray sent you his regards, by the way, Philip. The lad is coming along, you know. He got quite useful experience today, as a matter of fact. I went out of my way to give him a look inside."

Philip Dane did not turn forward; nevertheless, he was an actor and could do much with almost nothing, and he made it clear that Maule had scored. Maule was too experienced a hand anyway not to sense the slight relaxation, the slight rise of interest. After a suitable wait the eyes, followed by eyebrows and, eventually, head, turned upon Maule.

"Well?" Philip asked. "Go ahead. What did he see?"

Eight

Arthur van Zandt and his wife had tea together in a small room in one corner of their enormous apartment. It was the appointed place for tea, but it had received its commission much against Mr. van Zandt's will, for it was within enemy territory. That is, it was furnished according to his wife's taste, and with examples from her collection of Early American and English antiques. As the price for his concession here, Mrs. van Zandt was compelled to take her breakfast—she liked kippers and eggs, he *croissants* and *café au lait*—in another little room, amidst what she called his gold gewgaws (his ormolu clocks and *encriers*, his two silver-gilt *necessaires*), and those weak-faced Frenchwomen (his superb Boucher drawings) who hung upon the walls of this singular version of the breakfast nook.

Henrietta van Zandt was dressed so conservatively that Angélique de la Couronne d'Epines, for instance, would probably have thought she was a widow. Her suit was an Oxford gray approaching black, she wore no lipstick or rouge, and her only jewelry was a tiny pearl, more symbol than ornament, at the throat. A wisp of lace showed at each cuff, but Angélique would have surmised, and correctly, that she wore none at all elsewhere.

Thoughtful, she poured more tea from a quite ordinary teapot into a similar cup and handed her giant of a husband some macaroons on a common-enough plate—the cabinets in the room groaned with Chelsea and Worcester, but of course it was never used, not so much because she loved it as because she wouldn't risk it. Then she replied to the question van Zandt had raised five minutes earlier, but did so indirectly.

"Christ, I recall, spoke of how a person's love of possessions could lead him utterly away from spiritual things."

"Please, Henrietta. Leave Him out of this. You will make me so irritable I will get gas on the stomach."

"I believe it is true," she went on, suffering his crudeness to pass without notice. "I believe you love your collection at the expense of your soul, Arthur. You can hardly ask me to encourage that."

"And your collection?"

She directed her gray eyes into his. If a world of feeling lay behind those eyes, it was well hidden. "I do not have a collection, as you put it, Arthur. You know that."

"You're such a hypocrite, Henrietta. I wonder that you can contemplate other people's sinfulness and never realize the slightest thing about yourself."

"Arthur, I do not have a collection in the sense you mean. I have kept what my mother left me. I have even added to it. I do believe that I may be permitted, without being guilty of pride or the love of worldly vanities, to surround myself with the furnishings that befit my station in life."

"You call that new epergne such a furnishing?"

"Essentially, yes. It is also an investment. God has not forbidden us to increase the blessings that He has Himself bestowed."

"I call it a vanity, if you want to know what I call it. But, damn it all, I don't care. Anyway, how did we get off on religion? You never bring it up without a reason."

"I was about to explain that I will certainly *not* lend you money to buy another French painting, and particularly not one such as you have just described," she said gently.

"Your entire collection, Arthur, is nothing but the most *evident* vanities, made for the painted and ruffled women of a loose and lascivious age."

"Good God, Henrietta, where do you learn your speeches? I think you must take them out of some Salvation Army Handbook of Rhetoric."

"What I have said is a historical fact."

He put his cup down, his face contorted with anger. "Let me tell you something," he said slowly. "You've missed the point. I've got to have that painting. I'll do anything for it." Van Zandt slammed a hand down on the tea table. He shouted, "Anything, do you understand? Anything at all. And I'll get it. It would be easier if you would lend me the money, but I'll get it anyway."

"Frankly," said she, "I don't see how. Our affairs are rather mingled you know, Arthur." She poured herself more tea. "Our son did not return for lunch today," she continued, no change in her voice marking the abrupt change of subject. "He had not told me that he was going out," she said.

Van Zandt had slouched down in his chair and was staring at a corner. "Why should he? He's of age."

"He is of legal age, but his judgment is not much developed. And I consider his action today disrespectful. Will you speak to him, or shall I?"

"About what?"

"About his duty, Arthur. About good manners, and his duty to me, his mother."

The big man looked over at her. "You are too much, Henrietta. Simply too much to stand. The boy decides to stay out for lunch, and directly you're canting on about duty, insubordination, and endless blather like that. Jesus, let him alone."

She listened to him, then, with the sigh of the toilworn pressed once more into service, she said, "It is hard that I should have to do it all myself."

"Ugh," her husband said.

"Will you have more tea?"

"Will you have more tea?" he mimicked her. "No I will not have more tea. But if you hadn't somehow managed to get so much of our money tangled up, I assure you I'd have a divorce."

"Someone had to manage it," she said.

"Well, it strikes me you haven't done a good job."

"It will be there, Arthur, when other people's money is not."

"Oh, horseshit! Henrietta."

A look almost of ecstasy flickered across her pale face, although the gray eyes still showed nothing at all.

"Arthur, will you leave the room now, or shall I?" she asked.

Van Zandt left the tearoom and went to his library, a very much bigger room, where many of the best things he kept in New York were displayed—much of his collection was stored at his family's former summer place in Old Lyme. Here were shelves for objects, several cases, too, and storage cabinets for unframed drawings and prints. Behind the desk hung a large Rigaud of the Orléans Regent, profligate model to Louis XV; and the other walls had their Vernets, their Fragonards, their Paters and Lancrets and Greuzes. The desk itself had been made for Madame Elizabeth by Riesener, and had once stood in her apartments at Versailles. The entire room, in fact, was more a museum than a private library, and most people, once their curiosity about the van Zandt collection had been satisfied, were a little oppressed by all the dazzle; but it was here that the violent and coarse-looking man was most at home, for here was the very nucleus of all that he loved in the world. It was here, on a wall area now filled by a Nattier Diana, portrait of some marquise or duchesse, that he wanted the Watteau to hang.

He sat down and looked through his mail, selected a good-sized envelope to tear open, took out the auction catalogue for a sale in London that it contained, and went through it, making pencil notations on the margins. Suddenly he said aloud, "That woman!" and leaned forward to rest his forehead on a hand. He had no further arguments to say to her, and he was having to face his own ineffectuality.

Then he got up and went to a vitrine that contained only one object, a great porcelain potpourri in the form of a highly stylized ship, a Potpourri "Gondole," its upper part elaborately perforated to allow the scent of the dried petals and spices to pass through. He unlocked the case, lifted off the glass box that formed its top, then took the Sèvres porcelain with the utmost care and placed it on his desk. It was one of a pair that had once been sent to the Empress Maria-Theresa as a royal gift, and was suitably large and suitably decorated, its white reserves—the ground was *rose pompadour*—being covered with little scenes of shepherdessses doing inexplicable things with quantities of tiny flowers. Van Zandt touched it all over, feeling the glassy surface, following its outlines with his eyes closed.

To think they could both be contained within the same house.

Then he took a camel's-hair brush out of a drawer and spent a calming twenty minutes lifting off every speck of dust from the surface, his face now quite transfigured.

When he had finished, he replaced the fragile structure in its case, closed and locked it, then returned to his desk, where he wrote a note in longhand to Edward Maule.

"Dear Edward," it read, "I must be out of town tomorrow, and on Wednesday my doctors seem to want to keep me busy most of the day having some tests in the hospital. I trust I will be out on Thursday, but one never knows, when the doctors start, when or where they will end, so I wanted to send you this now to affirm my position. I am, as I said, extremely interested in your new painting. I would be most disappointed if you should sell it without prior notification to me, and warn you that it would terminate our long and cordial relationship, which has not, I hazard, been much less profitable to you than to me. Moreover, it is my understanding that I was the first person to whom you showed it, so that technical priority reinforces the claims of friendship. I will be in touch with you, and we can then discuss prices, ways, and means. Yours very sincerely, Arthur van Zandt."

He read it intently, decided it would do, sealed it in an envelope and put a stamp on it, then rang for a servant and ordered that it be put in the mail immediately, so that it would be delivered in the morning. As he went to his bedroom he passed the potpourri once again. He stopped to look at it with admiration and affection. He shook his head with wonder. And he thought: if it were ever a question of one of them breaking, the porcelain or the woman, she would be dead that instant. The idea brought a slight smile to his face as he passed on by.

Nine

She who had remained blasé through the popping of thousands of champagne corks scarcely heeded one more. She merely lifted her brows to show Theodore that he had filled her glass sufficiently. He was having vermouth, which Angélique never drank. She would occasionally have a dry Martini, but in general she always took the same simple cocktail as this evening's, unadulterated with bitters or sugar.

"You know, *chéri*, all the time I was at my *couturier*'s, and then later on when I was having my massage, and even at my hairdresser's, yes, even during the rather tormenting procedure of depilation, I have been able to think of only one thing today."

Little Theodore looked at this great beauty, whom everybody called his mistress, but who was not. "I wish I dared hope that it was of me," he said.

"In a way," she answered.

"In a way? What way?"

"More directly, I was thinking of that painting. It was so beautiful." She pointed to the space above her mantel, now filled with a mediocre oil of the Place des Vosges. "I kept thinking how lovely it would be right there. *Dans ce petit coin de France q'est mon appartement.*"

"Doubtless," Theodore admitted. "I should think it would be well on any wall."

"Here, Theodore, it would be at home."

Though he was horribly lovesick, Cariatis was nonetheless wary. "Doubtless," he said again. "Angélique?"

She frowned. "Oui, *chéri?*"

"I doubt whether you realize that as of tonight, the seventeenth of February, we have known each other a full year."

"That long? Can it be?"

"You think, as everybody does, that we have become good friends only during these last few weeks, since I arrived in America. Yet we have sunned ourselves at Eden Roc together, we have dined at the Palace in Monte Carlo, we cruised through the islands of the Aegean in the same group of amateur archaeologists, sailed on the Bosporus, finally kissed on the Golden Horn. . . ."

"It was on a dare."

"Nevertheless, we kissed—and all these things as if by accident. So you believed."

"You are right."

"Accidental, too, that we were together on my Acropolis under moonlight, the Jungfrau at dawn?"

"I hadn't thought."

"And as far as that goes, we happen also to have met at performances of Wagner in Bayreuth, Richard Strauss in Munich, Mozart in Salzburg, Verdi in Milan, Palestrina at the Vatican, and Elgar at the Albert Hall."

"Surely this is all leading somewhere," Angélique said.

"The memories are precious to me," murmured Cariatis sadly.

"Of course. But present your conclusions."

"Another woman, Angélique, with less than your sublime modesty, might have thought she was being pursued."

"But you have never made a declaration."

"I have been afraid to. Let me conclude, as you suggest. We have done all of these things together since we met, these and many more. You agree to that. But there is one thing we have never done."

She frowned again. "Which is?"

"We have never made love," he replied shyly.

"I have not forgotten that."

"I am as famous as you, Angélique, in these matters. I am known to be the most indefatigable womanizer, at least rich one, in the international set. What has happened between us is not like me, and I don't understand it. But I think it is this: I believe that you are destined to be the last great love of my life, the love in which all the others are somehow wrapped up, the love that is so great that it can only terminate a career, the love, my dear, that leads but to the grave."

"Theodore, do not be morbid."

"You are going to reduce me to a nervous wreck if you don't return my love, at least a little. Already I have neglected my family for you—I have hardly seen Ursula since I arrived. I have neglected my friends. Most serious, perhaps, I have neglected my business. I cannot concentrate on my refineries or my import-export business. Yet I seem to get nowhere with you. I cannot face failure, Angélique," he concluded menacingly.

"I am not afraid," said she, haughtily.

"I scarcely hoped that you would be. But do bear in mind that part of what I said that had to do with my love for you."

She fluttered her eyelids, which caused all the color to leave his face, emphasizing the artificial blackness of his eyebrows and mustaches, and of the fringes of his hair.

"You are making what is called an indecent proposal to me, are you not, Theodore?"

"Actually, no. I am willing to marry you, Angélique."

"*Theodore!*"

He sighed. "What can I do, then?"

She put a jeweled forefinger at the point of her chin. "I do not know," she said finally.

"I don't understand." He groaned. "Am I repulsive to you?"

"Not at all. You are *adorable, mignon.*"

"Am I not sufficiently attentive?"

"You are always here, now, when I need you. Often when I don't."

"Am I not adequately rich?"

"As to that . . ."

"Then I don't understand. Let us be candid with one another, Angélique. I am older now. I will not be importunate, not so often. I am not asking you for more than the minimum of passion on your part. Then—this apartment, all these luxurious appointments, your clothes, your jewels, your this and your that. You didn't get them working with your hands."

"I forbid you, Theodore, to speculate further upon what I did or didn't work with."

"But what is wrong? Why aren't you my mistress?" He rushed forward to embrace her.

She removed him gently from around her torso. "Before all this came up," she said, "we were talking about that painting."

He backed away, quite angry. "Frankly, mademoiselle, I was looking for a small present for you. Ten thousand dollars, maybe. Even twenty or thirty, considering that I am Cariatis. But not half a million. You see, I am a business-man in spite of everything. I know the difference between a sum one gambles and a sum one invests."

Her eyes sparkled. "That much for the little Watteau?" she asked.

"Probably much more. At least that much."

"And I, Angélique de la Couronne d'Epines, am being refused a gift from my would-be gallant because he won't meet a price?"

Theodore put his hands over his eyes, but left a space so that he could talk between the palms. "I'll meet it, Angélique. I'll meet it, whatever it is. But it is a gift one makes to one's established mistress, not to a friend."

"I am not for sale, Theodore. I am not a painting."

"Then there is nothing more to be said." The little man took his fingers away and stared at her, waiting.

Absent-mindedly, she picked up a tiny gold implement from the table, a kind of brush, and twirled it in her champagne to get rid of the carbonation. "Telephone Maule, Theodore," she said finally. She threw the full voltage of her glorious smile into him.

His tongue moistened his lips. "And tonight?"

"We will make love under Monsieur Maule's picture," she replied. "Nowhere else."

"I'll try to get him right now."

She watched him hurry away to the telephone, shrugged a little, and puckered her lips. "*Toutefois,*" she said softly, "*J'ai fait un bon marché.*"

Ten

It was most irregular for anybody to come to the door at so late an hour. Thackeray asked for a name over the communications system. "Oh, I'm sorry," he said, when he had heard it. "I didn't know Mr. Maule was expecting you back today."

"He wasn't," came the answering squawk through the little earphone. "I dropped by on the chance he might be in. I want to talk to him if he isn't busy."

"I'll see if I can locate him, Mr. McCaffrey. He could be anywhere. Even out," Thackeray said, just in case. "You come up, though," and he released the latch. When McCaffrey was in the reception room, he said, "I'll go and try to find Mr. Maule. Why don't you sit down?"

McCaffrey looked around. "Those aren't for me," he said of the spindly chairs, which were all the reception room offered.

Thackeray nodded. "We ought to have big armchairs for the gentlemen," he said.

"Somehow they wouldn't go here."

Thackeray gave McCaffrey a doubtful look and disappeared. Left by himself, the latter strolled around the room, glancing at the objects, at the view from the windows, finally at the desk, where he noted the appointments on the calendar. He turned toward the window again, but just as he did so he remembered the wastebasket. It was not a busy office. There was little in it besides the piece of crumpled paper on which Maule had written the telephone number belonging to the owner of the Watteau. McCaffrey just had time, as he heard the office door approached and opened, to lean over, snatch the paper up, and pocket it. Thackeray was back.

"Mr. Maule will see you. He wants to know if you'd like a drink. If you would, I'll go upstairs and get ice. Again."

"Please. But I've got only a few minutes."

Maule came to the door. "Well, Matt, where is your Mr. Kant?"

"He's at Radio City seeing the Rockettes."

"Surely he's seen them before."

"Yes, but he always goes. It's the discipline he likes, or so he says. Fortunately, it has freed me to come and see you."

"Fortunate, indeed. Let me just pour us drinks back inside here. The ice will be down in a minute."

"I know. Your virile receptionist just told me."

Maule smiled thinly. "He has some ability," he said. "And one likes to do what one can for them."

McCaffrey nodded. "We've just put one at our information desk, where he'd show. But I didn't come to talk about the race question. I came to talk about your Watteau. You haven't sold it already?"

Maule shook his head. "It's over at Tait's place. Nobody has seen it since you were here."

"Good. Good. You understand that I'm very interested in it. I think it's just what we want. You know—big name, chi-chi subject, and it doesn't take a lot of explaining. The only other even remote possibilities we've been offered are a Pieter de Hooch, which would put the newspaper reporters sound asleep, and the most dismal Poussin mythological piece you ever saw. No, I want your Watteau, and the price doesn't much matter. Barney can afford any price you put on it."

"Is it . . . relevant to wonder whether or not he liked it?"

McCaffrey smiled. "He thought it was a lot of money for its size."

"He should buy a Vermeer."

"Try to find one. Anyway, *I'm* interested, and I think I will be able to get my way. There are some politics involved, you see. I'll say just this much: we have a funny ruling. Our president is elected annually. It's always been the custom to re-elect the old one without any fuss—old Gloag was president for seventeen years. But Barney is a new man, newly arrived, newly rich, newly, and just barely, respectable. I got him put in over lots of objections, because I thought with all that as background, or lack of it, he'd probably give us more than a member of an old family ever would. You understand?"

"I'd heard rumors."

Now McCaffrey grinned broadly. "That's the way the world works, isn't it, Edward? The only problem is to see that it works for you. Anyway, I don't think he'll hold out against me and my brother-in-law, who's a big power on the board. Barney loves having the position, but there are a lot of people who'd like to get rid of him. We'll bring him around. Unfortunately, though, until we do I can't give you a firm offer. I can only say *I* want the picture, and I'm reasonably sure *we* will want it, at whatever price this mysterious owner sets. Is that good enough for you? Not to sell it out from under us?"

Thackeray appeared with the ice just then, so Maule waited until they were alone again to answer. He said,

"I don't quite see how I can give you a firm commitment if you can't make me a firm offer."

McCaffrey gulped at his drink. "I don't suppose you can. Only at least agree to this much, that you won't sell it without notifying me. We fly home tomorrow. I'll work fast."

The telephone rang, and Maule excused himself to answer it. "Oh, yes, Mr. Cariatis. I see. Yes, I understand. Well . . . No, but there are some problems. No, I'm afraid I couldn't promise anything. Please, Mr. Cariatis, you must understand my position. No, I simply cannot promise. It is up to . . . Yes. Yes, of course, I will let you know. No. No. Good evening, sir." Maule returned to McCaffrey.

"We were saying, Matt? Oh, yes. That much I can agree to. I will let you know when I am in a position to sell definitely. Others are interested."

"So I gather."

"Yes. Well, in a way, I favor your . . . cause. I would like to see it as the star at your opening. But one must weigh other considerations."

Each reflected upon those other considerations. Then McCaffrey said, jumping to his feet, "I've really got to go. I got about as much out of you as I'd hoped for, Edward. I'll be in touch."

Maule, too, stood. "Good-by, Matt. And remember me to Mrs. McCaffrey."

"I will. Cynthia adores you, you know. You're her favorite art dealer."

"What a compliment."

Maule waved McCaffrey into the reception room and, after he had gone, dismissed Thackeray, then sat in his office for a while. At length he went wearily up to his apartment, where he had another drink or two, supped on frozen foods, looked at a television show for half an hour, then tried unsuccessfully to telephone Philip Dane and went to bed.

Eleven

The first course at lunch had been a *pâté*, and Mrs. van Zandt had Artie's serving put at his place at dinner. He emitted his shrill, sad laugh when he saw it beside his soup. He looked to see if his mother or father had any such riches, guessing immediately what it was all about. "Which am I supposed to eat first?" he asked. He was in for it.

Mrs. van Zandt, who had not so far looked at him, said, "That was supposed to have been for your lunch, and I did not want it wasted. I had ordered it especially because I knew you liked it." She had changed clothes for dinner, but still gave the impression of out-of-season plumage.

Arthur van Zandt glanced over at Artie, more in sympathy than affection. He was a little tight, having had more than his usual number of drinks by himself in his sitting room, because the next day, with his tests coming up the day after, he was forbidden all alcohol. "Would you like me to interpret your mother's message, Artie, or can you get it by yourself?" he asked.

Mrs. van Zandt looked first at him, then at her son, as if at a loss which to sting. She decided upon her husband, whom she both hated more and loved less than she did Artie. "I will not have you undermine my position, Arthur, particularly not since you avoid all responsibilities for our son."

" 'I will not have you undermine my position, Arthur,' "

he repeated, imitating her. "That speech didn't come from your Salvation Army manual, Henrietta. It came out of the genteel tradition. Your preferred W.C. reading."

Mrs. van Zandt closed her eyes, but opened them almost immediately. "Where were you this noon, Artie?"

"I was kept later than I expected, so I had lunch downtown." The badgered young man had elected to eat *pâté* and soup simultaneously, and just as he answered, a sizable morsel of the *pâté* dropped off a piece of bread into the middle of his soup. All three at the table stared. He had failed his lie-detector test. He fished it out, put it back on the bread, and ate it.

"Kept by what? Lunch with whom?" his inquisitor went on.

"Oh, what's the difference, Mother? Nobody you know."

"Why didn't you telephone?"

"That's a rhetorical question, Artie," his father said. "I'll spell that for you. R-h-e-t-o-r-i-c-a-l. Which means that she knows the answer already. A cunning device for building a neat, self-righteous position. Clearly, you didn't telephone because you didn't want to. If she hasn't learned that yet, all she has to do is to listen to a mental playback of this conversation."

"Why didn't you telephone, Artie?" Mrs. van Zandt repeated.

Artie tried to dodge. "I wasn't near a telephone, Mother."

"That is not true. There is no conceivable place where *you* could have been having lunch that would have been too remote from a telephone for you to have called me."

Artie tried desperately to think of an exception to her

rule, working his spoon in his soup. "How about the Staten Island ferry?"

"There are telephones, I am sure, at both terminals."

"You're making a mountain out of a molehill, Mother."

"Not original, son, but apt," Mr. van Zandt said. "I was quite impressed by your Staten Island ferryboat. You've done better than usual so far. My congratulations."

Artie giggled. Not that anything was very funny, but it helped to have an ally. "Thanks," he said.

"Your father is supporting you, Artie, only because he is angry that I will not co-operate with him in a notable piece of extravagance. More explicitly, he is taking no more interest than usual in what *you* do. But he is more than usually determined to offend me."

"How cruel you can be, Henrietta. Where you claim to love."

"He wants to buy a very expensive painting, and I am seeing to it that he does not do so." The slightest touch of a cold passion entered her voice. "He will never own it." Again she spoke of lunchtime. "I am asking you to answer me, for the last time," she said.

Van Zandt decided to rescue their son. "You're a bitch, Henrietta. A real, prime bitch. Snuffling after ordure."

Henrietta van Zandt put down her napkin and rose at once, directing her empty eyes unwaveringly on Artie as she did so. "When you are ready to explain your conduct and to apologize, Artie, you will find me in my sitting room," she said.

"Aren't you going to finish your dinner, Mother?" Artie asked, getting to his feet.

She shook her head. "No. My cup is already overflowing."

After a period of silence, enough to let her get out of earshot, van Zandt said, "I suppose you'd better placate her eventually. Even if it means telling her whatever your secret is. Nice to confound her, though, if only for a little while."

"I don't want to tell her, Father, and I won't."

"No?" Van Zandt got up and went to the empty place left by his wife and rang for the next course. "Unfortunately, though, as I am learning: she who controls the purse strings, and all that."

Artie, freed from surveillance, played with his silver. "It's a girl," he said at last.

"That's a relief. I was beginning to wonder. What's wrong with her?"

"She's not Mother's kind. Mediterranean. Eastern Mediterranean."

Van Zandt whistled. "Oh-oh. I'm glad I'll be in Connecticut tomorrow—she'll find out no later than that, I'd guess. She's going to take it hard. Worse than my Watteau."

"That's exactly why I'm not going to tell her," Artie said. "I don't want to talk to her about this girl." He shook his head. "I won't do it. I just don't want to hear what Mother will say."

His father was surprised by his firmness. "By God," he observed, "you must be in love with her."

Artie nodded.

Twelve

After the movies, a Jean Harlow revival, Thackeray dropped by to see some friends, two young men who shared an apartment on the East Side. One of them came to let him in and took his coat.

"New?" he asked, holding it up by its mouse-colored velvet collar.

"Why yes. I never wear the same topcoat two seasons."

"Nice."

"Who is it?" called the roommate from the bedroom.

"It's the African Violet."

"Do tell. I'll be right out."

While he waited for his drink to be mixed, Thackeray wandered over to the window that looked across the side street onto another apartment building. The neighborhood wasn't very far from Maule's house, only a few blocks up-town and an avenue or two over. It was worlds less fashionable, however, though climbing out.

"What are these doing here?" he asked, lifting up a pair of field glasses.

"To look into the windows across the street, silly," said host number one, returning with the drinks.

Host number two now came in from the bedroom. He was dressed in a dark-green silk robe, with a comple-mentary red silk handkerchief in the breast pocket. On his head was a red wool nightcap. "Have you seen this?" he asked, pointing to it. "Christmas. From Charles."

They all sat down. "So what's new?" host number one asked.

"What a day," said Thackeray. "I'm exhausted."

"I didn't toil at all today," said host number two. "I telephoned in to the shop and said I had cramps." His sally was greeted with a good deal of laughter.

"I did," said host number one. "Like a demon. If *Leaf* ever opens on time, it'll be a miracle. By the way, a friend of yours asked after you today."

"I can guess who," said Thackeray.

"He wanted to know how often we saw you. He said you had him reduced to starvation rations. It's breaking his heart."

"He was getting so possessive," Thackeray replied archly. "I don't want to get involved. You know. How's it going to be, anyway?"

"What, my child?"

"*Leaf.*"

"Oh, it'll run for a while at least. At least that. The *Mirror* will like it; the *News* won't. The *Times* will say it is delightful and airy, about a more optimistic America, and a relief from the black despair that has marked so many serious productions of the season. The *Tribune* . . . let me see . . . The *Trib* will say that the cast is better than their vehicle. The *Post* will talk about the frivolity of late Edwardian society in America. The *New Yorker* will say, 'For the benefit of those who have the mentality of international chess champions, we will summarize the convolutions of what might, benevolently, be termed the plot. . . .' And so on."

"Is Philip good in it?"

"So you do care, after all. I'll tell him."

The telephone rang, and since it was a drunk friend calling from San Francisco, the two hosts went each to a separate telephone, one in the little foyer, and one in the bedroom. It promised to be a long conversation, so Thackeray switched off the lamp nearest the window, parted the draperies, then lifted the glasses and pushed them through an interstice in the Venetian blinds. One of his friends was nearsighted, it seemed, for Thackeray had to twist the knobs before he could see at all. Nearly all the windows in the apartment house across the street were dark, and among those that were not, most did not have a clear line of vision from where Thackeray was standing. But he began systematically to examine those with any promise, starting low and climbing. Suddenly he stopped.

"Well," he said softly. "*Well!*" He spied on, not noticing that the noisy conversation in the background was winding up with promises of transcontinental visits. "What in the world is he doing? And looking like that?"

He laughed softly. "My, my. Oh, for goodness sake," he said. "Oh, *no*. Yes, he *is*."

"Yes he is what?" said host number one, returning from the telephone.

"Here. Just look across the way into that window on about the eighth floor. You see?"

Host number one looked. "Oh, we've seen him before. He often forgets to draw his blinds. Isn't he hideous? An exhibitionist at least, though in a dull way. I suppose all artists are."

"He isn't an artist, not really. I know him," Thackeray said, exaggerating slightly. "Or at least he isn't a professional artist."

"What is he?"

"He's a restorer. We do business with him. He has his studio and office and things downtown, but he must live

71

over yonder. Here, give them back to me. I want to try to get a look at what he's doing."

"The glasses aren't strong enough to get much of an idea. Anyway, he's usually got his easel set so we can't see. But wait a minute and I'll get you our wee telescope. We've got everything."

When host number two came from the telephone, he found Thackeray still pressed to the window, but now holding a more powerful glass. He and his roommate watched Thackeray for a moment, then got bored. "Come back to the party," he said.

Thackeray didn't move or speak.

"Why, Charles, we've got a real Peeping Uncle Tom with us."

All three laughed, for here Thackeray was truly accepted as an equal, there being a community that quite transcended color; nevertheless, he didn't really think the remark was very funny.

Thirteen

Pearson Tait had always been a disciplined man, controlling his diet, his hours of sleep, his hours of work, his exercise, his relaxations, according to a plan and a schedule, slicing his day up like the statistical pie. He had worked hard to arrive where he had now arrived. Unlike almost everyone with whom he had to deal, he was not a worldling. Neither, on the other hand, was he precisely an ascetic, for his frugal outer and inner lives were not dedicated to any further end; they were, rather, the result of a feeling

72

he had about how he ought to be, and that was all. Put another way, as a method of containing that which he ought not to be, austerity had been successful. But there were signs that it was no longer working.

In fact, when, during the clean, pure, rational hours he spent in his laboratory and studio, he paused for a second to think about himself and the way he now spent his evenings, he was forced, as a scientist, to entertain the proposition that he was going mad.

At the same time, he considered it a good possibility that it would all pass. It seemed only likely, during those logical, clean daylight hours. But as night approached, and uneasiness uncurled inside his mind, yawned, stretched, blinked, and looked around, it didn't seem nearly so certain. Would he do it again? Or would he be able to resist?

After a simple dinner, whose calories he calculated without even thinking, he went to the same movie Thackeray went to, although Thackeray sat near the front of the house on principle and Pearson Tait sat in the rear, so they did not see one another. Thackeray took a long and leisurely route to his friends' apartment, with many stops to look in windows, so Tait, who left halfway through and walked directly and quickly home, arrived much sooner.

He went to his kitchen, drank a glass of milk, then returned to his living room, where he went through the mail that had come that day. There was a letter from his wife, from whom he had an amicable separation, postmarked from Tonga, the Friendly Islands. Mrs. Tait, a dedicated and also moderately affluent pteridophilist, was currently touring Polynesia and the Antipodes gathering specimens for her herbarium.

". . . Right outside my window at the guesthouse here is a fine specimen of *Adiantum capillus-veneris*, growing in a crevice on a wet shady wall, which is kept moist by some kind of seepage. I took one or two examples of the fronds. Of course one sees *Nephrolapsis hirsutula* almost everywhere on Tongatapu. It's a weed! The natives, who call it *laufale*, use parts of it for making different kinds of medicines. I have done most of the gathering I plan to do on this island, but I have arranged for transportation to 'Eua, which is a few miles away, is volcanic not coral, and has more forests left. I hope for rich harvests on 'Eua. . . ."

Tait put the letter down without reading it through, but not before it had evoked, in his normally none-too-active imagination, the image of a stout woman with metal-rimmed glasses, straggly hair, and very red elbows, slogging through marshes, one hand steadying the specimen box slung over a shoulder, the other slapping mosquitoes. He would retaliate in a day or two with a letter to her about the technical problems of the paintings he was now working on, which he must render even less interesting to her by withholding, as confidential, all names involved.

He went to his bedroom and undressed, then to his bathroom, where he brushed his teeth and washed, then back to the bedroom, and so between the sheets. It was 10:39 by his bedside clock. Ideally, he would be asleep by 11:00 P.M. He manipulated his mind, smoothing all wrinkles from its surface, imagining it an area that he could then erase clean. If there was nothing on it, he would be asleep.

It almost worked.

Unfortunately, just about eleven, his eyes suddenly widened, and his hands began to tremble ever so slightly, then to close and open, finally, unquestionably, to twitch. Beneath the light cover he used, even in the cold weather, his toes wriggled. Then his knees commenced to knock together, his belly to convulse like that of a man with hiccups, his breath to come in little gasps, his jaw to work, his eyes to roll, and his brows and scalp to jerk.

A hoarse, tortured whisper, "Let come what may." And he got out of bed.

Reaching out to steady himself from moment to moment, he left his bedroom, tottered down the hall, and came at last to two chambers that were kept under triple lock. He opened the door, after some false tries with wrong keys, and went inside. The first room was fitted up as a home laboratory, where in the past it had sometimes been his habit, since his wife had left him and vacated these rooms, to work in the evenings or on weekends. He went to a table where chemicals sat in their bottles, put a chunk of this and a pinch of that into a beaker, emulsified them in a generous splash of ethyl alcohol, added distilled water, took a deep breath, closed his eyes, tilted his massive, neckless head back on his shoulders, and drank.

His nerves quieted immediately, for now there was no turning back.

He went to a closet, where he passed by the white smock that hung there and dug on until he found a pair of black trousers of an archaic cut, pegged so much that he had to remove his slippers and push and twist his feet to get them through the bottoms. Then he took off his pajama tops and donned a shirt that had ruffles down the front and loose sleeves caught up at the wrists, which fitted oddly over his heavy shoulders and long arms. Finally, he reached to a shelf and found a velvet beret, which he put on his head. One would not have been surprised had there come a gentle knock on the door, and lo! Mimi.

When he was thus dressed, he went to a wall safe, opened it, and took from it a notebook, whose backstrip bore the title *Parodies*. He turned to a fresh page, sat at a small stainless-steel table, which was the nearest thing to a desk contained within his laboratory, and began to write. He headed the page "One of Life's Terrible Ironies." Then, indenting by a third of a line, he began:

"Today I was called to the offices of Edward Maule to see an important new painting he had just acquired and is going to offer for sale. I had a premonition from the time he telephoned, just from what he hinted to me. I was almost sure. Still, what a shock it was, when he took me upstairs and showed me his new 'Watteau,' depicting *a fete in the park of a country house.* (He calls it *Les Agrémens de l'Esté.*) Naturally, I concealed my feelings as well as I could, and proceeded to submit the painting to a suitable examination. . . ."

He wrote on for several paragraphs, then, with a flourish, terminated the entry, replaced the notebook, and from a cabinet took a palette. He put pigments on it, clutched some brushes with his free hand, and went into the next room, which was fitted up as a studio. Built into the wall was a storage rack for pictures, one half of which was sealed off and shut with heavy metal doors and another lock. He opened it. There were several canvases inside, which he stared at, his eyes now glittering strangely, his manner grotesquely different from that of daylight's Dr. Tait. He trembled now from a compelling inspiration. Now he was a man filled with a divine afflatus.

He pulled a certain canvas from the racks, placed it on an easel, and stood back. He moved forward. Back again. Forward again. He squinted. He turned his head to and fro. Then, with a sudden, imperious gesture, he plunged one of his brushes into a blob of pigment on his palette, raised its tip into the air, pointing it like an épée, and waltzed forward to the attack.

76

PART TWO

Monday,
a Week Later

One

Matthew McCaffrey handed the letter from Maule to the tall and lanky man in dark business clothes who had just come into the office. Will Nesbitt, McCaffrey's brother-in-law, a little horse-faced, like McCaffrey's wife, sank as comfortably as was possible into one of the Institutional Modern chairs, the style in which the office had been done over several years before, when McCaffrey was elevated to Director. He read carefully, for he was an attorney:

" 'Dear Matt, I wanted to write and tell you what a pleasure it was to see you last week, and to meet the new president of your board of trustees, Barney Kant.

" 'While it is virtually impossible these days to keep anything of quality on hand, I have one or two things that might do for your opening in the fall, which I could probably hold through that time, or sell only with the provision that they appear at your exhibition. Stop by next time you are in New York and we can discuss the matter further. Better still, plan to lunch or dine with me.

" 'Incidentally, Tait has finished removing the old varnish from the Watteau, and it seems to be, as it looked before cleaning, in miraculous condition. A few local scratches, and one little area perhaps half an inch in diameter, in an unimportant passage, where the paint film was damaged at some time. All the infrareds, X rays, etc., that Tait has done bear out what I say above. I'm sending you photographs under separate cover.

" 'Looking forward to hearing from you and to seeing you soon, I am, with best regards,

Sincerely yours,
Edward Maule' "

"A hint," said McCaffrey. "A prod. A nudge. He wants to know whether or not we're making any progress with Barney." He took the letter back. "The price won't have come down since the picture was cleaned, not if its condition is all that good."

"Did the photographs come?" Nesbitt asked.

McCaffrey nodded. "Pretorius has them." Suddenly he struck his forehead with the palm of his hand. "My God, Will, I'm getting feeble-minded. I think I have the telephone number of the mysterious owner of this picture, whoever he is. Now, what in hell did I do with it?" He thought back. "It must still be in that suit pocket, whichever one it was." And he tried to remember.

"What are you talking about? Where did you get it? I thought Maule was being so secretive."

McCaffrey explained, looking as guilty as a college boy caught stealing a kiss from someone else's date.

Nesbitt made a face. "Not too savory. Still . . ." He looked at McCaffrey curiously. "How in the world could you forget a thing like that?"

"Guilt, maybe. A parapraxis," McCaffrey answered. "The next thing is to find out if I still have it." He telephoned his house and asked to speak to his wife. "Chickie," he said, when she was on the line, "this is very important." Mrs. McCaffrey's real name was Cynthia, but to all her intimates she was Chickie, and had been since birth. "Do you remember the suits I took to New York last week?" He waited. "Good. Go through their pockets, would you, and see if you can find a little slip of paper with a telephone number on it. I'll hold on here." He dropped the mouthpiece away from his lips and spoke to Nesbitt. "The real reason I forgot is Barney, if you want to know. What a trip! The old grasshopper was something. I had to fight off call girls until four in the morning the night after I swiped this telephone number. I hope he and I don't have to travel together very much. I'm getting too old for Barney. If only his tastes were somehow surreptitious, like for red boots or Puerto Rican boys, so he'd have to leave the hotel suite, it wouldn't be so bad. But dizzy blondes . . ." He interrupted himself to listen once more to his wife, then picked up a pencil and wrote on a pad of paper.

"Chickie, my love, this is wonderful. It took real genius for you to guess not to send that suit out. I know. Will is with me right now, and he's already told me it's fixed up for tonight." He shot a quick glance at his brother-in-law, then said, "Now, darling, do be good and take it easy before we go out tonight. Right? Right."

He replaced the receiver. "She says Genevieve called to say that she's got Barney and some single woman for him for dinner. You tell Gen to be sure to take the ladies out after dessert and leave us to talk for a while, won't you?"

Will nodded. "She knows that much. She was going to be sure not to get an attractive woman to fill out, either, so Barney wouldn't get sidetracked." Casually, he added, "Chickie been all right?"

"I guess," McCaffrey replied. He looked at the telephone number written on his pad. "There's our clue, Will," he said. "Just for the hell of it, why don't I dial it direct? See who or what he is. If it's embarrassing, I can always hang up without speaking. Funny exchange. I don't recognize it." He waited, but legal counsel raised no objections. He dialed.

The relays clicked and twittered. In a moment, a female voice began to speak from the faraway city of New York, and a strange expression came over McCaffrey's face as he listened. He held the receiver out so that Will Nesbitt could hear, too.

". . . forecast for New York and vicinity. One o'clock temperature, thirty-nine degrees, relative humidity, seventy-one per cent. Winds from the northeast, five to ten miles an hour. Cloudy today, with highs in the mid-forties. Partly cloudy tonight, low about thirty in the city, to twenty-five in the suburbs. Tomorrow, partly cloudy, little change in temperature. This is the latest weather-bureau forecast for New York and vicinity. One o'clock temperature, thirty-nine degrees, relative . . ."

"That old pirate," McCaffrey said, laughing as he once more replaced his receiver.

"But why?" Nesbitt asked. "What is his game?"

"More innocent than it looks, I suspect. An elegant variation on the selling game. It can't be any real skulduggery. Maule's too reputable. He may be giving himself room to maneuver." He thought a moment. "You know, Will, this, in addition to his letter, begins to worry me. If there is no mysterious owner . . ."

"Which we don't know. We know only that he didn't talk to him the day you were in his office."

"Yes, well, in either case, I think Edward wants word from us." He picked up the letter. "Three paragraphs. Barney in the first, our opening in the second, his superb painting in the third." He tucked the piece of paper with the telephone number on it into the corner of his blotter. "I'll hang on to this. I don't know what it means, but it might be useful." He grinned at Nesbitt. "If Maule starts to dodge, we just might be able to use this to make him stumble." He looked at his watch—lunchtime. He stood up. "In any case, Will, no matter what he's trying to do, it's money that's going to talk," he concluded.

"It usually does," Nesbitt observed, following him from the office.

Forty-five minutes later they emerged from the executive lunchrooms of the museum, and McCaffrey led the way down a corridor. "Let's stop by Pretorius's office and have a look at the photographs of the Watteau, and hear what he has to say. Ammunition against Barney tonight." He lowered his voice. "We'll claim you have a prior engagement, Will; otherwise he'll wander on all afternoon."

Inside his office, Dr. Ulrich Pretorius was looking at the photographs of the Watteau, as he had been doing ever since McCaffrey had given them to him that morning. His words than had been, "I think it's a masterpiece, Ulrich, but it's up to you to see that my eye hasn't been led astray."

Dr. Pretorius was known as an Assistant to the Director, and was on the staff to provide such scholarly underpinnings as the museum needed. In the opinion of Dr. Pretorius, his Director had no eye to be led astray. In the opinion of Dr. Pretorius, only Europeans, and mostly only Germans at that, had eyes. And only Germans had both eyes and the ability to investigate what they saw scientifically. Dr. Pretorius recognized these facts, but as a humble man; for he also knew that while he could investigate, he could never make up his mind, hence he was where he ought to be in life and, homesick though he often was, perhaps even in geography—a place where what he could do was of value.

"You know my brother-in-law, Mr. Nesbitt, don't you, Ulrich?" McCaffrey said as the two men came into the office. It was a long, narrow room, almost inconceivably cluttered, in a traditional manner, with books and file cards and photographs. "Will here is a little pressed for time, but he wanted to hear what you've got to say about the Watteau." He winked at the learned doctor. "We're all dining tonight with Mr. Kant," he explained.

"So. So." Dr. Pretorius was very dark, about fifty, with thick hair and a very nervous manner. Through his mind flickered the thought that he had not dined with the McCaffreys in two years. "Well, where should I begin, Matt?" He waved at the spread of photographs over his worktable. "That is the painting as it is now, Mr. Nesbitt. And that is the ultraviolet, that the infrared. There are photographs of the X rays." He turned to McCaffrey. "They didn't X ray the entire painting. Often it is not done, but it is strange, considering Tait is cleaning it. However, perhaps he thought there was no point. You see the pentimenti here, where the artist changed his mind and had the young man put out an arm to the lady, instead of holding his hat, and then moved her to the left—I should think. One cannot be entirely sure. It is difficult to read."

Dutifully, Will Nesbitt bent his long body over the photographs. "Looks very nice," he said at last. "You think there's no doubt about it, Dr. Pretorius?"

Dr. Pretorius wagged his tousled head. "Well, of course, we do not have absolutely complete photographs of the painting since cleaning."

"You read Maule's letter, too," McCaffrey said. "He wouldn't lie."

"No, no. I suppose not," Pretorius admitted.

"So barring something unexpected," Nesbitt pursued, "there is no reasonable doubt about it."

"For such a picture, the pedigree is good."

Nesbitt straightened up, for with words and their implications he was more at home than he could be with photographs and what they stood for. "May I ask what you mean by your phrase, 'for such a picture'?"

Pretorius shifted on his feet. "I don't know. I . . . Let us say that its antecedents are informal. And it appeared, so! out of the blue. Still, it, or something like it, appears in the auction catalogues. But you understand, there can always be a question—is this the picture mentioned in the catalogues? Very probably. Yes, I feel safe in saying that much. Very probably."

Nesbitt looked at McCaffrey, who said smoothly, "But I believe there is more evidence than that."

Pretorius was pleased to elaborate, for scientific scholarship, as its scope enlarged, had a reassuring way of both clarifying and obscuring, often leading inevitably to no possible conclusion at all. "Yes, I am glad you mention it. An engraving of the painting, in reverse—that is usually the case, although not invariably—appears in the book published shortly after Watteau's death, which collected prints after his paintings. This picture appears there, engraved, probably by the Comte de Caylus, who was a noted *amateur* and also an engraver, although he was from the highest nobility, and under the old king, his mother had . . ."

"Yes, Ulrich. Yes, yes." McCaffrey looked at the clock on the wall.

"Or, let me put it more accurately. A picture identical to this one appeared in the collection, more or less identical. The plate is, after all, an engraving, the picture an oil, so one cannot speak of complete identity, you understand. Also, engravers take little liberties, sometimes, one suspects, quite unconsciously. They think to improve, they . . ."

"If I understand you, all that should make it virtually certain," Nesbitt said.

"Yes. It would. If we could prove that the painting from which the engraver took his plate is the painting that Tait now has."

"And why doubt that?"

Pretorius, his manner becoming more agitated, said, "But you must remember, Mr. Nesbitt, that a painting can be copied—by pupils, by followers. Also, an engraving can be copied. A forger might copy an engraving. Now, do we have *the* original, or do we have a copy after it?"

"That is, I believe, in essence, the question I am asking you."

"Well, you know, I don't like—I really couldn't say anything so much for sure at this point."

McCaffrey frowned. In spite of good resolutions, these conversations with Pretorius almost always ended by bringing out the commanding officer in him. "Ulrich," he said, in a tone of voice that brought his assistant's head around with a jerk, "Will and I have to face Barney tonight. You understand that. And we have to try to persuade him to put a lot of money into this painting, more than we have ever spent on a painting before. We must move fast. I have just . . . I believe Maule wants our offer. We must know whether or not to go ahead."

Pretorius breathed heavily. His eyes shifted.

"For God's sake, Ulrich. Just say yes or no. Nothing else will do."

Pretorius swallowed. At length, his voice constricted, he muttered, "I really . . . I really . . . I really . . ."

"Yes or no, Ulrich," McCaffrey said, raising his voice to a level far beyond the impolite.

Tears came into the scholar's eyes, for he knew that the rebuke, though unfair, was deserved; the demand, though impossible, was justified. He nodded his head.

"Good. Sorry to shout, old man, but sometimes you do need a little prodding to help you along." McCaffrey, his own amiable, boyish self again, clapped Pretorius on the shoulder. "Let us know if you ferret out anything interesting. Come along, Will, and see how the construction is going."

Outside the office the two men exchanged a look, but neither commented on Dr. Pretorius and his learned observations. Better to leave things where they were, at that nod of the head, with no more talk.

They walked the length of the museum, then out a side door and under a canvas canopy put up by the workmen who were erecting the new wing, thence into the gutless carcass of a hallway, where McCaffrey spoke to a foreman, and so on into the heart of the building. Nothing was finished. Wherever they looked there was raw concrete, steel reinforcing rods projecting like spines from its mottled surfaces, and a litter of dust, rubble, hoops of wire, broken light bulbs, piles of tiling and soundproofing material. Chaos.

"God, but this is depressing," Nesbitt said. "I can't believe it will ever get finished in time."

"They assure me that it's ahead of schedule. I no longer even think about it," McCaffrey replied.

They picked their way onward. "I saw Stu Adams over the weekend," Nesbitt observed, bending his long body almost at a right angle to get under some timbers. "He kidded me about Barney and how little he's done for the museum so far."

"Sour grapes."

"Maybe. But true. I don't know what it's all about, Matt, but Barney's in even worse odor downtown these days than usual. He must have taken away a lot of people's money somehow—I mean the wrong people. We don't hear much, in our offices. Anyway, Pierce is down on him, too."

"Stu Adams's family hasn't given this museum fifty thousand dollars all told since it was founded, and we're trying to nail Barney for fifteen times that, just for one little picture."

"I know, I know. Still, he hasn't come across, and I don't much like the way he's fooling around. Chickie said we'd never get anything out of him. Maybe she was right."

"Chickie thinks like Stu Adams, even if she is my wife and your sister," McCaffrey answered.

Nesbitt smiled. "There's some truth in that, if you concede in the first place that what goes on in Stu's head can be called thought."

They came into a large area with a slanted floor. "Now then, let me explain what they've done with the new auditorium so far, Will. That's the stuff that's going to be flooring, over there in piles. A sample stick of seats here. That goes on the walls and ceilings—accoustically ideal, they claim. The exit lights are going to be very fancy. Guaranteed not to shine in anybody's eyes."

"That suits me just fine," Nesbitt said. "The better to sleep by."

He stayed another few minutes to humor McCaffrey, then went back to his law office, glad to return to such a forthright occupation.

Two

Ursula Cariatis and Artie van Zandt were having lunch together again, in a restaurant where they were almost certain not to be seen, for Artie had asked for a very private talk. They were both struggling with veal shanks in Yorkville, and displacing, from time to time, mounds of red cabbage.

"Where did you ever hear of here?" Ursula asked. "It's of a supreme repulsion, Artie. Truly divine."

"I used to come here when I was in college," he replied. "I thought of it because it's out of the way and also near your appointment."

"That reminds me. I have to telephone about two o'clock to make sure. He said he might have to cancel today. For the first time. I nearly died or cried or something. He wheezed and coughed all through my hour on Friday. If I catch it from him, I'm going to make him treat me for nothing."

Artie laughed, high and hopelessly. "He'd say you caught it on purpose. That you wanted to bear his baby or something, and since you couldn't receive his seed in fact, you did it symbolically. His germs."

"Well, I don't," Ursula replied, giving up on her shank. "Not any more."

"I wonder if I want mine to bear mine," Artie mused.

"It's all mixed up with incest," Ursula said, not much to the immediate point.

"Speaking of incest, Mother's still in a terrible flap. She

won't speak to me, and I refuse to give in. She's started to refer to me as Arthur. I had a dream last night about it, and this morning it came out that I have terrible anxiety because it means that she is now identifying me with Father, and I'm guilty because I know that's what I ought to be doing myself. It's a fresh approach to castration anxiety. She calls him Arthur, too, you see."

"How do you know now which she means?"

"She doesn't talk to me. She talks to him about me. You can tell—with Mother."

"Consciously, you mean."

He nodded. Then he said, very seriously, "Ursula, I want out. I've been thinking over and over about what you said last week, and I don't think it really matters. Sometime we've both got to do something, even if it's not much. Won't you marry me?"

Ursula shook her dark head.

He, too, gave up on his veal shank. "Ursula, do you or don't you love me? I mean, within your limitations?"

"Within my limitations? I'll have to think about that, Artie," she replied slowly. "I'll take it up this afternoon, if he's there."

"Try to take it up right now," Artie said, a little sharply. "I'm proposing to you."

Ursula looked at him, hurt.

"I must admit I talked to mine about it this morning, and she finally said, 'Why don't you ask her?' I had the funniest feeling that she was bored."

"That's not very orthodox," Ursula said. "Interfering."

"I'm grateful for anything."

Suddenly tears came into Ursula's eyes. "Life is so *foul*, Artie. I *think* I love you, but I'm too mixed up to know. And the fact that I think I do makes me not want to, and knowing *that,* I think I ought to, and I know that thinking I *ought* to do anything will double back on itself, and I just don't know, in the end, at all."

"Ursula, I think we've got to hold our noses and jump."

"I know you do, Artie. But what if the water's been drained out?"

"A jump's a jump, for all that."

"So's a broken ankle," she answered.

They waited for their coffee. Then he said, "Ursula, I've also been thinking. Would you compromise? I mean, maybe if we just tried it out for a night, it would clear the air."

"Artie, how trite!" she exclaimed. "Like taking a trip when you're going to have a florid schizophrenic break-down."

"Mine once said a person had to have the courage of his conventions," Artie said.

"She sounds awfully verbal to me."

"You haven't answered my question."

"When? Where?"

"Tonight. Tomorrow. Any time. A hotel. Or we could drive out of town."

"I can't tonight. I'm going to the opening of *Green Leaf, Yellow Leaf.* With father and his new mistress. It's going to be awful. I haven't met her yet, and I know she'll be awful. They always are. They always are so *enormous* here." She pointed.

"Then tomorrow."

"I don't know. I don't know. This could be serious."

"I should think so." He reached for her hand. "Please, Ursula."

She drew it away. "I don't *think* I will, but I might. You telephone me tomorrow in the late afternoon, and I promise to have made up my mind. That will give me two hours to analyze what I feel. Which reminds me . . ." She checked the time. "I've got to call him right now. He said he'd leave a message with his answering service."

She got up and made her way to the telephone at the back end of the restaurant. A few seconds later, a middle-aged man with black jowls left the beer he had been nursing at the table right behind the young couple, put on a fedora, took his topcoat in hand, and followed her. He stood looking for a number in the directory, where he could overhear her conversation clearly through the wall of the booth.

"This is Miss Cariatis calling. Cariatis. Yes, C-a-r-i-a-t-i-s. Did Dr. Pond leave a message for me? He did. Same time as usual. Oh, thank you."

Ursula returned to the table, drank her coffee, then she and Artie left the restaurant together. The middle-aged man, who had gone to the bar for another glass of beer, saw them put on their coats and followed them out. When they separated, he trailed Artie, first into a bookstore, where Artie bought two primers on sex, blushing when he paid for them, then on a taxi ride. After Artie entered the van Zandts' apartment house, the stranger, in his turn, went to a telephone and called in.

Three

When Arthur van Zandt called to see Edward Maule, he did not have quite the brusqueness of the Monday before, nor was Maule quite so urbane, for each was older by the preceding week.

"I've just come from Tait's place—thanks for arranging

it for me. I saw the Watteau. Superb. First-rate condition."

Maule was gratified and said so.

"I can't stand that man, though."

"Everybody uses him nowadays."

"I know. Just the way everybody once had to have high-colonic irrigations. But he's never touched a thing of mine, and he never will. He hasn't got any feelings, and I don't give a damn for all the science. A picture wasn't painted by a chemist in the first place, and it shouldn't be restored by one." Van Zandt thrust his huge feet forward and slumped down into his chair. "Now let's talk business."

"I wonder if we should," Maule said.

Van Zandt ignored the remark. "See here, I've got to have your Watteau, no matter what. I've been thinking out ways and means. I can't give you a check for the whole thing today, but I can give you a check right now for fifty thousand, and the balance later. I've got to have that picture. I've thought of nothing else. I've looked at what Watteaus I could get to, photographs of others. It's a major work, absolutely major. No more important French picture has come on the market in years. It may be that none will ever come on again. I've got the best collection of the period still in private hands. The painting must be mine." He drew his feet back, stood up, and, putting a hand on either side of the desk, leaned over toward Maule. "How much?"

"I am unable to make a definite commitment."

"I should think I could get it for five hundred thousand."

Maule was disturbed by the figure. He lifted an eyebrow. "It's certainly worth more than that."

"It is, if you can get more. If you can't, then it isn't."

"What makes you think I can't."

"I'm no fool, Edward. I've checked into it, as much as I

could. There are lacunae in the provenance, especially recently. An immediate source you either can't or won't divulge. The museums may shy away from it—they don't want repercussions. I buy on the basis of my instincts, and they tell me it's worth half a million, and that's to a poor man like myself. But you keep playing footsie, and you'll end by selling it to some Texan for three hundred thousand."

Maule smiled. "Our Texan friends are so rich."

"They are, but they don't know the value of their money. Ha!" Van Zandt laughed harshly. "Now tell me who else is interested."

"You can hardly expect me to be that indiscreet."

"Why not? Edward, I've bought lots of stuff off you in the past. You owe me this picture. I should think you'd want to see it in my collection; you're not just a hawker, like the others."

"Perhaps it should go to a new man, just starting. One has to think of the future," Maule suggested, scrubbing a mustache.

Van Zandt was not amused. "There's none too much of that, I think," he said, "for you or for me." He paused, then said, "Well?"

It was true that van Zandt's collection was, in a way, the right place for the picture; but there was that new wing and that grand opening—reporters, the great world gathered together, full color in *Life*. Also the Kant bank account. "Another buyer has priority, Arthur. I'll be frank with you: if he should not want it, then perhaps . . . But a bit more than five hundred thousand, I should think."

"I saw it first."

"Only a technical point, Arthur, as you know."

"Is it Cariatis, God damn it?" van Zandt demanded, veering off.

"No."

"I'm glad of that." Van Zandt walked about, putting his hand on the head of the bronze Bacchus as he passed it. "That would rankle."

"The famous enemies."

"With reason. You know, when he began to buy things, he bought a couple of fine Saint-Aubin drawings right out from under me. Then he took a Hubert Robert away from me at auction. It was the night after I heard that that I saw him at some charity thing my wife made me go to, and I was drunk, you know, and angry, and I called him an oily little Greek in my usual tone of voice. Lots of people heard. He didn't like it."

"One can hardly blame him."

"Well, that's what he is. But that's beside the point. What I really didn't like was the way he was collecting. He was buying just because he had the money to pay. It takes the money, but if that's all you've got, then why not stick to the nineteenth- and twentieth-century stuff, the way others like yourself do? Why encroach on my territory? I don't mind rich fools spending money on Impressionists or the latest thing from some loft downtown. Somebody's got to buy that crap. But the Hubert Robert was lovely, and it matched a set of three I already owned—views of Tivoli. I'd waited twelve years for it to come up for sale. Guess where it is now?"

Maule shook his head.

"He gave it to some tart he was keeping, and she's taken it to her spider-ridden dump of a villa at Antibes, where she's retired, I suppose to die slowly of venereal disease.

I've tried to get it from her, but he tied it up. He gave it to her, but with the proviso that she can't sell it to anyone but him. Not to me, in other words. The greasy little head-waiter."

"Cariatis is interested," Maule put in.

"Probably for that French bitch he's seeing now."

"You seem to know a lot about him."

"I keep my ears open. Sometimes a man learns something useful. I think she was the one with him the other day when I bumped into him in your elevator. I should think she could take on two of him and sing the *Marseillaise* at the same time."

Maule laughed. "The lady would never sing that song. You seem uncommonly uncharitable today, Arthur."

Van Zandt passed a hand over his eyes. "Quite right. I've had a lot on my mind. Why live if you can't get what you most want? Why be charitable? Not many people really ever want anything the way I want that picture of yours."

"I believe that is true," Maule said, growing uncomfortable.

Van Zandt scowled. He stood in front of the Magnasco, his back to the dealer. "I'm going to be unfair, but again, why not? Let me tell you something. Do you know the story that that rascal Loménie de Brienne tells about Cardinal Mazarin? About the time he overheard the old sinner, just before he died, talking to himself as he walked through his gallery. Brienne was behind a curtain or something. First Mazarin stopped at a tapestry—after Giulio Romano, I think—and after looking at it said, 'I must leave all that. I must leave all that.' Up and down through that magnificent collection of his the old Cardinal went, barely able to walk, you know, but not wanting to leave it. Then he saw Brienne and asked him what he wanted, and when Brienne said he had some business to take up with the Cardinal, he was told to take it to the king, that Mazarin had other things to think about. Then, looking around again at his Titians and Correggios and all the rest, Mazarin said, 'Farewell, my beloved paintings, that I have loved so much and that cost me so dear.' Think of that, Edward. There was a collector for you. I suppose you're thinking though: well, what does it come to in the end? Nothing at all." Still van Zandt did not turn around.

There was a prolonged silence, while Maule considered the implications of the anecdote.

"I don't suppose I have to spell my meaning out."

Maule said nothing. He found himself, for some reason, not even thinking about van Zandt any more, but about the question: what does it come to in the end? One went on and on, and finally had one's heart methodically broken by some unworthy little Philip who doesn't ask one to come to his opening night.

Van Zandt finally turned, solemnly, his voice now very low and unlike him. "Suppose I handed you a check for— let us say six hundred thousand right now. And I said, there, Edward, now have Tait deliver the picture to me tomorrow. What then?"

"But you haven't, Arthur."

"I know. But it would make a difference, wouldn't it?"

Maule shrugged.

"Of course it would. There you are. Other reasons are fine, but the price has to be there, too. I know that. Christ, I'm tired. I'd better go or I'll sit down and fall asleep in your chair. I wouldn't want you to know what I'm saying in my sleep these days, either."

Maule was relieved. The van Zandt of this Monday was too difficult. "Are you planning murder?" he asked lightly.

"Not a bad idea."

"I'll warn poor Cariatis."

"Ha!" Again the harsh laugh. "Don't bother. He's safe."

Four

Out in a different time zone, the Nesbitts, the McCaffreys, Barney Kant, and a woman called Eugenie sat down to dinner. Her only topic of conversation seemed to be a jellyfish she had encountered in Florida several weeks before.

Well, at least Barney Kant was safe, Genevieve Nesbitt thought. "Is Mrs. Kant in Florida?" she asked him.

He popped an oyster into his mouth. "Naw. She's out west. Drier."

Chickie McCaffrey had been touching her fingers to the fringes of her hair. Suddenly she said, "Everybody seems to go west now instead of to Florida. Genevieve, when we were girls together, nobody went west at all, did they? I mean, really nobody went west, not in the winter. Did they, Genevieve?"

Chickie was already tight, Genevieve thought to herself, and soon would be plastered. A flicker of anger stirred within her at being brought so close to the problem; for now Chickie would start being rude to Barney Kant, and it would be up to her, Genevieve, to keep her sister-in-law under control. She ignored Chickie and spoke again to Kant.

"Mrs. McCaffrey and I went to the same school, and our families always had us down during Easter vacation. It is true, going west for the winter is relatively new. I'm sure it is delightful. I cling to Florida only through habit." She looked quickly around her table—Barney and Eugenie, outsiders. She, Chickie, and Will, real family. And poor Matt . . .

"I did look into Arizona when I had my cold last month," she went on. "Is Mrs. Kant in Arizona?"

"Thereabouts," he said. He wiggled his neck around in his collar and grinned. "She's learning to ride a horse."

"How nice."

"Nice? At her age? I think it's dumb, Mrs. Nesbitt."

"You're probably right. I learned as a child. I'd certainly never attempt to learn at my age."

"And you've still got the figure for it. Sally hasn't."

Did he wink?

" 'Sally in our alley,' " hummed Chickie.

Genevieve exchanged looks with Matt.

"We toured the new wing this afternoon, Barney," Will said, cutting across Eugenie to speak to the important guest. "Coming along fine, I should say."

"Matt's going to let me decorate the ladies' rooms," said Chickie.

"Now, Chickie," Matt said.

"A ladies' room should have a lady's touch, don't you think so, Mr. Kant?"

"Sure. And a bar ought to have a man's."

Chickie blinked, as did Matt. Will smiled ever so slightly, and Genevieve began to regret the entire dinner.

Chickie went on. "I want all the fixtures to be gold-plated. Wherever did you find the amazing ones in your house, Mr. Kant?"

"You mean the ones in the fancy powder room downstairs?"

Genevieve held her breath. The last time they had been together in that pink ruffled chamber, Chickie, who had been drunk then, too, had remarked that it was like peeing in a petticoat. Would she say it again now?

Chickie had forgotten. "That's the one. Those fixtures are so—so what? I don't know. I guess, so unbelievable."

Barney grinned. "Well, now, the decorator told me he bought those off the contractor who tore down your grandfather's town house, Mrs. McCaffrey."

Genevieve sighed and looked at Matt. Sweet Matt . . . Something would have to be done. It was just too often now. In any case, it would soon be time for the ladies to withdraw, and she might be able to suppress Chickie.

And soon it was.

Left to themselves, the men could settle down more comfortably. Barney took off his coat, with his host's permission, for it was hot in the Nesbitts' dining room, where a wood fire burned near the back of Barney's chair.

"I got a lot of photographs this morning from Maule," McCaffrey said. "Of the painting we saw. He sent a note, too. Said he'd be glad to lend to our fall opening. Put it in writing, which is nice. And he talked about what good condition that picture was in."

Barney turned to Nesbitt. "You're a businessman, or at least a lawyer, Will," he said. "What would you say to a man who wanted to sell you something but wouldn't say how much he wanted for it?"

"I'd probably make him an offer."

Barney grunted. "So would I—if I knew what I was buying."

"We're pretty sure about that, Barney," McCaffrey said. "I've had Pretorius working on it. You know how he is, but I pinned him down this afternoon. He's one hundred per cent behind the picture. Thinks there's no doubt about it."

"For that price I should hope not."

"You never know, that's all. You've got to be careful."

Will Nesbitt said, "Maule did give you some idea of a price, then, didn't he?"

"I guess that's what you'd call it—an idea. He said a figure 'well in excess of six hundred thousand.'" Barney poured himself more brandy. "That would be the income on about fourteen million dollars of endowment, if the museum had it. A lot of money."

"Good paintings aren't cheap," McCaffrey said.

Barney guffawed. "Not if you're paying for them."

"It's a painting I'd like to buy for myself," McCaffrey said.

Nesbitt said, "Only one man connected with the museum has enough to buy that picture. You, Barney."

"Me?" Barney grinned. "That's true. I've got enough. I don't know if I'm the only one."

"I mentioned it to Stu Adams. Nothing doing."

"Adams couldn't buy it right now if he sold everything including his cuff links and the pin holding up his diapers," Barney said.

"Possibly. But he's got a vote on the board."

"So have you," Barney said, still smiling.

"One."

"Meaning?"

Nesbitt shrugged. "If there's one man I know smart enough so I don't have to fill in outlines, it's you, Barney."

"Well," Barney said, still smiling, "it's nothing I didn't know when I took the position. Still, there's a question. Is this the right picture?"

"I think it is," McCaffrey said.

"We have to be guided by the experts," said Nesbitt.

Barney thought a moment. Then he said, "I tell you what I'll do. I'm going to be in New York again on Wednesday. Matt, you telephone that Maule fellah tomorrow morning and tell him I'll be in to see him. To negotiate, you understand. To negotiate."

"I'll tell him exactly that," Matt said.

"Fair enough," Nesbitt said. "Now I think we ought to rejoin our ladies."

McCaffrey raised his brandy glass and finished off the contents. "To the ladies, God bless 'em."

Barney said, "Yeah? Not that Eugenie. I wonder where the jellyfish nailed her. Any more brandy and I'd probably ask." As they went to the door he said, "Well, it isn't the first time I thought I was invited for dinner and had it turn out that I was the one who had to pay. I'll say one thing for the scale you do things on, Will: the tab's never been quite this big before."

Five

If dinner lasts one more second, I'll scream right out in the restaurant, Ursula thought to herself. She *is* simply awful, although she looks beautiful, and those little white orchids and French violets are pretty on her great big whoosis; and what's more, there's something funny about the way

Daddy acts around her. She's different in some way from the others. I've got to think how.

She occupied herself with the question while conversation limped on. Cariatis had planned the little dinner and theater party so that Angélique and Ursula could get acquainted. It was an ideal time, for dinner would have to be quick and early because of the opening night curtain, and if they all had to talk afterward, they could talk about the play. Unfortunately, the schedule had worked all too well, and they were left with dinner over and time still to pass.

"I saw a rather fine enamel at the dealer Edward Maule's place late this afternoon, Ursula," Cariatis said. "Ursula has a rather nice little collection of Byzantine enamels," he explained to Angélique.

"I should adore seeing them," Angélique replied, already bored.

It's so awful, Ursula thought. He's unhappy, and I'm unhappy, and I imagine she is unhappy, too. And I hate his little mustaches.

"It was Middle Byzantine," Cariatis went on. "Of Saint Gregory of Nazianzus, from the cover of a known manuscript of his sermons, probably, so Maule says, commissioned by Constantine Porphyrogennetos as a gesture to some monastery off down in Cilicia."

Angélique fanned herself with her hand. "*Oh, là là,*" she said. "How they make my head spin, all these barbaric names."

"I'm sure one of your rude ancestors helped sack Constantinople," replied little Cariatis, smiling slightly.

"It is true, *chéri!*" Angélique cried. "Have I not told you? It was my ancestor Childebert, who was called, as we were then, the Comte de la Tour Noire. He took a famous relic from one of your churches in 1204, brought it

103

home, and renamed his estates after it, so we became the Couronne d'Epines, and that is how. It was an object of veneration to all France; but alas! the cursed Protestants, when they marched up the Rhone Valley, captured both the relic and the poor curé, who had remained to harangue them and lead them from error. He was tormented, it is said, by being made to sit upon his own relic, which piety had long since sheathed in silver." She opened her purse and began to powder her nose.

"One does not forget those things," she added.

When, a few moments later, Ursula excused herself and went from the table, Angélique said, "She is an over-powering child, Theodore. So large. So voluptuous-look-ing, yet not. And as yet unmarried. I do not understand. Has she no gentlemen friends?"

"I believe not. One day I will choose her husband."

"And whom, then, does she see? Girl friends?"

"I don't think so."

"Then that is the trouble."

"I saw Maule again this afternoon, as I said. Still no de-cision."

Angélique sniffed. "You bargained with him," she said. "Remember, to bargain with him is to bargain with me, and I do not bargain."

"No. No, I didn't. I finally offered to let him set his own price. But I don't think he wants to sell me the painting."

"In that case our love affair will end before it begins."

"Marry me, Angélique," he said, desperately.

"This is no place to begin joking again, Theodore. We are in a public restaurant. An Italian restaurant, too."

"I'm not joking." Cariatis attempted to kiss her arm.

"It is no place to propose marriage. Anyway, you are

104

already married, for the third time. You are also a schismatic."

"I am separated. I will divorce my wife. We can have a civil ceremony."

"I am a Catholic," she replied proudly. "It is forbidden. If you obtain the Watteau, I will become your mistress, but I will never marry you. My Church understands weakness, but it will not forgive disobedience."

"Shhhh. Here is Ursula. How strangely she looks at us."

Ursula, as she returned to the table, had had an insight.

Angélique read aloud from her program. "Act One," she began, once they were seated, she on Cariatis's left, Ursula on his right. "The butler's pantry at Sickert's Hotel, Saratoga. Act Two, Wanda Sickert's bedroom. Act Three, the veranda at the Sickert. Act Four, Wanda Sickert's bedroom." She blew her breath out. "It is impossible," she cried. "What does it all mean?"

"The lights are going down," Cariatis muttered.

"How I detest the American theater. In France one can at least understand the jokes." She snapped on a little flashlight and reread the settings. "What is this Saratoga, Ursula?" she whispered, leaning around Cariatis.

"It's like Vichy," Ursula said.

The answer was inspired, for Angélique was silent thereafter through the entire first act.

When the curtain came down, Ursula said she had to telephone and ran up the aisle to reach the phone before there should be a line. She was the first there, and she called Artie, on the private number his mother had allowed him to have put in as his twenty-second birthday present.

"Artie," she said, without preliminaries, "I've already decided I will."

"Wonderful, Ursula." He wriggled so hard that the literature he was studying—his books bought that afternoon—scattered around him. "When? Tomorrow? I've been reading." He giggled. "It won't be so hard."

"I can't tomorrow. I promised to play bridge with Daddy."

"Couldn't you cancel?"

"It would look funny. Why not the day after? But where?"

"I've been thinking. I think a motel would be better. More traditional, somehow. Out of town, but not out of the state."

"But where?"

"I've thought about that, too. I think maybe Nyack."

"How awful. All right. When will you pick me up?"

"About seven o'clock. We'll have dinner, too. Ursula?"

"Yes. Hurry. I see them coming."

"I do love you, Ursula."

"I've got to run, Artie. And Artie?"

"Yes."

"This new one *is* awful. And do you know what I think? They don't do it. I just know they don't. I wonder if Daddy has become impotent."

Six

A very short while after the third act (The Sickert Veranda) began (Wanda Sickert, and Philip Dane as handsome summer help, acting together as if nothing had happened in Act Two), Henrietta van Zandt's telephone rang. She was half reclining on a firm couch in her sitting room, and she, too, was reading—a life of Thomas Hooker. She finished her sentence, placed a finger in the book, and reached for the telephone. Almost at once her book, too, dropped from her hand, and she took a pencil and paper. She made a note or two, asked several questions of Mr. Mulligan on the other end, thanked him, replaced the receiver, and burst into tears.

A singular occasion.

She then accused herself. Had she no inner strength? No light? Self-apostrophe was not uncommon in her inner dialogues. She dried her tears and began to think of what she might do.

Step number one, she decided, was to attempt to enlist her husband, no matter how offensive he would surely be. With him, now, she did have a lever, too. She rose, tidied herself, and went to the door of his library, where he usually stayed reading until quite late at night—he was a bad sleeper, obviously because he had a bad conscience. She knocked.

Inside, Arthur van Zandt put down his book and looked up at the clock, scowling. "Who the devil is that? Artie?"

"It is I. Henrietta."

"Well, it isn't locked."

She entered the dimly lighted room, where her huge husband lolled vulgarly in a leather armchair before a fire whose flickerings lent life to all the loathsome rococo that curled and twisted on hearth and mantelpiece, shelf and pedestal. She began to talk even before he could see her.

"We face a major family problem, Arthur. Else I would never have come here."

He waited until she was in view. "Any change could only be for the better," he said, hating her drab robe.

"Be serious, Arthur. It is a deadly serious matter."

"Nobody ever jokes. But go on."

She looked about for a suitable chair, but, aside from her husband's, they were all tapestried and carved, not to her taste. Finally she perched on the edge of one near him, a Poor Clare at Versailles.

"Our son is courting disaster," she said.

"Artie? I rather suspected he was courting, but I didn't know the girl's name."

"Arthur, I cannot endure your facetiousness."

"Nor I, Henrietta, your clichés."

"Let me be quick and factual, so that we can then talk and I can return to my room."

"Agreed. Let us be quick and factual. Above all, let us be quick."

"He has been seeing a woman who is . . . unacceptable. And now he has made plans for an assignation."

"How do you know this?"

"I have my sources, which I cannot disclose."

Van Zandt stared at her. "You wouldn't," he said. Slowly he shook his head. "Yes, I think you would. No one will stoop so low as the righteous."

"They are planning to go day after tomorrow to a . . ." Now that the word had to be said, Henrietta faltered. "To a motel, Arthur. Our son, to a—*motel*."

"Well? We live, after all, in a car culture."

"And to a motel . . ." She faltered again. "A motel in *Nyack*."

Van Zandt snorted. "That is a little odd, I agree. It would seem to indicate a deficient feeling for aesthetic consonance. Still, if you're going to a motel, I don't suppose it matters where it is. You don't go for the local society, or as far as that's concerned, for the general *mise en scène*, do you, Henrietta? You go for the sex."

"Arthur!"

"But surely you knew that."

"He knows nice girls, Arthur. He is favored by heredity on my side of the family, and even your ancestors were at least good Dutch farmer stock. He will be of adequate fortune. I can't see him throw all that away on this creature. This creature with the name of Cariatis."

Van Zandt sat up in his chair. "Cariatis, did you say?"

"Ursula Cariatis. The daughter of that millionaire you dislike so."

"Huh. I don't know that I approve of this myself."

"I do not see how you can hesitate even for a moment. It is a nightmare. *Our* son, and a woman named Cariatis."

"Do you know if her father knows?"

"They have been meeting in secret."

"Well, if it's any consolation, I don't think he'd be any more pleased than you are."

"Whatever he felt would be of no concern to me, unless he were able to prevent this horrible arrangement from taking place on Wednesday night."

"Frankly, Henrietta, whatever the pros and cons may be, if Artie wants to take some girl to a motel in Nyack and there lay her, I don't know of anything we can do about it. Or have you some ideas?"

"We could speak to her father."

"You might. I couldn't."

"I don't think I could either. Perhaps an anonymous letter?"

"Better see your lawyers first."

"I know. I asked a friend about that a minute ago."

"A friend?"

"A friend in need. Anyway, I think we ought to work from our side of this unfortunate liaison. On Artie. Bring him to his senses. Make him see his folly."

"But is it so important, Henrietta, really? Isn't it safer to let them get it out of their systems?"

"Never. *Never!* There is not only the social issue, there is also the moral one. Never."

"What do you plan to do?"

"I want you to talk to him. Bring pressure. Use every argument you can think of. Order him not to. You have some influence. I won't say he respects you more than he does me, but he is interested in what you have to say. With me, recently, he is merely rebellious."

Van Zandt considered this. "Why should I? I'd prefer it weren't Cariatis, but I don't feel very strongly about it." Suddenly he laughed. "On the other hand, maybe it's a good idea. It's a lot worse for the girl's family, particularly thinking about their women the way those people do— half Orientals, they are. Cariatis would be furious. My son enjoys his daughter. Ha! I like the idea, I think."

The results of the conversation were, so far, much as Henrietta had thought they would be. Now she drew out her lever and applied it. "Arthur, I believe you still want to buy that painting?"

He was made very angry merely by the question, but he contained it, and only glared silently at her as she sat primly upon the edge of the Louis XVI chair.

"Your collection means a great deal to you. Artie means as much to me. As for that painting . . . I have thought it might be arranged somehow. It would involve selling securities and spending capital, and it would, of course, diminish your own income somewhat. But it could be arranged, if I were willing to co-operate." Her expression-less eyes did not waver. "It could be arranged," she re-peated coolly.

"Bless my heart if I'm not being offered a bribe."

"Call it what you wish."

It took some thinking about, and he worked at it de-liberately. Then he took the poker and thrust it savagely into the fire, so that sparks flew and the flames burst forth again.

"What must I do, Henrietta?"

"That is up to you. I am attempting to buy real effort from you, that is all. If, through your agency, this disgust-ing relationship is terminated, then you will have your Wat-teau."

"I don't know whether to laugh or vomit."

"That does not concern me, either. I believe we have been quick, and we have at least established the cogent fact, Arthur. There is nothing more to talk about. Now I will leave, as we agreed." It was evident that she felt in some way triumphant when she spoke her last two sentences before opening the door. "I remind you that there is very little time," she said. "Artie is in his own room."

Van Zandt continued to reflect before his fire until it was almost midnight. Then, with a sigh, he heaved him-self out of his chair, turned out the lights, replaced the screen, and slowly walked to the central hall. It was a du-plex apartment, and he climbed the stairs and went to his son's door, where he hesitated, one hand raised to knock. Inside he heard a turning of pages, and a giggle. Then—something, it struck him, he had never heard before—he heard Artie hum to himself. He let his hand drop to his side and went on to his own bedroom. He would sleep on it. Tomorrow, perhaps, he would see what he could do.

Seven

Thackeray waited until some of the crush had disappeared after the final curtain call, then, putting on his topcoat, he sauntered down the stairs from the mezzanine to the orchestra, one glove on, one glove off. Now and then he nodded, for Dane and he had many friends in common, and the house that night was filled with them.

"How'd you like it? Marvelous, wasn't it?"

"Sheer delight."

"That place where Wanda discovers that Philip's just a servant after all. So *complex*. A real twist."

"A tour de force," Thackeray said.

He reached the lobby. "Ah. *Bon soir*, Mademoiselle," he said. "Good evening, Mr. Cariatis." He went past them, finally assuming the dangling glove.

"Who was that, *chéri?* Diplomatic?"

Cariatis lifted his shoulders. "I haven't the remotest idea," he replied. "A little too *au lait* for the United Nations, I would guess."

Outside, under the marquee, Thackeray met more friends. "It looks like Philip's got a job for a while," someone said. "Yes, he was damn good," said someone else. A third, rather cattily, said, "Of course, the role was created for Philip." "And Philip for the role," said a fourth. A fifth: "True. In any case, his career is made. He'll be somebody when the reviews come out." "Finally," said still another young man. There was general laughter.

"Are you going to the party?" somebody asked somebody else.

"Why not? For a while. Let's catch a cab on Ninth Avenue. We'll never get one here."

But they were going to a different party from the one Thackeray was invited to—theirs was being given by the chief angel of the new hit, his by his hosts of a week before, one of whom was an assistant to the stage manager. At the latter the guests wouldn't be as important—no stars from the cast, at least not until much later—but everyone would be prettier or more handsome, certainly younger, possibly with promise. Thackeray walked to the subway, got off at Fifty-ninth Street, and then took a taxi to the door of his friends' apartment.

No particular decorating had been done for the celebration, and the living room looked much as it always did, except that there were some flowers in it, and a billboard was set up in the little entrance hall, covered with photographs of Wanda Sickert's bedroom, Wanda lying in bed hugging a tea cozy to her fading cheek, et cetera, et cetera.

"Thackeray, you dog, come on in," host number one crowed from the doorway. "Wasn't it marvelous?"

"Sheer delight."

"*The* most bitched-up plot ever devised."

"A tour de force," said Thackeray.

He progressed into a room already filled with people. Host number two spied him from near the window.

"Come hither, Black Mischief," he called, "and try our new telescope. Much stronger than the other." He held it out.

Thackeray wove delicately through the crowd and took the telescope. He focussed it and trained it on Pearson

Tait's window. "My, my," he said, "he's got his easel turned so I can see tonight. And just *look*. Just look at it. Dr. Tait, of all people. What a scream!" He laughed.

A girl standing nearby turned around. "What is it?" she asked. She held out the delicate hand of a ballet dancer for the instrument. "It's heavy," she cried. "You hold it up for me." Thackeray did so, and she, too, watched Pearson Tait at work. "My, but he's intense," she remarked, "and funny-looking." She pushed the eyepiece away. "Is he a famous artist?"

Thackeray shook his head. "Maybe he ought to be, though."

"Don't you work for an art gallery?" she asked. "Why don't you show him?"

"I was just thinking that I might speak to my chief about that," Thackeray replied, smiling. "In due time."

She wandered off, but Thackeray stood at the window for another five or ten minutes. Finally he put the telescope down, then circulated for a while, nursing a drink, for he was quite abstemious. Eventually he worked through to the bedroom, where the coats were piled up, and put on his own. It so happened that he encountered his theatrical host on the way to the door.

"Thackeray. You aren't leaving yet. We've hardly begun. And Philip is stopping by just as soon as he can get away from the drearies."

"I have lots on my mind to do tomorrow," Thackeray said.

"He'll be heartbroken. He's really only coming because I said you'd be here."

Thackeray's nose went ever so slightly into the air. "Tell him I congratulate him. But tell him he didn't come along in time, and I had to go home."

"Well," his host said, watching him leave. "We're certainly high and mighty these days. *Well*."

Thackeray turned for a postscript. "Tell him I just don't have the patience to wait very long—not for anybody." He was miffed, a little, that he hadn't been asked to the larger, more important party, and Philip, if he'd really tried, could have arranged it. Perhaps they were drearies, but it would have been nice to have found that out for one's self.

Eight

Spent, drained at last, the frenzy over, Pearson Tait nevertheless continued to paint a little while longer, for he felt the work of the night was a rare success.

"There," he muttered, dabbing at his canvas. "There and there and there. How is that for a shadow? Ah—lustrous! Ha. So, my pretty, we moisten your lip. There." Another dab.

But at last he could go on no longer. The inspiration, whose vehicle was the potion that he stirred himself in his beaker, had evaporated. He was left mere man once more. He put down his brush and easel, pulled the velvet beret off his oversized head, and stepped back for a final look. How mysterious, thought he, were the ways of creation. The trembling antennae of his psyche were drawing back like the filaments of some sensitive plant at the approach of an alien body—the workaday world. He was but Pearson Tait once more.

He had to clean his tools, tired as he was. Then the canvas on which he had toiled so magnificently had to be replaced in its locked metal cabinet. He noticed a spot of lavender on the tile floor, got turpentine, and cleaned it up. Then he withdrew to the next room, changed back into his regular clothes, yawned, and let his head rotate forward—since he had no neck, there was nothing to let it hang down by. He longed for sleep. He felt as if there were lead weights sewn into his solar plexus. But there was one more duty he could not avoid.

He took out the notebook, *Parodies*, dated a fresh page, and wearily scratched in his entry for the night.

"Tonight I truly felt the presence of a great artist at my elbow, as if guiding my fingers with his energy and his mammoth appetites. And his courtesy, too. We belong to the aristocracy of greatness, he and I. A momentous collaboration.

"The painting is filled with Sabine women. What a rape it is! They are everywhere, running, hopping, leaping, tumbling, all in the wildest distress, their plump cheeks puffing out as they gasp for breath, their great breasts heaving free of the gauzy draperies that fail so adorably to conceal their masses of voluptuous promise to the libidinous eye of the marauding Romans.

"A thousand tons of hot flesh, all woven into a rollicking tangle. Oh, what a rape!

"I worked tonight on the blonde in the left foreground, who is just being caught by one lusty follower of Romulus, and whose buttocks swell almost out of the picture plane. I flushed her cheeks with hot and frantic blood, while my august companion clucked his approval. Then, my hand trembling, I dipped my brush into the blue, and laid on a glaze under her armpit. One could almost feel the moistness within that shadow. Finally, I touched her lips with saliva. Nearer to a cry of distress nobody could possibly get in paint.

"I was almost overcome with emotion. I painted like a madman. I am utterly exhausted. And tomorrow I must rise early and go to my official studio and work on the 'Watteau' in spite of everything."

He drew his usual little squiggle under the last line, closed the notebook, and put it away. He was by now so exhausted that he considered sleeping with his head down on his arms, but eventually got up. Then, thinking of an aphorism, he returned to the notebook, and in it wrote: "The scientist must labor so the parodist can eat."

When he got to bed he realized that, tired though he was, his mind was still too agitated by the evening's activities for him to sleep, particularly given his now almost constant worrying. How much longer, he groaned, could he keep up this double life he was leading? What was right, what wrong; what was truth, what falsehood? He got up, went to his bookcase, and took out a book on the Civil War; but when he opened it a flower fell out, a pressed flower, left there, he did not doubt, by his wife. He then remembered that he had another letter from her written from Tonga, which had come that day, and which he had not opened. He went to get it.

"My expedition to 'Eua was a great success, although our little boat nearly capsized trying to make its landing. But I got ashore safely with my specimen box, and spent a heavenly day roaming the moist, secluded forests of the eastern slope of the island, where the heaviest growth is preserved. Among others, I collected: *Angiopteris evecta* (the fronds I took were three meters long—my faithful native had to carry them, poor soul, and preserving them will be a problem); also a sweet *Trichomanes minutum* frond only about a centimeter long; lots of others, including one rarity, *Asplenium obtusatum,* a terrestrial fern (the *Trichomanes* is epiphytic—I got it off a tree trunk in a particularly moist area). I collected an extra specimen for you, as I am sure you would want it."

He made a *moue.* His wife, in spite of years of marriage and finally a necessary separation, had never been able to comprehend that he detested ferns almost more than any other single thing, and that if there was any state of fern he liked the least, it was the dried specimen, examples of which he had constantly found in his scientific books, where she had put them, then forgotten to remove them after they were pressed. His *moue* became a pout.

"Don't bring me any," he said. "I won't take them."

He read on: "Soon I'll be seeing more of the *Asplenium,* I suppose, since I must leave on the next boat for New Zealand, where it is fairly common. I dread the trip, because of my propensity for seasickness, which even affected me on the little passage from here to 'Eua and back. I'm a land plant, not a water plant, there's no doubt about that, although a good swamp doesn't bother me any, and I can hardly wait to wade right in. Write me in Wellington. The name of the hotel is on the list I left with you.

"Well, the odor of roast pig is floating through the jalousies, so I must close this letter and be off to dinner. . . ."

Tait, too, closed it, and thought about his absent spouse. Tonight he rather wished she were nearer. She was obtuse, she was a bore, she blundered, but she also had a kind of superb simplicity, a way of floundering through difficulties where he, with his more scrupulous intellect, got stuck. He wished he could confide his problem to her, for, with that innocence, she might see a solution. He didn't, after all, want his wonderful and terrible life to become some-

thing ugly, dangerous, criminal. He was what he was—
but how could he have foreseen the accident that had happened, and which he still could not explain? He did not
want to have to confess, but neither did he want to betray.
Betray the trust of his nighttime companions, his beloved
Old Masters.

He shuddered, for there was no turning back the ship
of fate from its course; then once more he turned out his
light and, after an hour's tossing, went finally to sleep.

PART THREE

Wednesday,

the Same Week

One

"You heard from McCaffrey what I was coming about, I guess," said Barney Kant on the other end of the line. "I would have called sooner, but my plane was late."

A little quiver went through Maule, the physical response to excitement now, in his approaching old age. The fox was in sight, tallyho! as he had been wont to say of the consummation of an important sale back in the days when he dealt in Stubbs. "Yes, Matt telephoned."

"When can you see me? It'll have to be this afternoon now. I've got business through lunch."

"Any time that would be convenient. I have no appointments that can't be rearranged."

"You're ready to get down to brass tacks, eh?"

No reply.

"Umm. Well, it shouldn't take long. How about four thirty?"

"That late?" Maule said.

"Well, four o'clock then."

"Four thirty will do very nicely." There was a pause. "Now, what about the painting? Do you want to see it again—it would commit neither of us, of course, but I could have it brought over, I suppose."

"Me? Naw. Any reason I should?"

"Well, sometimes people do."

"I don't. It's not like buying it for myself—if I do buy it. So long, Ed."

"Good-by, Barney." Maule replaced the receiver and

called for Thackeray to come in. "Don't bother to keep a transcript of that, Thackeray," he said, for he had bidden his receptionist listen in. "Nothing for the files. He's coming at four thirty, as you heard. We'll want the usual ice."

"Yes, Mr. Maule." Thackeray folded his sheet of notes several times preparatory to discarding them. "Mr. Maule?"

Something jarred the dealer's nerves. "Yes?"

"I've been wanting to talk to you."

"Could it wait? I've got lots on my mind today."

"Yee-es. It *could* wait."

"Then it will have to," Maule said testily. "Maybe tomorrow. Yes, tomorrow." He fingered his mustaches. "And he doesn't even want to see it again," he muttered. "What a world."

"Isn't it?" Thackeray said, spinning lightly around. He tossed his employer a sour look as he left the office.

Meanwhile, Barney Kant sat in the office down in the financial district, where he had made his call, and scratched his cheek with the tip of a wrinkled forefinger. Then he beckoned to the secretary who had been making notes from the extension telephone in the same room. "Toss 'em out, honey," he said. "Nothing there." He watched her while she tore the paper out of her stenographic notebook, shredded it, and deliberately allowed the fragments to trickle into the wastebasket. "Say, what's your name?" He grinned at her, disclosing teeth just a little too perfect for the weather-beaten face they graced. "Do you like the Rockettes?" he asked.

Two

The New York offices of Cariatis Enterprises were also located downtown in the financial district, but at the very bottom of it, in suitable adjacency to the harbor. They were on the tenth floor, corner, and the choice room with double exposure was, in fact, the private office of Theodore Cariatis himself, basileus of all the vast and profitable empire that bore his name. Its chief decoration was a series of murals, high up on the walls, depicting the stages in the cultivation and harvest of the olive, the gift to mankind of Athena, who presided in the form of a marble bust above the door.

Cariatis's dark eyes were cold and his soul well shielded when Arthur van Zandt was let into his office. He stood automatically, almost an act of forgetfulness, but he did not offer to shake hands. He had not forgotten, nor would he ever forgive, or so he thought, the insults of this great, dangerous buffoon who faced him now—a re-enactment of some ancient confrontation of rough barbarian and subtle Greek trader.

For his part, van Zandt thought how unappetizing the little man was, in his continental clothes, his hair too sleek and swept back too fast, with his smooth mustaches and puffy eyes, lids almost shut now in hostility, waiting, watchful, like a tiny musteline predator that specialized in some prey such as the nestlings of doves. Thank God one was too strong to be taken by the throat.

"I suppose I need not tell you, Cariatis, that it isn't friendship that has brought me to your office." Van Zandt's visual curiosity asserted itself, and he craned around to look at what might be on the walls. He skipped over the murals, hesitated at the goddess, and returned to his host. "Or that I wouldn't be here at all if I didn't think it was essential."

"You are at least candid," said Cariatis, feeling himself made somehow smaller than usual.

"Blunt, you mean to say. Such is my reputation."

"Or a part of it."

"May I sit down?" Each of them took a chair. "Good, that's better. Well, we don't have much in common, you and I, Cariatis, I should think, but one thing we do have right now: a devil of a problem."

Cariatis's little slitted eyes became still narrower. He found himself wanting desperately to twirl his diamond ring, but desisted. "A problem in common," he managed to say at last. "I don't know of such a problem—unless you mean . . ."

"Unless I mean?"

"Have you by any chance come here to . . . ? But why? To what end?"

"Speak up, man. If you know what I'm here for."

Cariatis hesitated, feeling outmaneuvered. "It's only that the last time I saw you was at Maule's place. Has this visit anything to do with . . ."

"So that's it." Van Zandt exhaled noisily, glowering. "You're *still* after it. Maule's playing a complicated game. I wonder why."

"Usually, when people play such games, there is one reason: that they hope to get more money that way."

"A little crude for Maule. I don't quite have that impression."

"Or"—here Theodore waved a hand, his glittering diamond embellishing the complexities of his thought—"it could be that there is a conflict of cupidities involved."

"Odd thing to say."

"A conflict within Maule himself. Money is rarely the unique force behind any significant move, don't you agree? And Maule is not, after all, a poor man."

"I don't know whether or not I understand, Cariatis."

"We Greeks tend to express complex ideas in appropriate language. But in any case, I take it he hasn't promised the picture to you, van Zandt. Now, just how is it that your visit here affects what you refer to as our common problem?"

"It doesn't affect it at all. That wasn't the problem I came to talk to you about."

Cariatis drew back. "You led me on," he accused.

"What if I did? Anyway, it doesn't make any difference. What I came to talk to you about is your daughter."

"Ursula? You came here to talk to me about Ursula?"

"If that's her name. Yes, I believe that was the name my wife mentioned. Funny name for a Greek girl."

"And what about Ursula?"

"It's about her and our son, Artie. My wife's having a fit about them. Do you know about them?"

Cariatis shook his head.

"Well, it seems they've been seeing a lot of each other. And somehow Henrietta's found out that they intend to go off together tonight. Sleep together, you understand, in a motel in Nyack. Ever heard of it?"

Cariatis nodded. "It was mentioned in the lyrics of a popular song some years ago."

"Strange fact to know."

"I used to go dancing," came the whispered reply. Then Cariatis got his voice back. "No," he cried. "No, it must not be. Not *my* daughter." He glared furiously at van Zandt. "And *your* son."

"Precisely how Henrietta feels about it."

Cariatis shriveled into himself. "You mean she objects because the girl involved is my daughter?"

Van Zandt was a little embarrassed. "Well, I mean, Henrietta'd object no matter who the girl was; but I don't think she'd be quite so unreasonable about it if the girl was —well, you know. What is it they say? A wasp—white, Anglo-Saxon, and Protestant. That idea."

Cariatis said nothing.

"I don't object so much myself. As far as I'm concerned, Artie can have an affair with anyone he wants to. I don't care if he goes off to Nyack with . . . with a belly dancer. What's the difference, once the lights are out? But I'm trying to oblige Mrs. van Zandt. Also, I suppose you feel differently about it. The girl probably loses more than the boy when they go to Nyack, don't you agree?"

"We think she loses everything, van Zandt."

"I know that. So you've got to stop her."

"And why don't you stop your son?"

"Well . . ."

Cariatis sensed something. "Aren't you the master of your house?"

"It isn't easy to come here and see you, Cariatis, but I decided I preferred that to the other. I don't like to tell him not to do something I would have done myself. I mean, not your daughter, but a girl like her, when I was Artie's age."

Cariatis said, "You mean, you would have taken a girl outside your circle to Nyack. But you marry a—Henrietta."

"Yes, God help me."

"Why should I oppress my daughter so that you can spoil your son? Keep him at home tonight. Forbid him to go out. Or haven't you that power, van Zandt?"

"I don't want to crush his independence." He was silent for a moment. "Personally, as I say, I don't care anyway. I care a hell of a lot more about that Watteau than I do about Artie and your daughter."

The mention of the Watteau recalled Angélique to Theodore's mind, and she appeared there in a condition that his outer eye had never beheld. Then her place was taken by Ursula, as he felt obliged to stick with that problem. Ursula as a desirable woman—he really had never thought of it. Ursula grown up. Ursula planning an affair. Ursula rupturing the orderly routine of life, such as it was. He sent her back to her room. It would never do.

"In my own country," he said, "we are careful with our girls. But here they are allowed to run free. Ursula was raised here—I sent her over at the beginning of the war. I think it is twenty years too late for me to control Ursula as I would like."

"Well, if you can't control her, and we can't control Artie, I don't see how we can stop it from happening. Nyack is in New York, you know. They aren't planning to leave the state."

Cariatis stood up from his desk, went to a window, and looked out over the harbor, where, like an ungainly cow, one of his own ships was being dragged to a berth somewhere in Brooklyn. "How did your wife find out about this plan?" he asked.

"I don't know. I suspect she has used private detectives."

"There could be a child," Cariatis mused. "Disastrous."

"Artie has been doing homework. I saw the books in his room this morning. I don't think we need worry too much about that. Our children may be inexperienced, but they are not innocent."

"Your attitude toward my daughter is offensive," said Cariatis.

"I don't even know your daughter. I have no attitude toward her."

"I have heard your son is a weakling."

Van Zandt was obviously determined not to quarrel. "He is. I admit it. But now he seems to be showing a little spunk, and I hesitate to squelch him, even if I can."

"My daughter has been going to a psychoanalyst. There was a time not long ago when she was quite confused. An incident with deep water—too far out—a boat came by in time. I, too, have reasons to hesitate, van Zandt."

"It's more serious than just Nyack, Cariatis. Henrietta's spies have heard some mention of marriage. What if they got married, man? Think about that."

"I detest your wife for spying on them."

"That's the smallest part of it," van Zandt said, "although I suppose it would be easier if you spoke respectfully of her." Suddenly he said, "Have you talked to Maule today?"

Cariatis shook his head. He watched the progress of his ship. She would be leaving in three weeks to return to the Aegean, Homer's sea. There came to him the vision of Sounion and its temple, of the Piraeus lying ahead in the sun. Perhaps he would go with her and take Ursula along. He came to a decision.

"I will try to reason with my daughter, van Zandt, but only on one condition. You must give me your word of honor that you will talk to your son. I am not a servant, nor she some poor man's daughter, that you should seek to divide them only by confining her in some way."

"I suppose that is reasonable."

"And I have your word?"

"Yes. I'll speak to Artie. I won't tie him to his bed."

"And I will not lock Ursula in her room."

Van Zandt hauled himself to his feet. "Fair enough."

Cariatis let him go to the door by himself, then called out, "Van Zandt. One more thing. I have a message for your wife. I want you to tell her that I will do what I can to stop this only because I find the connection unworthy of my daughter."

Van Zandt almost smiled. "I'll deliver that message," he said.

After he was gone, Cariatis turned again to the window. Half the world, he thought to himself, licks my boots because I am so rich; half the world despises me because I am little and dark and my walk isn't exactly right. With these I am powerful, with those helpless; for they despise me not for something I do, but for something I am. The one half worships my money, but the other half despises my self, my essence.

He looked down at his little feet in their pointed, shiny black shoes. And yet, it isn't my essence at all, he thought sadly, but it is as near to it as anyone gets. For with me, as with everybody, the shoes are more important than the feet, the body more important than the soul, and manner blocks access to mind. He watched them slowly turn his ship around. He nodded to himself.

"And so it is," he said aloud.

Three

Artie and Ursula were holding a last meeting to plan the night's stratagems.

"Mine made an interesting remark just now," Artie said. "She said that the people who think they grew up easily can never have any idea how hard it really was."

Ursula sipped her Bloody Mary, her dark brows wrinkled with concentration. "Like imagining what it would be like to be an Eskimo."

"More or less, if you really were one, but then had repressed all memory of snow, for instance. I think she meant that we may have more insight than the others, though, because we know it isn't easy at all. If we can survive, we may be better off. Anyway, we know we've got the problem. We work out ways to deal with it. Cover-ups, mostly."

Ursula followed him. "Like words. Words like *terrible* and *awful*. I've discovered I use them all the time to hide what I really think of something. Hide it from myself, too. When I really am thinking: that's a story I didn't want to hear, because it means that so-and-so doesn't really like me, and that means I'm not really likable, then I say 'Oh, how *awful*' instead, and don't have to think what I mean. Does that make sense?"

Artie nodded, his Adam's apple rising and falling as he swallowed his own drink. "To me it does," he said.

"Using words like *awful* is awful," Ursula went on. "Having to, I mean."

He nodded again. Then he said, "I think we're manufacturing conversation right now. What's really on your mind? Right this second."

Ursula smiled. "I'm wondering what's in your package."

Artie blushed. "Nothing much," he said.

"Well, you asked me what was on my mind. That was."

"I'll tell you. It's a pair of pajamas and a new bathrobe." He continued to blush. "For tonight."

"Oh, Artie," she said, and two tears soon stood out upon her lashes.

"It'll be all right, Ursula." He worked hard for a moment at removing a lemon seed from his glass. "You know, I've been thinking," he said finally. "This is what's really on *my* mind. Suppose it works. Suppose it works out just fine. Then, you know, we'll have a *real* problem on our hands. From the first one, tonight's, we go on to a second. What do we do then? Have you thought about it?"

"Uh-huh. But I think it's a screen."

He shook his head. "Not completely."

"Then let's just say it's tomorrow's problem, Artie."

"Agreed. Another?" When she shook her head, he then said, "Is there anything special I should bring? Maybe a bottle of Scotch?"

"Yes. Yes. And I'll be ready at seven, Artie. I'll wait downstairs for you. I'm going to have to go now."

He nodded, suddenly miserable. "Won't it be embarrassing? I mean, in front of the doorman? I mean, with an overnight bag?"

"I don't see why. He won't know."

"They always seem to know everything they shouldn't. At least ours do. I'll bet he'll guess."

"Artie, do shut up. You aren't making it any easier. What an awful thing for you to worry about at a time like this."

"You used *awful*." He managed his dispirited little laugh.

"I know." She smiled slightly and moved from her seat, then turned to him. "Artie, what color are the pajamas?"

"Blue. Striped."

"Don't bring them."

"What?" He blushed again. "But Ursula . . ." He jumped up to follow her.

"I bought a pair to give you, as a joke," she said, not looking at him. "Awful ones, with sayings written on them, like 'Too hot to handle.' The kind of thing people hide in the suitcases of newlyweds. You know. Corny but universal."

"What size?" he asked.

"Mediums."

"The legs will be too short. They always are."

"Maybe not. I got extra-long mediums. Seven o'clock, Artie."

"I'll be right on time."

They parted in relief outside the door. Although the sands of their cherished childhoods were running out, they had yet six or seven precious hours when each could still remain a discreet organism.

Four

"All favorable. And four out of the five specially favorable to me. Hollywood's already nibbling, and I'll probably do it out there when we close here in New York. Things are looking up in *my* scrapbook," Philip Dane said.

"Congratulations," Thackeray replied. "I wish I could say the same thing."

Dane beckoned the waiter and told him to hurry with the sandwiches. He had a matinee, he said. Then he turned back to Thackeray. "What's the matter? Isn't Uncle Edward treating you right?"

"Well enough. It isn't that. But I'm not getting anywhere, because there isn't anywhere in that office to get to."

"You mean you're tired of being a receptionist?"

"And *fac*totum," said Thackeray.

"What do you have in mind?"

"Well, what I really want, Philip, is a gallery of my own. Just a little one, to start with. I was talking to some kids the other night who know something about it, and they all said the same thing: there's no future in these old pictures. All the future is in contemporaries. I think I know enough now to do something like that. You know, run a little gallery of my own. I've learned words and phrases and the way you have to do things."

"But—you need money."

Thackeray nodded his shapely head. "That's it. And some help, like advice, to begin with."

"I don't have any money, not that kind, anyway."

"Oh, I know that. I wasn't hinting to you," Thackeray assured him. "Uncle Edward has the money, but he wouldn't want to spend it like that, I suppose. His basement is still unrented, you know. That's just the size place I'd need."

The close passage of the waiter brushed the Dane coiffure, and Philip growled under his breath; then, when the sandwiches had been deposited in front of him and Thackeray, he raised his arm and repaired any mischief that might have been done.

"Maybe," he said, "just *maybe*, someone could do something for you, if you were willing to do something back."

"Like what, for instance? And who?"

"We're going to have a good run, but we have to change theaters in the summer. There'll be about a three-week interval between the time we have to give up where we are now, and when we can open in the new one. The beginning of August. I'm going on a holiday," Philip said. He nibbled at his bacon and tomato. "I was thinking of Portugal." He was watching Thackeray closely now, who was gazing off into space. "But I don't want to spend three weeks in Portugal alone."

"Won't there be a few Portuguese there?"

"Who needs them? I'll have enough money by then to pay for the type of companionship I like. All expenses."

Now Thackeray began to munch his own sandwich—he had wanted chicken, but had ordered beef on principle. "Someone's going to be lucky," he said.

"How would you like to be that person?"

"Me? I have a job to keep."

"I can handle Uncle Edward."

"Also," Thackeray said, "I might not like Portugal."

"But what if you were returning to this new gallery, the one you want to open?"

"Why then, I guess I *might* like Portugal."

"So I thought."

Thackeray grinned. "It *could* be diamonds and emeralds," he said.

"We'll see, we'll see, we'll see." It was a noteworthy line from Act Three of *Green Leaf, Yellow Leaf*.

"I'm kind of in a hurry," Thackeray said. "I have to make plans."

"Well," Dane replied, "I can't talk to Edward this afternoon. I've got a show to put on." He pulled some brochures on Portugal and its beach resorts out of his pocket. "I picked these duplicates up at the American Express, just in case anyone was interested. Hotels and things like that. Look them over."

Thackeray took them and tucked them into a pocket, and later, when he was back in the offices of Edward Maule and Company, he looked through them. Then he sat and thought for a while, balancing one thing against another. He was not unaware just how hard it was for any Negro, having come so far, to get much further, or, put differently, how easy it would be for him to get hung on dead center. He didn't really like Philip very much and, if it were a question of getting to the top by certain methods, would as soon have done it directly through Maule; but Maule wasn't interested in what Thackeray could offer. A colored boy needed a real boost, just about now, and Philip Dane could give it.

He looked once more through the bright little leaflets. "And it does look nice," he said.

Then he dialed a number. "Hello, Momma. How are you today? How is the foot? Oh, I'm glad of that, Momma. That's good news. Oh, nothing much. Pretty quiet, but things'll be happening soon, I expect. I had lunch with a friend of mine, and Momma, he wants me to go to Portugal with him this summer for three weeks. What? Yes, I know that, but he's willing to pay for it. No, no, Momma, I said he was a *friend*. I'll be going to keep him company. I've got some advertising on the hotels and beaches, and it looks real nice. Why? Well, you see, he has three weeks off, and he wants to go to Portugal, and he doesn't want to go alone. He's got lots of money, so he's willing to pay to have the right person along, that's all." A moment later, he interrupted her comments. "There went the buzzer, Momma. I'll have to sign off. Bye-bye."

Five

"Tell your boss that Barney Kant is here to see him, son," said that gentleman, whirling his hat onto a chair and following it with his coat.

Maule came to the door. "Barney! Come right on in."

"I guess I look just like a square meal to a hungry man, is that it, Ed?"

"I had quite a good lunch," Maule replied distantly. "But following along that line of thought, don't you think we might have a drink? It's only four thirty; still, I'd like one myself."

"Count me in. No reason to stop now—I've been at it since before lunch. Nothing like a working day. I may say a few things I shouldn't, so don't make it too big."

"Well, you know, Barney," Maule said, intensifying a certain British edge to his accent in order to point up his epigram, "our anticipated indiscretions are never the harmful ones."

"Bull," Barney replied. "Just put about three ounces from that bottle into a glass, will you?"

"Is that the way you like it? Soda? Good. Now, do sit down."

"Thanks, Ed." The old man dropped lightly into a chair, without spilling anything from the glass in his hand. "Let me do some talking first, right off. Okay? Now, I'm known to be a sharp horse trader in the circles where I'm known at all. But in this situation I'm pretty well out of my depth. I don't know what we're bargaining for, and I don't have much of an idea of what it's worth. I'm dumb, the way you'd be on the commodities market. Do I make myself clear?"

"So far."

"What I'm leading up to is this: don't bother to do any dance around me. Just tell me what's what. How much do you want for this picture, and how do you want to be paid if I buy it?"

Maule scrubbed a mustache. "All right, Barney. So be it," he said. "I want seven hundred thousand for it now. It might have been a little less before, but since it's been cleaned . . ."

"Never mind that. I don't care what it might have been."

"Seven hundred thousand dollars, as I said, is the price. I would want some small sum now as earnest, the balance to be paid when the painting is delivered, either to you or to the museum, whichever is the more convenient."

A grin appeared on the wrinkled old-farmboy face of Kant. "So that's how it's to be, is it?" he said. "A lot of money, Ed."

"Yes, it's a lot of money, Barney."

"And this owner. Do I meet him? Can I talk to him?"

Maule was prepared for the question. "He insists on anonymity. I am free to negotiate as I please."

"Well then, I guess I'll have to do a little talking to you," Barney said. "I suppose you know how I happen to be the president of McCaffrey's museum?"

"I presume it is because you were elected."

Barney waved an impatient hand, and this time did spill a few drops. "Come off it, Ed," he said. "You know what I mean. I was made president so I'd ante up. They wouldn't have done it if they hadn't been in a spot, either. I've got lots of enemies."

"Any successful man has enemies," Maule murmured.

"Do you have enemies?"

"Only a few. But then, I'm not successful as you are."

"Huh! Anyway, what you may not know is that they're going to be in a real tough spot, and there isn't any old Gloag to fish them out any more. He's dead. He's given all he's ever going to give, Ed. And they've overextended, with their silk walls and their marble trims; and the city fathers are irritated at them, and they're going to be madder than hell when they find out how much more of a tax slice it's going to take to keep this new wing open. Now, who comes to the rescue? The trustees of course. That's why they're trustees, isn't it?"

"Wealth brings responsibilities," said Maule.

"Bull. It so happens that these rich men are tighter than hell. So enter Barney, who tells the wrong kind of jokes at the wrong time and all the rest, but who's flush. But old Barney, he's already on the scene to the tune of quite a hunk of glue for your picture. Now, the way I figure it is this: they *want* the picture, but they've *got* to have cash, and this year, too—this tax year, I'm thinking. McCaffrey knows it, but he won't face it head on. He'd ramble on about the cultural role of the museum in the city and stuff like that, and pretty soon you'd forget that it's a simple question of red ink, not red herrings. Then, there's Nesbitt, his brother-in-law. He may have something up his sleeve, but I doubt it. Best family in town, he is. More likely, you see, it's Barney who's supposed to provide the cash, too. Well, I'm not going to do it, not just for fun. I'm willing to do what's fair, but I'm not going to do everything."

Maule frowned. One knew about this kind of thing, of course, but wasn't it preferable never to say it?

After a pause, Barney digressed. "Funny thing," he said,

"I know it was really McCaffrey who got me on the board. But I don't trust him. When we were here last week, I wondered if he was maybe going to get a kickback from you."

Maule raised a hand in horror.

"Oh, I know he isn't. If he was, I could handle him easier. I'd know the rules. You see, that's part of my problem right now: I'm not always quite sure of the rules. Telling a dirty joke at the wrong time—that's clear enough to me. But there are others. Well anyway, McCaffrey and Nesbitt are my supporters, but I wouldn't trust either of them. and I don't trust the others either. I'm not about to give them a pile of money my first year in office and then suddenly find myself bounced while they laugh at me. Maybe I'm crazy, but that could happen."

"I'm sure they will be grateful for anything you give."

"More bull, Ed, and you know it." He held out his glass for whisky. "Right now Nesbitt and McCaffrey treat me the way you would a man you were trying to get to come and fix a leaking toilet on Christmas Eve. They've just plain got to be on my good side, because the pee is just about to run all over the presents. But when the toilet's fixed, they'll remember I'm just a plumber, see? Well," and he suddenly turned more serious, "before I'm through, when I whistle they'll jump, let me tell you. I'll own 'em, and they'll jump."

Maule tried to interrupt, for Barney had gone quite far enough, and more talk of this sort would compromise the dealer's relationship with both McCaffrey and Barney; but the old man overrode him.

"No, no. Let me talk on. I feel like it. This has been quite a day for me. I feel like talking, yes, I really do. I suppose you wonder why I care about being president of that board, don't you? I don't know anything about art, and I don't much care. Well, Eddie, I'll tell you why. But first, you tell me why a man gets rich."

Maule drew the corners of his mouth down and pondered the question. "A special talent for making money," he said at last.

Barney waved his free hand. "Yeah, yeah. That, and it takes luck. But most of all it takes the will, and it's different from the will to *stay* rich. It's the will to have something you don't have. See?"

Maule nodded.

"But why the will? I'll tell you why, why you want to have that particular something, namely money, which you don't have. If you're tired of having people pay no attention to you, then you want them to sit up and look. Money! People look down on you because of where you came from or something and you want them to kowtow. Money! They don't bother to listen to you, and you want them to beg you to talk. Money. You're ugly, like me, and you want to be like Clark Gable. Money! Once I didn't think I'd ever get enough rich food and expensive liquor; now I've had enough of them, but I'm still hungry for what you'd call position. Sure I'm conceited, I'm shot full of vanity, Ed, just plain self-love, and oh, man! it needs to be fed. Money!"

"I see." Maule didn't envy McCaffrey.

"When I got started, I worked for old Gloag. You didn't know that, did you?"

"I didn't know Mr. Gloag either."

"No. Well, I did. He was an ornery old devil, too. I was just a kid, but I worked hard, and he smelled my ambition and liked to prick me when he could. But I watched him, you see. I know how he did things. I learned a lot from him."

"And now you're president of his museum."

Barney nodded. "Old Gloag, he really ran our town by the end of his life. He wasn't much to begin with either, but by the end he ran everything, or damn near." Barney jumped up. "So will I," he cried. "I've got maybe fifteen years to go and it's plenty of time. One of the ways he did it was to get into all the things like museums and libraries and the local university. He knew the women. He'd help them out with their hospitals and book funds. Do you know what?"

"No. What?"

"I'm taking music-appreciation lessons on the sly. I've got my eye on the Symphony Board, too." He cackled. "Ever hear of *Wozzeck?* Well, I can hum it, Eddie." He cackled again. "Now I'm sure you think I'm crazy."

"You don't fit my definition of crazy," Maule said, but he thought to himself that by one definition Barney was indeed crazy, like all rich people. On the other hand, his money was real, and it lay at the center of his vision, so the world left him out of its asylums.

"We're a long way from your picture, which I'm going to buy," Barney went on, "but not *give* until I've got the board committed to re-elect me, not once, but for three years. They can modify that rule. It's their own."

Maule nodded.

"I'm going to buy it according to my own plan, though, Ed."

Maule always sat erect, so it cannot be said that he stiffened in his seat. "And what is that?" he asked.

"Time. I want some time to pay you. I'll give you twenty-five thousand right now, but the rest will have to come a while later. You can keep the picture in the meantime, if you want to." He wagged a finger, and grinned again. "I couldn't raise seven hundred thousand right now if my life depended on it. I just got through hocking just about everything."

Maule sat quietly, but he found himself close to panic. What was this all about? Why had he kept on listening? Call Cariatis. Call van Zandt. Get this old nut out of the office. Or was it a joke? A manner of speaking? Calm down, Edward; you're an old hand. Don't show anything. He smiled. "Am I to understand, Barney, that you really came here today to ask me for a small loan?"

"You might say for a small credit. Six hundred and seventy-five thousand dollars' worth of credit."

"I'm hardly in a position . . . Besides, it isn't my painting."

"Neither you or the owner will lose. Here's what I'll do. I'll give you the twenty-five thousand right now for him. But to sweeten the whole deal for you, there'll be another twenty-five thousand, face value, in a certain stock that's going to be issued, and that's going to go up quite a ways. And when it does, you'll get the balance of the money. And I'll not only be *a* rich man back home, I'll be *the* rich man."

"What if your plans don't work?"

"I default. You repossess. Or keep on keeping the picture."

Maule grimaced. It was all sticky, vaguely unethical, distasteful, and slightly dangerous. "Why should I do this? I could sell the painting for the full price immediately by lifting the telephone."

"I'm going to be president of that museum for at least three years, and maybe a whole lot longer. I operate big in a couple of other cities with museums. I may start helping them buy a few things. Naturally, I'd have a whole lot to say about where they got them—or didn't."

Maule got up and paced the floor of his office. "I don't like it, Barney," he said.

"Wait till you see what this stock is going to do," Barney replied. "And fast. You'll have the certificates in ten days."

"I don't know. I just don't know." The next time Maule turned toward Barney, he found he was writing out a check. His pacing brought him within reach of the busy hand. "I just don't know," he repeated.

Barney held out the slip of paper. "Here, Eddie. You won't be sorry. Neither will that owner."

Maule wheeled around and paced the full length of his office several more times. Yes, it was distasteful; but, on the other hand, there really wasn't any risk. With the stock market behaving the way it was, the securities could go up ten, fifteen, twenty times. And capital gains, too. What about McCaffrey? Not his responsibility. Maule stopped in front of his Magnasco and stared at it. He felt old, tired, confused, indecisive.

His sleeve was twitched, and when he looked around, he found Barney at his side, still holding out the check. Barney winked, Maule took it, and the interview was over.

Except for Barney's final remark, as he lifted his glass to drain it. "If you begin to wonder why I've shot my mouth off as much as I have today, Eddie, wonder why I trust *you*, well, it's because I figured that just about right now you'd be in it as much as any of the rest of us, and you are." He drank. "Here's to the Kant Collection," he said, winking once more.

Six

"To my great regret, Angélique," Theodore Cariatis said, "I cannot go with you as we had planned to the reception." They were talking together in the Cariatis apartment, where Mademoiselle de la Couronne d'Epines had come for her glass of champagne before going on to the reception. "It seems that Ursula is planning to elope, in a manner of speaking, tonight, and I must do what I can to dissuade her from it."

"*Mais c'est de Marivaux!*" cried Angélique, swizzling her cocktail. She looked gaily through her veils. "And with whom?"

"It is quite serious," the little man said. "With a boy named Artie van Zandt, whose father is my worst enemy."

"Ah, then. It is no longer Marivaux; it is Molière."

"Neither Marivaux nor Molière, but Madness. And it must not happen. In any case, Ursula has been out all afternoon, and I must await her here. I have checked with the maids. She did not take a suitcase with her, so she must return to pack. I am sorry."

"No matter. It is not the kind of function that requires an escort," Angélique said. "You must not be too sorry about Ursula, either, Theodore. I think it is well that she should be showing an interest."

Cariatis was hunting through the cigarette boxes for the one that contained his Turkish cigarettes. "I understand

hat point, but I do not intend that she should do this thing.
I intend that she should be respectably married. I will not
have her become someone's concubine."

"Theodore!"

He had found the right box, but now he dropped it. He
turned. "Angélique," he said. "I am so sorry."

"Cupid," she replied, "plays many a curious prank."

"I know, I know. I hear the telephone." He stopped to
listen, and then a maid came in and said it was for him, a
Mr. Maule. Theodore excused himself and went to take it
in an adjacent room, leaving Angélique alone.

"So sorry to bother you this late in the day," the dealer
said smoothly, and Cariatis knew that he had lost the painting. "But I did have a matter to speak to you about and
thought it best not to wait."

Cariatis's voice was expressionless. "Yes?"

"Have you thought over that enamel I showed you, by
the way? I do think it has good quality."

"I am sure you didn't call me to repeat an offer of sale
you have already made once."

"No. Quite right. Ah." Maule cleared his throat. "I'm
afraid I've got some disappointing news for you, sir. Or
perhaps you're not really interested in that little French
picture any more."

"Which little French picture?"

"The one attributed to Watteau. You recall?"

"Perfectly."

"Well, one of the persons who saw it earlier has decided
to take it. I'm afraid that it has, for all intents and purposes,
been sold."

Cariatis shook with anger. It was not just a matter of
love, a matter of Angélique; it had become a business deal

at which he had been bested. "You cannot do this to me, Maule. You cannot sell that out from under Cariatis. You cannot sell it, do you hear?"

Maule became frigidly polite. "I'm afraid that that is precisely what I have done," he said.

"I offered you money. I offered you whatever you wanted. Why have you done this to me?"

"I assure you, Mr. Cariatis, that there is nothing personal. I would have been delighted to let you have the painting, but you weren't the first in line, you see. There was a bit of a queue, and first come, first served, don't you know."

"He is first in line who has the most money, Maule, and we both know it."

"Sometimes, perhaps, not always. Not everywhere."

"Yes, everywhere. In Greece, in the United States, in Sweden and Patagonia and Albania, in Red China and the Soviet Union, and in Hell. Also in Heaven. If there is a Truth, that is it: that he who has the most is first in line. I know it and you know it."

"You are illogical, sir. If yours is the only truth, then I must sell the painting to you. But I have not sold the painting to you, therefore yours is not the only truth."

"I do not want to drain my passion with words, Maule. I am an angry Theodore Cariatis, and when Theodore Cariatis is angry, he is a dangerous man. I warn you, you had better reconsider."

"Mr. Cariatis, your tone of voice is unacceptable, and so are your threats," Maule replied.

Theodore Cariatis began to wave his arms and do a little dance of rage to the extent that the telephone cord left him free to do so. His accent became much more pronounced. "I will tell you why you have done it. You have done it because I am Theodore Cariatis and not tall. You didn't want to sell it to me because I wear a diamond ring on my finger and would give it to my French whore. I know, you see. That is so, isn't it, Maule?" Cariatis was now quite beside himself, and utterly forgetful of the fact that with his voice raised as it now was, Angélique could probably hear him from the other room. "That is it, isn't it? You have done this thing to me because I am an oily little Greek."

"Mr. Cariatis, I assure you that nobody could respect Greece more than I," Maule said.

"Because you like boys? You think that is respect?"

There was a pause, then Maule said icily, "You are offensive."

"Thief. Coward. Pederast," Cariatis shrieked.

"There is no point in continuing this conversation. I wish you a good evening."

"Wait. Tell me this at least: have you sold it to van Zandt?"

"No." Maule hung up the receiver.

When Cariatis had collected himself—he had gone to his bathroom and bathed his face and hands, then put some eau de cologne on a handkerchief and inhaled it several times—he returned to Mademoiselle de la Couronne d'Epines, who was sitting where he had left her.

"Here comes a man with a matter on his mind, I am thinking."

"I have just quarreled with Edward Maule," Cariatis said.

"And was that wise?"

"Why not? He has sold his Watteau to someone else. There is nothing to be done about it. He is my enemy."

"My poor Theodore," she said, smiling up at him. "This is a difficult day for you. Ursula, Edward Maule, and now, I fear, Angélique."

"I had no choice. It was not my fault. I offered him anything, any price, but he wouldn't have it."

"I can imagine. Yes, perhaps you did, but not in time. In any case, as I told you, without the Watteau I would never become your mistress. I keep my bargains, Theodore."

"But that is unreasonable, Angélique. I did what I could."

"And—failed. Perhaps it was fated that way, Theodore." She looked at her wrist watch. "I must leave soon. The Minister is supposed to arrive at six and leave at six thirty."

Cariatis rushed from the room and returned a moment later holding a small box. He opened it and showed the contents to Angélique—a necklace of fleurs-de-lis wrought in platinum and set with precious stones.

"It is very pretty," she said.

"Take it. It's for you. I had it made in Paris for you many months ago, but I have waited until now to give it to you."

She raised a hand, but then drew it back. "No, Theodore. That would not be fair. You have made an error. A bargain is a bargain."

"Bargain!" he cried, in anguish. "Do you not hold love as something above the market place?"

"I do not love you, Theodore," she said, "therefore it is in the market place where we must go to do our business."

"But I love you. Oh, Angélique," he begged, "just try me." He came toward her, but she put out a palm and pushed him away. "You will never be sorry. You will never have to enter the market place again. You will never have to answer your own door." He referred to the fact that she could afford only part-time maids.

"For that improvement, you are not the unique way."

"No, but I am here. And I am very rich."

She shrugged. "No, Theodore."

He wrung his hands. "I don't understand," he said. "I simply don't understand. What are you, Angélique? What makes you do what you do? Why do I like you? You are a great hetaera. A great one, I agree; nevertheless, a profession is a profession. Have you no values, then? I will even marry you. I will turn you into my Empress Theodora. Yet you say no to me. Me, Theodore Cariatis. Because of a painting? No, that makes no sense at all. Avarice is a kind of madness, it is true; but if you are merely mad with avarice, then surely marry me you must."

"I will talk to you now, Theodore, before I go. You compel me to tell you some disagreeable things. Is there just a drop more champagne? Good. Please agitate it for me." She watched him and saw that his hand shook. "Poor Theodore," she said again. "You know much about the world, and much about business, but there are many things you can never know. You were never raised in a cold and damp old house in the country, and not really so very big a one, a house whose very rats went back to the Dark Ages, because there had never been enough money since then to exterminate them. You never had to hide in your room when richer relatives came to call, because you didn't have a dress nice enough to wear before them. You didn't walk by the *boucherie* in the village and look with great child's eyes at the trickle of blood running out into the street from the carcass of a fat calf, and know that there would be no meat on your plate. Those things, Theodore, I can never forget. My days are filled with satin and champagne, but at night it is those memories that still fill my dreams."

"My poor Angélique," he said, attempting to clasp her again, but again receiving her palm in his chest. "Shall I tell you something? Something nobody else knows? I am not even a true Greek. I was born in New York. I pass the house I was born in when I glide down the West Side highway in my limousine on my way to the offices of Cariatis Enterprises. I can look across and see it. It is an old-law tenement. There, in the midst of every squalor, was born Theodore Cariatis."

"How did you get where you are?"

"My father returned to Greece to make his fortune, taking me, a baby, with him." He approached her once more, but this time stayed out of range of her hand. "And so you see, Angélique, I do understand what you have experienced. And I can banish rats from your house forever."

"But not, Theodore, from my dreams."

"I will be beside you when you awaken."

"No, Theodore."

"Why, why, why?"

"Must I tell you? Very well, then. Because you do not appeal to me."

His eyes moistened. "Does that really matter?" he asked quietly.

She nodded. "It does. You see, I am not just any woman. I have my *éthique*, my *système*, one might say my *idéologie*."

"And can I not be fitted in somewhere?"

She shook her elegant head. "No. Nowhere. I am not intransigent. I gave you one chance—with the painting. All other roads are closed to you, Theodore."

"You will kill me."

"Possibly. Let me go on, however. I have had many lovers since I left the broken-down estates of my ancestors, although not so many as you probably imagine—for I rather think that men multiply the lovers of their mistresses in order both to diminish and to increase their pride of conquest. Nevertheless, I would not describe my amorous existence as circumscribed. But think of those men whom I have loved, or of such as you know."

"I am thinking. Should I name them? You might be surprised. My agents have investigated."

"Don't bother. But do you see a pattern?"

"A German, an Italian, a Scot, two Poles . . . No, no pattern, except, perhaps, cosmopolitanism."

"You make it difficult for me. I had hoped . . . However, I will say it. They have all been young, dashing, handsome."

Theodore lowered his eyes. "But you, too, are at least older, if not as old as I. Am I otherwise unworthy?"

Angélique considered his question. "Would you ruin yourself for me?" she asked finally.

Cariatis thought of his olive groves, his refineries, his mills, his villas and palaces. He hesitated.

"You see," she said. "How can I love you, old and little as you are, when you would not even ruin yourself for me if I asked you to. I am not rich, but I have enough to spare myself that. I may be a courtesan, but I am also a Couronne d'Epines. Indeed!" She got to her feet.

"No," he cried. "I beg of you, Angélique."

"Theodore, it must be so."

With a groan Cariatis fell back on the couch. He still held the handkerchief on which he had put the eau de cologne, and he spread it out to cover his eyes.

"And now, farewell, Theodore. No, don't move. It is better so. Adieu."

"Will I not see you again?"

"Perhaps, *chéri*," Angélique said from near the door. "After Easter, perhaps—I mean our Easter, not yours." Without a backward look she went out to the hall and through the front door. Downstairs in the lobby she met Ursula. "Ah, little Ursula," she said. "Your father is eager to see you, but you had better leave him alone for fifteen minutes to recuperate."

"What's the matter with him?" Ursula asked.

"I have just broken his heart," said Angélique.

Upon hearing this, Ursula went around to the kitchen entrance of the apartment, let herself in there, and got to her own room without encountering anyone. Thus she did not see her father until she was packed and ready to take the elevator downstairs to wait for Artie. Theodore Cariatis did not move on the couch until he heard her coming.

Seven

After fortifying himself with whisky, Arthur van Zandt felt able to talk to his son. It was late, after six o'clock, and if he didn't do it soon, he wouldn't have the chance. Knowing Artie and how he was likely to vacillate, the elder van Zandt had waited deliberately, so that should he be able to change his son's mind, the latter wouldn't have time to change it back again. His heavy knock was greeted, from within Artie's bedroom, by a kind of squeak. This the father took to be the son's invitation to enter. He opened the door and went in.

"Oh, it's *you*," Artie said, relieved.

"Yes, Artie." They stood and looked at each other until the son blushed. "Ha!" said his father.

He looked around to see how far things had gone. There

was a small suitcase pushed under a chair, and an open book pushed under a pillow. "Let me first present my credentials, Artie. Or should I say, let me claim the cover of my agency, cowardly though it be. I am here at the request of your mother, my wife, our burden."

"Here to do what?" Artie asked, backing toward the couch and pushing the book further into concealment.

"Here to talk to you, as man to man." Van Zandt sat down heavily. "Or father to son, if you like. Not that I'm going to try to tell you that you have or have not to do anything."

"Does it have to be now? I've only got a few minutes."

"I know."

"You know?" Artie's eyes went to his suitcase, to his overcoat, to the book, then back to his father. His Adam's apple worked.

"I know everything. We know everything. *She* knows everything."

Artie sat down. "Then I was right. I suspected she knew. But I thought maybe I was just being paranoid."

"Where your mother is concerned, Artie, it never pays to decide that too quickly. Any outrage is possible."

"Outrage?"

"Spying. Private detectives."

"So that's how. I was thinking more about her knowing than about how she found out. I guess I never got that far in my fantasies."

"Had I been you, that is where I would have begun. However, all this is avoiding the question. Let me ask you—do you know what you are doing?"

"I think so. I hope so."

"Do you know what you may be jeopardizing? I am no longer very rich, but your mother still is. You realize that scorned, she may well be sufficiently outraged to do something drastic. I couldn't stop her."

"I know that. But supposing you had my choice, Father. What would you do?"

"Say rather, what will I do?" the elder van Zandt replied. "But that isn't a fair question. You're not in it as far as I am." He smiled at Artie's puzzled expression. "Couldn't you find some girl your mother would approve of? It would be so much simpler."

"But do you really think it's her snobbery that's the matter with her? I mean, there's psychology . . ."

"I prefer to look no further. In any case, it would disarm her if the girl were well connected, we might say. A scorpion with no sting is still a scorpion, but one can ignore it.

"I am in love with Ursula."

Van Zandt stared at a school pennant that hung on one wall, after so many years, because nobody had bothered to take it down. Artie had not got through college. "Even though you say that, I do want to ask you one question. It's up your alley, as a matter of fact. Are you sure, in your heart of hearts, that you aren't doing this thing tonight just for spite?"

"For spite?" Artie repeated, astonished.

"Revenge. To get even with your mother. Perhaps with me."

Artie looked down. "I've been all over my reasons with myself. I've thought about it. No, I'm not. That's behind me now, I think."

"You know, Artie, other people really rarely betray us, not the real flesh-and-blood other people; and when they do, they can be dealt with rather simply. It is the imaginary person we build in front of the real person who be-

156

trays, who doesn't live up, who lets us down, who disappoints and saddens. I have learned this. You should, too."

"Don't talk like that, Father. Let me go ahead and do what I've planned to do. Ideas like that are too paralyzing. Who could ever do anything?"

"I didn't finish. I was going to add that sometimes, sometimes, mind you, we must take an action even though it may be directed at the envelope, not at what's inside. We have to risk it. I'm not making very much sense, though, am I? I mean, it's all quite a long way from you—if, as you say, spite is not involved." He looked strangely at his son. "I do not urge you too strongly to stay home tonight, because I would just as soon you left. But there will be consequences."

"I know that. And I'll face them."

"Why then, Artie, be on your way. I will face them, too. More than that, I may just effect a few." He stood up and laughed. "Into operation goes Plan B," he said. "But first of all, I wait to see if Cariatis has had more luck than I. For, Artie, my boy, he's supposed to have been at work on his end, too. Your Ursula may never show up for your journey to Loveland."

Artie picked up his suitcase and tucked the book under his arm. "If her father really tries to make her stay home, then I'm not worried."

"Will you telephone me immediately if she doesn't go with you and it all falls through? It's important."

Artie promised he would.

As he left his bedroom his father remarked, "There is something so downright wistful about the inexperienced wisdom of you poor young people, who see life darkly, through the clouded glass of psychology. It reminds me somehow of the child seminarians one sees in Italy and Spain, who choose their terrible profession before they can know what they are giving up."

"It's better than nothing," Artie replied. "Good-by, Father."

Van Zandt went into the main drawing room and looked around it as carefully as if seeing it for the first time. He went to each of the doors to listen, in order to have an idea of how much noise could be heard from the kitchen, the dining room, and the hall. As for the outer hallway, only if he stood with his ear pressed to the door of the apartment could he hear the elevator; hence, he assumed that from the corridor outside no sound from the apartment would be heard, particularly not if the inner doors were closed. Then he walked over and stood below the balcony that projected at the top of the stairs leading from the first floor to the upstairs hallway. A good drop, a sufficient drop, he estimated; for the apartment house was old, and extravagant with its space. Quite all right. He then walked upstairs and noticed that in the sitting room Henrietta's new epergne was sitting on a table with some papers under it. She had been cleaning it, perhaps to calm her nerves during the crisis over Artie. Beside it was some lacquer with which she was surfacing it to halt oxidation. Van Zandt looked closely at the spidery structure. "Ruining it, of course," he muttered. Then he snapped his fingers. "Perfect!" he said.

He then went into another part of the upper floor, to a small storeroom where various household things were kept. Henrietta was too parsimonious ever to throw away anything potentially useful, and here she kept, in a box, all the little bottles of drugs that any one in the family had ever had left over from an illness. He pawed through them, found the two bottles he wanted, then restored what order there had been in the box. As he came down the hall toward his own bedroom, fingering the little bottles in his pocket, he encountered the butler.

"Oh, sir, I was looking for you everywhere. There was a telephone call for you a few minutes ago."

"Mr. Artie?"

"No, sir. The gentleman left his name—Mr. Edward Maule."

"What did he say?" van Zandt asked sharply. "What did he want?"

"He said he wanted to talk to you, but that he couldn't be reached and would have to telephone you later in the evening."

"Thank you. Thank you." Exulting, van Zandt turned into his bedroom. He smacked his huge hands together, for he had a premonition. "This is it. This is it, I know it. I *know* it is," he cried. "He's going to offer me the picture— if I can raise the price. He's called to say it's mine." An odd look came over his face. "And I will be able to tell him, Henrietta, my dear," he said to his absent wife, "that, one way or another, the money is virtually between my fingers at last." He went to his closet and, after a moment's thought, took out his dinner jacket, which he usually refused to wear for simple dinners at home, to disoblige his wife.

"Tonight I will dress for you, Henrietta. A little celebration. I'll humor your innocent pretense, just for tonight, Henrietta."

Eight

"Edward, how exhausted and positively ancient you're looking. Do come right in," Philip Dane said. "It's going to be chaos, unfortunately, and I'd hoped to have a quiet bite with you. But some journalistic type telephoned and simply has to have an interview, and this is the only time twixt mat and eve performances. She'll be along soon. Drink?"

Maule nodded. "Whisky and soda. Not too strong."

"Umm. I can't, unfortunately."

Maule noticed the newspaper clippings strewn about. Timidly, he drew some from his coat pocket. "Philip," he said, "I thought perhaps you could use copies of your reviews. I cut them out of my papers."

"With your own tiny hands? *How* thoughtful. I'll send your copies to my mum way off in the Lone Star State. I've got that place on my mind—this reporter's connected with a newspaper down there. You know—famous-son stuff."

Maule smiled. "I always forget you come from Texas, Philip."

Dane plumped his scarf and flicked some lint from his blazer. "One *has* done a good job hiding Texas," he said, approaching the mirror and favoring it with his reflection from several angles in sequence, left to right. "And it's so big, too." He turned his back and craned around to see that aspect as well. "So. I'm ready, but where is our scribbler? Oh, I'd better order our supper from the delicatessen. They have enormous corned-beef sandwiches on Jewish rye. Want one of those?"

"I think I'll just have my drink now. I'll pick up something at a restaurant later. I'm a little upset—nasty telephone conversation with a disappointed client."

"I envy you—dinner, I mean. This is my sandwiches-only day, until late tonight, and I could really go for a spot of *la cuisine française* this instant, too. But if I did, I'd undoubtedly open my mouth for my entrance line, and out would come a great thundering belch to rattle the bridges of all the lady buyers in the front row."

He telephoned, and then the doorbell rang and he skipped off to answer it. "Come right in, Miss Carroll," he cried enthusiastically. "My chambers are a mess, but I'm moving into much larger soon." He followed a plump girl in her mid-thirties, wearing horn-rimmed glasses, back into his living room. "Miss Carroll, I'd like to introduce Edward Maule. Edward, this is Miss Carroll. Mr. Maule is a famous art dealer."

"How nice," she exclaimed, in the accent of her native region. She took out a pad and pencil. "I know you're rushed, Mr. Dane, so I'll hurry. I just want a couple of quotes."

"Cue me, honey, and I'll give them to you," said he, seating himself in a chair opposite her.

"Well, what does it feel like to be in a big Broadway success?"

"It feels like being elected Governor of the State of Texas."

She giggled. "They'll adore that," she said. "By the way, what has always been your ideal? To do just what you're doing?"

Dane considered the question, cocking a curried eyebrow. "Well, yes and no. Of course, any actor wants to be in a good play. But I think I'll confess to you what my real secret ambition is. I want to play the classics. Shakespeare, no less."

"What roles?"

"Hmm. I guess I'm a little old for Puck, and young for Falstaff. But I might do for Romeo."

"*I'll* say, Mr. Dane."

"And Mark Antony—thanks, honey—and Hamlet. And while I'd hate to offend the racial feelings of your readers, I'd also like to play Othello. And of course, Macbeth. Yes, definitely, Macbeth."

"Who would you want to play Lady Macbeth?" Miss Carroll asked, writing swiftly.

Dane smiled. "I should think any Broadway actress who'd been panned in the reviews of her last couple of plays would do," he said, snug in his recent triumph.

Maule, who had been listening with some distaste, got up quietly and tiptoed into the other room of the apartment and closed the door. It was then that he tried without success to talk to van Zandt. Afterward he noticed some brochures on Portugal lying on the desk, and he picked them up and looked at them. By the time he had finished, the interview was over, for he had looked carefully, not only at them, but also at some jottings on a notepad— prices for accommodations, a suite with double occupancy, American plan, out on the Atlantic. Dane came in to get him.

"She's gone, our lady reporter. She said to say good-by to you. What *have* you been doing in here, Edward? Oh. You've been looking at the Portuguese flyers." He laughed. "Doesn't it look marvelous?"

Maule forced himself to be casual. "Are you planning to go there, Philip? I noticed you had hotel prices."

Dane was offhand. "I might," he said. "I just might, in

the summer, for a few weeks. We have to close for a bit then."

"I . . ." Maule didn't look Dane in the eye. "I should rather like to join you there for a while. I haven't anything on for the summer. Unless you have other plans."

Dane frowned, and when he went to answer his doorbell, which had rung again, he made a face that Maule could not see. Then he called, "Come on in here, Edward. That was my sandwich, and I don't want to eat it in there." When Maule was with him again, he had composed his answer. "I do have other plans, Edward, to be blunt. I was hoping to go with someone we both know."

"Who is that?" Maule asked.

"Thackeray."

"I see."

"Still, it's not hopeless."

"Hopeless?"

There was the sound of lettuce being torn in teeth. "Actually, one of the things I wanted to talk to you about tonight," said the actor, his enunciation clear in spite of his full mouth, "was Thackeray. I had lunch with him today. Another sandwich."

"Yes?"

"He's an ambitious boy, you know, Edward. He wants to get ahead. Actually, what he wants to do seems pretty smart to me. He wants to open a small gallery and sell contemporaries."

"Then he must be planning to leave my company."

"Oh, not so fast, not so fast. Actually, I told him I'd speak to you about something. I guess he's diffident. You know. I told him that I'd try to talk you into something that would make you some money."

"And that is?"

"To set him up in business. You have that basement, which isn't rented yet. Why not set him up in a little gallery there and oversee him while he gets started. He's up and coming. He'd make a go of it, I know."

Maule was outraged. "How dare you make such a suggestion," he said. "And how dare you discuss me with that little Negro pansy?"

"Now, now, Edward, don't get violent. Remember your heart, old thing. And nobody to take care of you if you should get sick."

"I think I will go out and get my dinner now."

"If you must. But you didn't hear everything I had to say. I was going to say this, that if you and Thackeray were going into business together—nobody would need to know it, incidentally; you could insist on that, and to gossip wouldn't help him out at all—what more natural than that you should take a little vacation in Portugal, to come talk to him about it. Probably tax deductible, too. You'd be welcomed by him, in that case, and what was welcome to him would be welcome to me. You could even stay in our hotel."

"I will go where I please and stay where I please," Maule said, hearing his own voice, as from a distance, the voice of a petulant, helpless old man.

"True. But not with me. That is my offer, Edward. Set little Thackeray up in bizz and you've got yourself companionship for your vacation. Plus future gratitude, for whatever it's worth. Refuse, and I'm afraid you're out of luck."

"Philip, you've become absolutely heartless. After all
. . ." Maule caught himself.

"Ha-ha!" Dane cried, brandishing half a sandwich. "You were going to say, after all I've done for you, including all those other summers, weren't you, Edward? I've read too many trashy plays to be much smitten by that line, my boy. Besides, who was it taught me the great principle of *quid pro quo?* You, Edward. True, with you, in the old days, the rewards preceded the favors."

Maule put his head in his hands. "How has this happened?" he said. "How has it happened that you have come to hate me, Philip?"

The crunch of lettuce. "Oh, nonsense. I don't hate you. But about Thackeray again—do think it over."

Maule stood up. "I will never mention the matter to Thackeray. Good-by, Philip." He hurried from the apartment while he still had will power enough to do so.

Dane popped the last bite of sandwich into his mouth. He shrugged. He thought a moment of that last question—why had he come to hate Edward. Did he? No. But he did rather despise him. Edward had been his first protector in New York, and had, in fact, sent him through drama school. In those days Edward had been a figure to admire, a successful man with money and position. But in recent years the tone had changed. Who could really like an aging character actor who wheedled for one's smiles? One put up with it, but one had learned by then that one's favors commanded a price. As for the summer, Edward would come around. He was too lonely not to.

Maule himself went directly back to his apartment, took some medicine to calm his nerves, then sat in a chair to let it work. He thought about Philip, about the past. About the stripling he had found, the young man he had helped to mold, and now . . . It was true, in a way, what Philip had said. A relationship based on bribes granted and favors asked. And the account of each was paid up. But there was one thing Philip had overlooked, that he was still the emotional axis of Maule's life, a life not much given to close friendships. What did a man do, Maule wondered, when the only important relationship he had was based on *quid pro quo*, and he no longer had much to give? Why then, thought he, in helpless disgust, I suppose a man sets Thackeray up in business, and thereby gets through the terror of another vacation.

Maule could not eat, but he had several more drinks. Then he remembered Arthur van Zandt and telephoned him once again to tell him that the painting was sold. This time van Zandt himself answered the telephone.

Nine

Ursula came through the room and found her father on the couch, a handkerchief over his eyes.

"Who is it? Ursula? Are you just coming in?"

"No, Father. Are you all right?"

"Ursula, you are my only acknowledged child," he said.

"I know. I should have been a boy."

"That is neither here nor there."

"It's the classical situation."

"In Freud's sense, perhaps. Not in Cariatis's," he replied.

"Didn't the old Greeks leave girls out to die on hillsides?"

"You were not a child of ill omen. You were the child of love."

"Don't be so naïve, Father. As if the one excluded the other."

He sat up, removing the handkerchief from his eyes at last. "Ursula, I think your psychoanalysis is causing you to have undesirable thoughts." He noticed that she had on a very becoming black dress, which set off her swelling figure. In addition she wore a silver serpent coiled around her neck, its two ruby eyes directed into the cleft of her bosom, as if it would slither down and coil in the warmth. "You are dressed to go somewhere," he said, looking at the snake's eyes and marveling at the ingenuity of the designer.

"I'm going to spend the night with a friend."

"I have neglected you. I have let you spend too much time by yourself. I have let you make too many decisions for yourself. You have need of a father's guidance."

"It depends on timing," Ursula said. "It's too late now."

"I am informed about everything," Cariatis said.

"I guessed that somehow. But how?"

"I was told by the boy's father."

"So they know, too."

"They think you are unworthy of him."

"In a way, I am," she said. "And vice versa."

"It is the vice versa that I believe in," her father cried.

"Well, actually, I'd say we were about evenly matched."

"You are about to throw away something whose value you don't even know, young and innocent as you are. I must intervene. Ursula, my daughter, I must forbid you to go away with that young weakling."

"But you can't. I'm an American citizen, and I'm of age. You can plead with me, but you can't forbid me to do anything."

Cariatis warmed to his new role. He jumped to his feet and paced the floor in front of her. "What does your psychiatrist say? Surely he has told you that you are a fool."

"Oh, often. That is, he hasn't said it, but I know he has thought it. But not about this."

"Why am I paying him?" her father asked shrilly. "He

is there to guide you. He should say: no, Ursula Cariatis, do not go off like this."

"That's what you should say. It's not what he should say."

"I'll have him put in jail," Cariatis cried. "I'll have him barred from his profession."

"It wasn't his idea, Father. It was Artie's."

"Have you considered the consequences? You will no longer . . . No longer be a virgin."

"That's the least of them, I guess."

"The least! How could it be the least?"

"Don't be so awful and old-fashioned, Father. What if I have a postcoital breakdown?"

Cariatis waved his little hands in the air around his ears, the diamond sparkling on his finger. "I don't understand you. I don't understand. You don't know what you're talking about. You say all these shocking things, these words, but I don't think you know what you're saying or what they mean. I have lived longer, Ursula. I know what they mean. I will not let you destroy yourself, no matter how much you think you deserve it."

"Deserve it?" she repeated quickly.

"Deserve the freedom. Deserve the right to do so."

"Oh, is that all. I thought for a moment that you had had an insight." She noticed the clock. "I have to leave now, Father."

"No," he said. "No, no, Ursula."

"I must." She went to a mirror and looked at herself. She brushed her dress smooth over the hips, then picked up her coat.

"I may not have legal power over you, Ursula, but there are other kinds of power. You are not accustomed to poverty."

"I have analyzed all that, Father. Anyway, there is enough in our own names to keep us alive. And I am your only child, so you'd come around. It's the bluff of the impotent."

"Impotent?" he cried. "Who has said that I am impotent?"

"I didn't mean that way. You Mediterranean men worry about such silly symbolic things—virginity, impotence." She put on her coat and started to leave the room.

For the second time that day her father found himself trying to take hold of a woman and keep her near him. He seized Ursula's free arm. "As your father, then, let me beg of you to stay here with me tonight. At least think about it one more night, and stay with me now. Do not leave me alone, tonight of all nights."

She twisted from his grasp. "It's an awfully obvious thing to have to say, Father, but I spent too many vacations alone at boarding school as a little girl and too many hours talking about them the last few years to be reached by that appeal." She moved on, and when he ran after her, trying to take her overnight bag, she lifted it out of his reach.

"Please, Ursula, please. Stay here with me tonight. I beg of you. I appeal to your mercy. Don't leave me alone."

Her hand was on the doorknob. "Really, Father, even though you're not analytically oriented, I should think you could see how incestuous this all is." And she left.

Theodore Cariatis recoiled, a look of horror on his face. "Incest," he whispered. *"Incest!"* Slowly he crossed himself—up, down, right, left—then said an oath in Greek, and slowly drew back into the interior of the apartment.

Ten

When Henrietta van Zandt saw her husband, she said, "I see you have dressed for dinner tonight, Arthur. You are doubtless celebrating your unsuccessful talk with our son."

He was mildly surprised. "You have always had a genius for finding out things that make other people uncomfortable, Henrietta, but how do you know that I have had an unsuccessful interview, or any interview at all? I haven't seen you since, and I am sure he didn't see you either. It's true he's gone."

"It is all recorded on tape," she said.

Van Zandt did not swear as he would have liked, since he didn't want to risk driving her to her room. "I suppose there's a virtue in being thorough, if you're going to go in for that kind of thing at all," he said. "You do think of everything."

"The stakes are high," she said. "My only son."

"I spoke to Cariatis this morning," van Zandt went on. "I judge he had no luck with Ursula, since Artie didn't call me back. They are on their way."

"Yes."

"You don't seem sufficiently upset, Henrietta." He looked at her curiously.

"What do you know of that?"

"Anyway, I did what I could," he claimed, without much conviction. "I brought myself to see Cariatis, and I did talk to Artie."

"I hardly consider that you fulfilled your part of our

agreement—you virtually urged him to leave. And of course, your speaking to him as you did of me is unpardonable. In any case, it is not up to me to condemn you. Perhaps losing your painting will lead you to some much-needed self-examination."

He looked fiercely at her. "Losing my painting, you say. Our agreement, you say? Well, I had a call from Maule. He's going to call later, but I'm sure it was to tell me that I can have the picture if I can raise the price. I must have it, Henrietta."

"Must you?"

"Let us say I am giving you a last chance."

She did not reply, but it seemed to van Zandt that she ate with more gusto.

"You are quite enjoying this, aren't you? I mean my disappointment, as well as Artie's disobedience—if you want to call it that. How I detest a God who has made it possible for people to be proud of their moral states. Pride in something like achievement—a building erected, a book written—that isn't so bad. Even pride in physical beauty is at least founded on the palpable; and that one person is beautiful does not make all others ugly. But spiritual pride—bah! It revolts me, and so does spiritual humility. You can't have one without the other, and the world would be a better place if neither had ever been created." He pushed away his soup, which was cream of asparagus, which he disliked, as she knew, and as he knew that she knew. "Odd that they should be the occupational hazards for Christians," he said, "from Jesus and Saint Paul right down the centuries to you, my sweet, long-suffering, and self-righteous spouse."

"The condition of your soul quite precludes any nicety of spiritual observation, Arthur," she said.

" 'Nicety of spiritual observation,' " he repeated after her. "I am more worried about the condition of my body right now. If you have veal coming after that filthy soup, I shall go out for dinner." He caught himself, for that was the one thing he could not do. "Or rather, I ought to."

His wife was silent while the soup was removed and veal chops appeared.

"I see you somehow guessed when you made up this menu how my efforts would turn out," her husband said when they were alone again.

"I have spent much of today thinking, trying to discover the flaws within me that might have led to Artie's attempt to ruin himself," she said. "To discover wherein I have been lacking, or what I have done wrong."

"Well, I can answer that. What you did wrong was not to order in a ball and chain when you were getting all that electronic equipment to spy on him," van Zandt answered.

"I concluded that I had been cowardly all these years in dealing with him. I should have faced the problem squarely. I should not have let him come so much under your libertine influence."

"Oh, my God," her husband said.

"Your drawing collection alone. Those suggestive and wicked Frangonards, for instance."

"The female types?" His mind leafed through them—*la coquette, la femme tendre, la prude, la dédaigneuse.* "How could they do anything but elevate the soul of anyone?" He thought of something. "Odd, Henrietta, how in our relationship we seem to return to the same subjects, over and over again, to bicker with each other. Even tonight when we have a truly new thing to talk about—Artie's defection." She did not reply, and he continued. "But here we are, back on the subject of my collection, and soon we will be on the subject of yours, I imagine. It is like the way in which second-rate eighteenth-century composers always solve the compositional problem by using their overworked formulas once more. Our life together is an endless Boccherini quartet, marked *con esasperazione, molto brutto e stupido*, and *da capo per l'eternità*. We are simply second-rate composers, Henrietta, in the area of human relations."

It was a summing up, and Henrietta did not quite know how to answer. Finally she said, "I consider our failure as one of the chief vexations I must endure. The ways of the Lord are unfathomable, Arthur." She rang for dessert.

Another pause while there were servants in the dining room. Then, hardly noticing the stewed rhubarb she had ordered as his final gastronomic persecution, van Zandt said, "You are so religious, Henrietta. I wonder something. Just what do you anticipate when you are dead? I mean by that, do you expect to have to live in some spectral relationship to me? Or apart from me? Or do you believe you will be dissociated from personality entirely?"

"It is not for me to pass judgment," she said, "yet I can hardly believe that, whatever the basis of judgment, we would spend forever near to each other."

"What you mean is, you think there's a fair chance that you will be in heaven and I will be in hell."

"Let us just say we will be separated."

"It will be the only sure proof of the Lord's mercy."

"You will not scoff on That Day," she said.

"Good enough. Now another question. Do you regard yourself as in a state of grace, whatever that means? I mean right now, for example?"

"Why are you asking me these things, Arthur?"

"Idle curiosity," he replied. "Also, I can't help but feel

that Artie's action has somehow marked a change, something new, something that more or less opens up possibilities. Doesn't it, Henrietta, exact some new confrontation, for which one should prepare? I don't know. Anyway, aren't these matters more interesting than, say, your taste versus mine, or money, or social standings, or any of our usual themes?"

"I try to remain as nearly in harmony with God as is possible," she said. "And I . . ."

She was interrupted by the butler, who informed her that a Mr. Mulligan wished to speak to her on the telephone, and said that it was urgent. Henrietta left the room, and while she was gone, her husband jumped to his feet and went to her place at the table, took out a little pill, pulverized it against his fingernail, and let it fall, powdery, onto the dish of rhubarb, which he stirred around. Then he took his own rhubarb and went to a cabinet, opened it, lifted the top off one of his wife's Chelsea tureens (in the form of drakes) and dumped the stewed fruit into it, then returned to his seat before she came back.

She noticed his dish. "You have learned to like rhubarb," she said, spooning up her own.

"I didn't think it was as bad as usual," van Zandt answered, watchful. "At least, it is a powerful flavor."

When Henrietta had finished, she stood up. "We will have coffee in the upstairs sitting room, I think," she said, an edge to her voice that indicated agitation. "I have news, and want no ears nearby."

She waited until the butler brought the coffee up before she told the substance of the telephone conversation. "It was about Artie," she said, pouring out the coffee. "From the man I employed to assist me in keeping track of him."

Van Zandt took his coffee and put it on a table by his

chair. "Don't you think you should check the hallway?" he asked. "I mean, if you're going to give away secrets."

"You might look for me," she answered, sipping. "How strong it is tonight."

"Yes, I complained before dinner. It's been too weak." He added, "Check yourself. I'm not one to distrust servants: and furthermore, the secrets are not mine."

She got up, the gun-metal taffeta of her dress rustling dismally, and went to look out the door and up and down the hall. While she was standing with her back turned, he quickly dropped another pill into her coffee and stirred it. "Nobody there," she said. "I wonder if Martin isn't dependable anyway."

"Nobody is dependable."

She yawned. "God is a mighty fortress," she said. She drank her coffee quickly and poured more. "I must have plenty. I do not want to fall asleep."

"And yet you must," said van Zandt.

"Only after I have done my duty."

"I'd swear I heard someone in that hall," he said.

She was too suspicious not to get up to have another look. This time she closed the door behind her before she returned. Meanwhile, another little pill had been put into her fresh cup of coffee.

Her husband then poured himself a measure of brandy in a glass so large that it virtually concealed his face from his wife when he sniffed into it. When he tipped it up to drink, only his eyes showed above the glass rim. If she noticed a wild glitter about them, she probably attributed it to reflections.

"So, Henrietta," he said, "I am not to have my Watteau because Artie has fled the matriarchal roof."

"That is correct." She made a little face as she took more coffee. "I shall countermand your order tomorrow."

"Yet, over there, you have your epergne. Am I to believe it your justice that you will buy yourself whatever you want, while I must be content with nothing?"

"You have your funds; I have mine."

"Somehow I seem to have lost out in their mix-up."

"We have talked about this already. What was it you said about how we always talk about the same things?" Involuntarily she emitted a deep sigh, which terminated in a gasp for breath. She looked surprised.

"*Da capo. Sempre da capo*," he said. "What about the telephone call however?"

"Telephone call? Oh, yes. Let me think."

"You are vague, Henrietta. It isn't like you."

She passed a hand over her forehead. "Drowsy. So drowsy. It has been such a terrible day for me. This will help that." She drank more coffee. "I will tell you," she said, clearing her mind with an effort. "You have come to nothing, Arthur. I mean, your plans have come to nothing. He won't get away, and you won't have your Watteau." Her head wobbled slightly when she craned forward to try to see his face. She straightened up. "The call was from Mr. Mulligan."

"So it was. So it was."

"He has traced them to a restaurant on the way to Nyack. They are presently drinking cocktails there—still. He says each of them has had three Martinis so far. Three." She blinked. "Your influence."

"It is more than my influence, it is my legacy, Henrietta. You probably never knew that by the time our marriage ceremony took place, I knew something of what was happening to me. I got drunk."

176

"They have not yet ordered dinner," she went on, apparently not hearing him. "They will drink more, Mr. Mulligan estimates."

"What do you intend to do about it?"

"I'm not sure yet."

"Have you no plans?"

"I'll think of them . . ." She yawned and put a hand to her eyes. "I'll think of them later."

"Why not now?" he asked, looking closely at her, testing for the extent of her stupor.

"Later. Later." She started. "I said later."

"How do you know that I won't take revenge for your depriving me of my Watteau? I might damage something in your collection."

"What . . . could you do? Arthur, you are ineff . . . ectual. I have known that for some time."

"You are mixed up, and what's more, you don't know what you're saying, do you, Henrietta?"

She considered the accusation, her head nodding. "No. I mean yes. I'm saying that you can't. Hurt anything. That's what."

"I might, for example, drop a jasper-ware vase on the floor of the dining room and blame it on Martin."

She was weaving in her chair now. "And why couldn't Martin just as well drop your *bleu du roi cachepot?*" she mumbled. She hiccuped.

"If he did, I would take my Caffiéri firetongs and pulverize your Staffordshire Pew Groups," van Zandt said.

"I have always wanted to obliterate your wicked Sèvres scene from *Les Bijoux indiscrets,* after a model by Falconet," she replied, producing the latter fact with triumph. "It ought to be done anyway. I think one of my Paul Revere tankards would be the right weapon." She hiccuped again.

"But consider, fair Henrietta, what I might then do to your two candelabra by Gabriel Sleath. Right down the incinerator, just like that," and he pantomimed opening a door and tossing something down a chute.

She was weaving badly now and hadn't long to go. It took her several minutes to understand what he had just acted out. Then she said, "To be followed almost at once by . . . by . . . by the little gold stuffbox, no sssnnnuff- box you prize so much. Decorated . . . with . . ."

"Decorated with scenes after Vernet."

"Vernet."

"By Poitreau."

"By Poitreau. No. No. Not followed." She almost pitched forward on her face. "Not incin . . . Toi . . . Down toi . . ."

"How vulgar, Henrietta. And you do seem sleepy to me. You seem very sleepy. Are you asleep yet, Henrietta?" he whispered, leaning forward eagerly.

"Asleep yet Henrietta?" she repeated. "I . . . bite . . . Vincennes . . . teacup."

"That would hurt, I'll admit," he said. "Not as much as Artie hurts, though, Henrietta. And you're never going to get Artie back now, no matter what you think. Do you hear me? Are you still conscious, beloved Henrietta? Never will you get him back."

"Never get Watteau," she mumbled, slumping until her head was on her knees.

"Artie is mine, now, not yours."

"Artie mine. Artie never yours. Artie never your son."

Van Zandt jumped. "What do you mean?" he asked

sharply. "For heaven's sake, Henrietta, wake up enough to explain that remark."

"Artie son of . . ."

"Of whom?"

She swallowed several times with effort. Finally she was able to say the name. "Lord Coyne."

"Coyne? Coyne? You mean that fellow who visited Philadelphia just after we were married?"

"Dear Oswald. I sinned with Oswald. Artie son of Oswald. I couldn't resist . . . his . . . quarters."

"I think you mean his quarterings."

"Artie my son, Oswald's son."

"I don't believe you."

"Letters. Desk. Proof. You unworthy me Artie too."

A look of great regret came over van Zandt's face. "So," he whispered. "So. If I had only known. Henrietta?"

No answer.

"Henrietta, I say. Are you out yet?"

No answer. A snore.

He got up and leaned over her so that he could speak directly into her ear. "Hsst, Henrietta. Would you wake up if I told you, for instance, that I was going to pick you up in a few moments and carry you to the balcony and drop you head first onto the floor below? You'd be killed, Henrietta. And if the first time didn't do it, I'd pick you up and carry you back and drop you again. Oh, yes. And your precious epergne will go with you to wherever that place is where you will spend eternity separated from me. It will appear, Henrietta, that you were carrying it toward the stairs, only you'd taken one pill too many to quiet yourself in all this crisis over Artie, and you stumbled, you slipped—that little rug you've often said should be nailed

179

down in some way—and in your efforts to save the great epergne you fell over your own balcony, carrying it with you. A collector's death, Henrietta. Do you hear me, Henrietta? And nobody will ever know. The maids have left and this is Martin's night at AA meeting." He stopped and glanced over to the telephone table. "I'd better answer that damned thing. Better do it. It might be Mulligan, needing to be put off. It's things like not answering the telephone that get your average murderer into trouble." He left his supine consort and went to the phone.

"Hello?" His manner became eager. "Maule. Yes, I got the message you'd called. You're going to sell it to me, aren't you? I'll have the price—have it without any trouble at all. Easy as falling down stairs." He was silent while Maule talked. Gradually he became incredulous. Then, "What?" he cried. "No. No, I don't believe it. I was so sure. Edward, you can't do this to me. I must have it, especially now. It belongs to me already, in my mind. Who's taken it? Not Cariatis? Reconsider, man. You must."

He sat down, his eyes on his slumbering wife. "But Edward, my plans are all made. I can't go back now. Edward, nothing else would ever have got this statement out of me that I'm going to make now. I'm begging you to reconsider, because if you don't, you will be inflicting almost the only truly grievous disappointment possible on a dying man, a man who has been your good customer and your good friend. Dying. Yes, dying. I hinted at it the other day. The Mazarin anecdote. Well, it's true. Not tomorrow or the next day, but it's all worked out in the doctors' minds. They just haven't set the date yet. Probably in a year or two. Nothing to be done. I don't mind so much, not really, but it's made me want that picture more. To try to perfect all that I must so soon leave, don't you see?"

He listened while Maule talked. "Final?" he said slowly. "Deposit?" His voice dropped. "I see. I see. And there's nothing I can offer you, nothing more I can say, is there? I've already said as much as a man could, I think." Suddenly he turned red in the face. "God damn you," he shouted, and slammed down the receiver.

He sat for perhaps five minutes staring into space, then, noticing some gurgling sounds coming from his wife, he went to her and dragged her to her feet and off to her own bathroom. She was sick there, and he stood by watching, and wondering if he shouldn't go through with his plans for her anyway.

"Better not," he finally said aloud, as if informing her of her reprieve. "Even though I don't have much to lose, it would be sheer bravado, showing off. That's not too nice to see in a man my age."

She was pawing the foundation of the toilet groggily, and he left her at it while he went to the storage closet to find some stimulants. On his way back to her bathroom he remembered her earlier hint about letters, and went into her study, where he flipped open the drawers of her desk— a thing it had not occurred to him to do in all their years of married life. She hadn't even bothered to hide the Coyne correspondence. It was there, about twenty letters, tied together with string—no ribbons for Henrietta. He opened one and scanned it. "Quite enough right there. No need to kill her at all." Then he returned to the bathroom, got her to her feet, doused cold water in her face, and forced her to take more pills. He dragged her into her sitting room and propped her up on her couch. "I think you must have been drinking on the sly," he said. He left her alone, for he was sure that she would be up to no more mischief that night.

But the old warrior in her roused itself, helped by the stimulants he had given her. She began to make at first futile efforts to come to her senses. Then, while he read downstairs in his library from the *Mémoires* of Saint-Simon, Henrietta got herself to her feet, staggered to her bathroom, and got under a cold shower with her clothes on. After ten minutes of this, she was able to get back to her dressing room and change. She lurched out to her sitting room and read the dial on the clock there—she could not yet focus on her wrist watch. Nine thirty-five. Mr. Mulligan would probably not yet have called back, if his predictions about the evening and those Martinis were correct. She hadn't missed him. She realized, at first dimly, then with all the sharp clarity of her hatred, that she had been drugged; but she assumed that her husband had done so to prevent her from further moves against Artie.

Eleven

Ursula hummed a phrase from the tune that had just been coming—muted violins, saxophones—over the tiny speaker beside their table. A revival: "Tiptoe Through the Tulips." "I wonder what it means," she said. "Tiptoe through the tulips. Where? What tulips? Think of anyone tiptoeing through tulips. It's so surreal."

Artie was paying the check for cocktails and dinner, with faltering hand and unsure calculation. They were at a steak house decorated with the mounted heads of longhorn cattle, each with a kind of lobster bib around its neck; but both he and Ursula had had fowl, which had seemed lighter, more digestible, somehow. The waitress, he was sure, had been scrutinizing them both.

"Do you know what she was thinking?" he asked, when she had gone away with his money.

"No, what?" Ursula whispered the title of the song again. "Tiptoe through the tulips. You know, Artie, what makes that line so obsessive is that everything is repeated—like *tip* and *lip*, and then *thru* and *tu*, and almost *toe* in that group, and *th* and *the*," she said. "It's all a big poetic device, that line. Poetry bent to an inferior end."

"She was thinking: they've come up here to—you know," he said.

Ursula smiled, flashing her white teeth. "She was thinking: they've come up here to bend themselves to an inferior end," she said.

"I'm sort of drunk, Urse," Artie confessed.

"I'm plastered." She got out lipstick. "But that doesn't matter. I don't have to do anything." She blushed. "Oh, I'm sorry, Artie. I didn't mean—I mean, I meant things like driving the car. You know. Damn. Right on my front tooth."

"It's all right, Urse. You haven't said anything I haven't been thinking." He squirmed his way to the edge of the seat of the booth. "Let's go on."

"You're calling the moves," Ursula said.

At the door, where they stopped to take several little mints designed to purify the breath, the hostess, from behind her revetment of cosmetics, said her customary "Good night, folks" to them, which caused both of them to giggle as they picked their way across the icy parking lot. Neither of them noticed a fattish man with heavy black jowls, definitely "folks" from the looks of his fedora, who sauntered out of the roadhouse after them and went to his

183

own car, which was parked near theirs. He stopped to light a cigar on the way, seemingly quite at his leisure. Until, that is, their car was started and they pulled away from the lot. Then he moved like a boxer, quick and sure, into his own car, turned on the motor, backed swiftly around, and followed them at a distance of half a block as they slowly progressed toward the motel that Artie had selected.

It had an office in the center, and rows of cabins on each side, separated one from another by car ports, almost all of which were empty; for it was late winter and there wasn't much doing, as the old woman who was tending the office observed. She had to be roused from her television set and her knitting in order to give Artie the blank he had to fill in—Ursula remained in the car outside. His name aroused some interest.

"A Dutch name," she said. "Not so many of them around any more."

"My ancestors were farmers from upriver here," Artie said.

"We're probably related, in that case. Take Cabin Five, North. Turn right as you go out the door." She shoved her needles down into a basket and went to a panel, where she flicked on a switch. "That's your outside light. You can turn it off from inside when you go to bed." She walked over to her television set and turned the sound back up. "I suppose you know it's supposed to snow," she shouted.

"No, really?" Artie said.

She nodded, sitting down. "A couple of inches."

He got back in the car and drove it to Five North. "It's supposed to snow, Urse," he said. "Maybe we'll get stuck here."

"Damn. I didn't bring boots."

"Well, here we are."

"Yes. Here we are," she said.

They got out of the car and went into the cabin. The red neon sign advertising the motel's name—The Riverview—flashed on and off out on the highway and on the walls of the cabin before Artie found the switch for the inside lights. He left Ursula alone to look around while he went out and got their suitcases. When he came back in, he found her looking at a print on the wall above the tiny table. She was crying.

"Isn't it awful?" she said.

Artie put an arm around her. "It doesn't matter," he said. "We didn't come here to look at pictures."

"I looked out the back window, Artie. It doesn't have a river view."

"They never do. It's only a name."

"How do you know?"

"I just said it to say something. I don't know."

"Oh, Artie."

"There's nothing to cry about. I don't care about a river view." He giggled. "Nerves," he explained.

"I'm not crying about the picture or the cabin," she said, "I'm crying because I just remembered that I forgot to bring the pajamas."

"Urse!" he cried, stepping backward.

"It's going to be just like going to a movie when there aren't any short subjects before the feature," Ursula said.

Artie was grim. "Stop thinking up elaborate things like that to say, Urse," he said. "It's a lot worse than saying *awful* all the time. Anyway, I've got my bathrobe." He went to his overnight bag. "Let's have a drink, first of all."

"Oh, yes," she said. "I'm dying for one."

"After all, there's no hurry."

"No, we've got plenty of time," she said.

Outside, the portly man with the jowls took his listening device from the door, made a note in a notebook, and tiptoed back to the other end of the line of cabins, where there was a pay telephone in an outdoor booth. He felt in his pocket, cursed, then ran to his car, which was parked down the highway a hundred feet or so, its dim lights on. He felt on the tray above the dashboard, where there was some change, found a dime, and returned to the booth. He used it to dial the long-distance operator.

Henrietta van Zandt's telephone rang, and she reached out a languid hand to lift the receiver. She had to swallow several times before she could speak into it. "Mr. Mulligan," she said, struggling to get upright. "What? I am having trouble hearing, so do speak up. What? I see. I realize there's a rush. Yes. Your assistant. Yes, I understand. I will somehow manage to get downstairs in five minutes. Yes. Good-by." She stood up, then groggily collected some warm clothing to put on, and started toward the door, but stopped as she thought of something. Her husband must be kept out of this, but there was another parent involved, who would be her ally. She looked in the directory and was relieved to find that Theodore Cariatis had a listed number. She called him.

After she had identified herself, she said, "I know that you, like me, do not approve of what is taking place between our children. There has been another development to which I am privy." She told him of Artie, Ursula, and the motel. "They have begun to drink again. My informant believes there will be time to get to Nyack and put a stop to this folly. Speed is essential, although Artie has always been a congenital dawdler. I leave at once, and have called to suggest that you join me there. With each family represented, they will surely be tractable. The motel is called The Riverview."

She waited while he answered her, an expression of contempt gradually appearing on her face. Finally she held up a hand, which the little man could not, of course, see.

"Enough," she said. "I do not intend to waste precious time listening to your abusive language. If you do not care about your daughter, I yet care about my son. This conversation has only convinced me the more that it is an intolerable liaison. If Artie is to take a mistress, then I pray that she may at least be the daughter of a gentleman."

She cut him off, seized her pocketbook, and hurried out.

Only a few minutes later the telephone in the van Zandt apartment rang, but this time it was answered, eventually, by Arthur van Zandt himself. He had put aside Saint-Simon, and was giving a more careful reading to the Coyne correspondence.

"Cariatis," he exclaimed. "What do you want?" When Cariatis had answered him, he replied, "But I assure you, I know nothing about it. I would have stopped her. In fact, I thought I'd done so. In fact, I can hardly believe that in her condition she could get anywhere. Hold the line and let me check." He ran out of his library, took the stairs two at a time, and burst into Henrietta's bedroom. She was gone. He picked up the telephone there and said, "She's escaped, all right, though I can hardly believe it. I wonder. She'd taken a lot of medicine, and maybe it's affected her sense, such as it ever was. Quite right. Oh, quite right. Of course it's outrageous, but I see no way of stopping her now. Above all, it is so cruel. Poor things." Suddenly he shouted, "Hey, Cariatis, there is one chance. Let's go on up there ourselves. We might be able to intercept her, although she's got a head start. In any case, we might be able to help a little. If we can't head off the dragon, we may be able to pull her out by the tail. Why the hell let the villains in this world always get their way? You have? Good. I'll put on a coat and come right down. You know the address here? Right."

He ran for his overcoat and hat, then remembered the letters, returned to his library and locked them up, and left the apartment. Theodore Cariatis's limousine arrived almost as van Zandt got out of the elevator.

Twelve

As the new car drew silently up behind the car already parked, a figure emerged from the bushes whose black jowls were half concealed by a heavy muffler. His fedora, lightly dusted now with falling snow, was pulled low. His breath puffed out into the air, a cheerful detail.

"O'Toole?" he whispered in through the ventilating window.

The driver of the new car leaned over. "Check," he said.

"Where's the client?"

"Back seat."

"Oh." The man outside opened the rear door. "Come on out, Mrs. van Zandt," he whispered. "But keep your voice low, and don't slip."

Henrietta unwound herself from an old army blanket. She extended a hand, which her agent took, and emerged from the body of the car. She had been sitting as erect as possible all the way from New York, and now she was stiff with cold. She pawed the ground with her feet.

"The heater is defective," she complained.

"They never do work much in the back seat. You ought to have ridden in front."

"In front?" she said. "Mr. Mulligan!"

He had shifted his attention to his colleague. "You wait here, O'Toole, to cover our rear. Blink your lights if anything comes up. And don't play your radio. Got it?"

"Check."

Henrietta and Mr. Mulligan crept down the road, then cut over toward the row of semidetached cabins across the white earth that reflected the red of the neon sign.

Mulligan stopped. "That's it," he said, pointing a round gloved hand toward Five North. "They're in there."

Henrietta, shaken deeply, began to slip and slide. She was rescued by the beefy arms of Mulligan, who lifted her clean off the ground for a second, as the best way of stopping her without danger of knocking her down.

"Careful," he said disapprovingly. "We don't want any accidents."

"Not now," she replied. She stopped. "How can I ask you this? How can I put it? Yet somehow I must, Mr. Mulligan. Am I . . . ? I wish to say, is it . . . ? In a word, are we too . . . late?"

Mulligan averted his face. "No, ma'am, we aren't," he said. "I'd have told you right off if that had been the story. But they're still talking. I've got a transcript of some of it." He tapped a portable tape recorder. "I'd take you back to the car and play it, but it might be embarrassing in front of O'Toole; and also, sometimes in cases like this nothing will happen for hours, and then all of a sudden they begin to move fast, and in a minute it's all over but the lawsuits."

"Hurry. Hurry, Mr. Mulligan," Henrietta cried, once more moving forward, this time at a less unwise speed.

Soon the sluff-sluff of feet treading upon snow and grass

189

gave way to the crunch-crunch of feet over snow and gravel. Then she and Mulligan slowed to a creep. He pulled another piece of equipment from his bulging pocket, a kind of stethoscope. "Put these earpieces over your ears," he said, "and hold this disk tight against the door and listen." He started to give her the instrument, but kept it long enough to take a clean handkerchief from his breast pocket and wipe the earpieces. They mounted the step up to the concrete platform on which the cabin was founded. Mulligan thought of something. He had her turn her back to the cabin, now only a few feet away, and whispered into her ear.

"Will you be wanting pictures?"

Now that the climax to all her plans was approaching, Henrietta, partly, no doubt, because of the combination of soporifics and stimulants she had taken, was feeling giddy, even confused. She looked uncomprehendingly at the detective.

"Pictures?" she said, slurring slightly.

He tapped his other pocket. "Camera. Photographs," he explained.

"Why would I want a picture? Oh, I don't think so."

"Right, ma'am. But I thought I'd better ask."

He propelled her noiselessly across the concrete apron until she stood by the door. Then, after fitting her with the headpiece, he guided her hand with the hearing disk to the thin wooden panel and pressed it tight. Then he stood back.

She frowned, then stiffened. "Abominable," she said noiselessly. "Drinking, too." Then, "Detestable." Finally, "He says such a thing about me to her," with wonder.

She started to retreat to consult with her man, but curiosity got the better of her and she returned to listen some more. "No, Artie, no." She drew away from the door and beckoned to Mulligan.

"What will we do?" she asked. "I fear that in spite of certain problems that I cannot discuss with you, they are perhaps drawing toward an irrevocable act. Am I clear?"

"I got the whole picture before you arrived," Mulligan answered. "In my experience, with kids it's always either fast, slow, or never."

"They may not succeed, Mr. Mulligan," she said, frowning, "but they may try. What shall we do?"

Mulligan organized the possibilities. "Well, ma'am, we could interrupt them. I mean I could. I could knock on the door. Then when they answered it, I'd pretend it was all a mistake and that I was a drunk looking for another cabin. I might even try to get in there, swear they were stealing from me, or something like that." He smiled shyly. "I can put on a pretty good drunk act. Sometimes I do it at parties."

"Yes, yes. But why do all this?"

"Because I have the feeling, begging your pardon if I'm blunt, that after an interruption like that, from what I heard, your son isn't going to be much good the rest of the night." He brushed snowflakes from his eyebrows. "Or I could pretend to be the police. That's dangerous, though. Still, I doubt if it would occur to them to do anything about it."

"Shouldn't we hurry?" she asked.

"Maybe, maybe not. You know, maybe my camera's really the best thing. I could knock, then when he came to the door, I'd hold the camera up and flash it through the crack, then run. They'd never need to know who or what I was, but they'd be too shocked to do anything more tonight, those two would. I've met 'em who wouldn't even stop what they were at for fifteen seconds when a flashbulb went off, but these two aren't tough like that."

Henrietta collected herself. "Mr. Mulligan, you have gone too far."

He hung his head. "I'm sorry, ma'am. I forgot myself."

"Please do remember that in the matter of this case and its relation to your other cases, the distinctions are far more significant than the similarities."

"I know it. Still, there is the problem, what are we going to do? It's cold, getting colder, and now the snow."

"It is up to me," Henrietta replied. "I will go in the cabin myself. If a mere flashbulb might end it all, think what my appearance will do."

Mulligan remembered a few of the things he had heard the two in the cabin say about their respective parents before Mrs. van Zandt had arrived. "I imagine," he agreed, "that they will then give up for sure."

"I will knock first," said Henrietta.

"Best to do so. Your son—well, maybe I'd better not say it."

"If it is relevant, and not merely ruminative, then you must go ahead and say it, Mr. Mulligan."

"Well, your son doesn't have on pajamas, ma'am."

"Oh." It was a little cry. "Mr. Mulligan."

"An oversight," he said. "Anyway, I'll stay out here to stand guard, just in case anyone comes. I'll knock three times."

"Thank you, Mr. Mulligan."

"Not at all, ma'am." On an impulse he reached out and took her hand and shook it.

As Mulligan faded away into the shadows of Four North,

Henrietta van Zandt resolutely approached the door of Five and knocked softly.

Inside, Ursula, whose head was out of the covers, whispered, "Artie, what was that?"

"I didn't hear anything."

"Pull the damn sheet off your head. I'm sure someone knocked."

"It must have been the heating pipes."

"No, it wasn't. Artie, I know someone knocked. Maybe it was that old woman you talked to in the office. Maybe you filled something in wrong on the card."

"Urse, you know you're being silly." He stuck his head out. "It's so cold in here I wish the heat *would* come on. Are you sure it wasn't the pipes? Anyway, unless you calm down, Urse, I'll never manage, no matter how I try. You know how anxiety communicates itself."

There was another knock, this time louder.

"Who's paranoid now?" Ursula said. "You'd better go to the door."

"Let's wait a minute. Maybe it was a mistake."

They waited, but the knock came again, this time still louder and repeated more often.

Artie threw his long skinny legs out of bed. "Where did I put my bathrobe?" he muttered, feeling around the armchair in the dark. "Ouch. God damn it. Here it is. I'll see who's there, Urse, and get rid of them." But she didn't hear, for she had gone into the bathroom and closed the door.

He felt around for the light, then changed his mind and instead left the interior of the cabin in darkness. He found the knob and opened the door just enough to peep through.

"Mother!" he cried. It was audible to the faithful Mulligan over at Four North.

"Yes, Arthur. Mother," Henrietta said, pushing the door ajar so that they faced each other, after she had ascertained he had on a bathrobe.

"But how? Where? I mean, what are you doing here?"

"I have spied upon you. I have employed private detectives. I have humiliated myself. I have come to fulfill my responsibilities. I am here to stop you from consummating your affair with that woman."

Involuntarily, he looked behind him, and in the flashing red light saw that the bed was empty, the bathroom door closed. He opened the front door wider so that his mother could see into the cabin. "What woman are you talking about? There isn't anybody here, and you can see it. You've gone mad."

In reply, Mrs. van Zandt held up her eavesdropper.

"What's that?" Artie asked.

"It hears through closed doors. I have been listening for the last half hour," she lied.

He blushed. "You mean you heard us talking? You heard that . . . Mother, how really low of you."

"You dare— Artie, I heard, among other things, you tell your friend that her . . . that her thoracic development made it possible for you to dissociate her from me. How dare you!"

"But that's psychology, Mother. Nothing personal."

"Psychology. You speak to me of psychology at a time like this? Perhaps you are right, and I really am going mad. Or sleeping. Surely I will awaken—Artie, close your lower jaw, you look half-witted—surely I will awaken any moment and find this has all been a terrible dream, that I have you back again, safe in our home, that we will meet . . ." She became vague—the pills. "Where? Over kippers and eggs in a few hours."

"If that is your dream, you need some analysis your-self."

"Let me in. I am nearly numb with the cold out here."

He began to, obedient to years of training, but caught himself. "No. No, I won't. You got yourself into the cold, so you can get yourself out of it. But you can't come in here."

There was a sound from behind him. "Let her in, Artie. You might as well. She's won this round and we both know it. What will we ever be able to do now, even if she does go away?" Ursula's voice was hard, not tearful.

"I won't do it," he replied. "She has no business in here."

"Business," Ursula said. "What does that have to do with it? She's rather obviously ill, I would say."

Artie looked in exasperation first from Ursula to his mother, then from his mother to Ursula, breathing through set teeth. At last he stepped back, and his mother came into the cabin, there to confront, for the first time, Ursula Cariatis. Her opening speech was no longer very appropriate, but she had planned it, and she delivered it.

"I have come to take my son back from you."

"I don't think I ever got him away. Not that I tried very hard," Ursula said, searching for a cigarette. She had dressed while in the bathroom, which Artie thought unfair. "Artie, we'd better go on back to the city," she said.

"But Urse, I won't give in like this. Not after all the preparations we made."

"Do as she says, Artie," Mrs. van Zandt commanded.

"I won't. Mother, I want you to leave. If you don't, I'm not going to see you again, ever."

There was a soft knock on the door, three times, which nobody inside the cabin noticed.

"Yes, kippers and eggs," Henrietta said dreamily, as some

new chemical combination achieved dominance in her circulatory system.

"I'll be having breakfast with Ursula," Artie insisted.

"I don't eat it," Ursula said, puffing furiously on her cigarette. From behind a cloud of smoke came a question, an afterthought. "God, do you really eat kippers for breakfast in your house? How simply awful. No wonder you used to be sick in the mornings."

"Come, Artie. Just leave her. Come away home with me," Henrietta rambled on, covering the second set of three knocks. "In a year or two we will find you a suitable young lady to marry. You will forget entirely both tonight and this person when once you will have entered into the legitimate satisfactions of a worthy marital alliance."

"My daughter is not a 'person,' " said a voice behind her.

"You are never at a loss, in your speeches, for an appropriate sentiment, Henrietta," said another. "I am interested to know that the legitimate satisfactions of a worthy marital alliance are what I have endured all these years."

Henrietta froze. "Pinch me, Artie. Those dangerous things your father gave me have brought on hallucinations."

"Mr. van Zandt," cried Ursula.

"Mr. Cariatis," cried Artie.

"Artie, where have you learned ventriloquism? Did this woman teach it to you?" Henrietta said.

Artie sat down on the bed and put his face in his hands. "It's an inversion of the primal scene, Urse."

"What are you doing here, Father?" she asked. Now she did begin to cry. "How awful everything is. Everything."

"At least it can't get worse, Urse. We've run out of parents."

She crept over and sat down so that Artie partly hid her.

"You save us," she whispered. "I just can't carry this off. You'll have to try." She hid her head under a pillow.

Henrietta looked at her and sniffed.

"My daughter has collapsed with chagrin," said Theodore Cariatis, coming all the way into the cabin and hurrying to Ursula. Behind him came van Zandt, and behind him, Mulligan.

"If she has collapsed, it is from shame, not from chagrin," said Henrietta, turning at last to face the men. "You are real after all, Arthur. It is no trick of your poisons. How could you have let this happen?" she demanded of the unhappy Mulligan.

"I knocked twice, ma'am. I tried to warn you."

"Take off that preposterous hat, Mr. Mulligan."

He removed it. "Sorry. The cold . . ."

She turned to the other men. "This is an outrage," she said. "There will be repercussions." Suddenly she felt faint, and put out a hand to steady herself against a wall. "Let me warn you both."

Mulligan had sidled up next to her. "Pictures now, ma'am?" he whispered into her ear.

"Pictures!" she cried.

"Honestly, ma'am, it never hurts to have them."

To the astonishment of everybody, she fell to her knees. Her husband said, "By God, she's going to pray," but he was wrong, for she fainted and sagged slowly to the floor.

Mulligan dropped to her side, but van Zandt said, "Just let her lie there. We can settle things better without her."

She, not her husband, however, had retained Mulligan. He searched around in an inner pocket and found a phial of smelling salts, another tool of his trade, and applied them to her nose. Soon she revived, and Mulligan drew her to a sitting position and gave her more of the fumes from the salts. She shivered, blinked, and turned once more to face the group.

"What have you come for?" she demanded of her husband.

He shrugged.

Cariatis, who had been stroking Ursula's shoulder, now spoke. "I have come so that you cannot humiliate my daughter. I am also here to take my daughter away from your son. I do not want the child of my flesh defiled by the child of your flesh, Henrietta van Zandt. To say nothing of my enemy, your husband."

"Don't worry about the latter," said van Zandt, obscurely. "But come now, Cariatis, let them alone."

"Never," said the little man, beginning once more to stroke his daughter's shoulder.

"Stop that, Father," she said. "It's awful."

"Well, take your choice. Side with my wife or side with them," van Zandt said.

Seeing his dilemma, Cariatis cursed.

Suddenly van Zandt seemed to weary of the situation. He walked over to Artie and put a hand on his shoulder. "Sorry," he said, "but I thought that, bad as it is, it still might be better to have me here than not. I tried to block her earlier. I almost closed the whole dossier in fact, but I didn't, partly through fastidiousness, partly, I suppose, from prudence. I should have gone through with my original plan." He looked over at Henrietta, sitting on the floor, supported by her detective. "If I had foreseen all this, I probably would have. I might have paid for it, but you would have had more of a chance. In any case, Artie, what happens from now on is up to you, I think." He stepped back.

Artie leaned on an elbow and nodded. He encountered

Ursula, and with his free hand patted her on the knee. Then he said, "That's true, isn't it? It's up to me." He sat up. "Very well, then, this is what I have to say. Get out, all of you. Let us alone. Go away. You, whatever your name is, take my mother away with you. Father, you go, too. It was nice of you to come, but enough is enough. Mr. Cariatis, I'll come and see you tomorrow morning, but tonight you must go away. There. It's all settled."

"Good for you," said the elder van Zandt. "I'm off."

"But I am not," said Cariatis.

"Don't be an ass, Cariatis," van Zandt said. "It's another generation, and it has to float or go under, finally, according to its own laws. Besides, this is Nyack, and you can't have your own way here."

"Come, Ursula," said Cariatis.

"Get under the covers, Ursula," said Artie.

Now the decision was Ursula's, and everyone looked at her. Deliberately, she removed one shoe with the other, then the first with her freed toes, and slipped beneath the blanket. Whereupon van Zandt took Cariatis by the arm and pulled him to the door and out of the cabin.

"One moment," said Henrietta, standing. "I have no intention of going."

Artie looked at her a long time, then shook his head regretfully. He stood up and removed his bathrobe. "Stay if you want to," he said, "but we are going to bed."

Henrietta lowered her eyes. "Artie!"

"Surely you want a picture now, ma'am," said Mulligan.

"A picture?" cried Henrietta, staggering out the door. "I need no photograph of what I have just seen, Mr. Mulligan. It will remain forever in my memory."

Her husband, hearing her, called, "You'd better have it enlarged," and he took Cariatis off toward the car.

Artie watched the departures from a chink in the blind. "Well, Urse, that's that. Maybe I'm not much, but just this once I did what had to be done. And you didn't leave me. That matters more than whatever else does or doesn't happen, that we each did what had to be done. Mine says that, after all, the most you can ask of people is that they do the best they can with what they've got."

"Oh, Artie."

"Little Urse. My little she-bear . . ."

Mulligan left Henrietta near his own car, then went to dismiss O'Toole. When he came back, he found that she had let herself into the back seat. He shrugged and started off, although he had trouble with the snow. "We'll go down the Jersey side, I think," he said. "Less danger of an accident." He could hear her teeth chatter.

As he climbed a hill and made a slow turn to the left, following the markers to the Palisades Parkway, he felt himself begin to slide. He tried to change course, but slowly, sickeningly, the car went off into the ditch. He got out, but there was nothing to do but sit and wait for someone to stop, and in a short time a truck did so. The driver, too, looked the situation over, and said he didn't have a tow rope. He offered to stop when he found a garage open and tell them to come and help, but that might take a lot of time, and it was cold. Didn't Mulligan and the lady want a ride in the cab of his truck?

Mulligan asked Henrietta, who leaned over and looked out of her window at the monster pulled up beside them. It was carrying sausages from Albany to New York City, according to the signs painted on its side. She shook her head.

When Mulligan got back in the front seat, he turned the motor on to run the heater. "Real shallow ditch," he remarked. "No snow, and we could get ourselves out."

He received no answer. Then he turned around. "Look, ma'am, are you sure you wouldn't be more comfortable here in front with me?" he asked. "We're likely to have quite a wait."

Another silence, then the trembling Henrietta got out of the back seat by herself and came around to the front. Mulligan unlatched the door for her and she got in.

"Why not, Mr. Mulligan?" she said. "Why not? Everything else in my world has been turned upside down tonight. I have lost the only person who matters to me. I have failed, and I don't even understand why. And so, why not?"

"You did your best," said Mulligan.

"It's kind of you to say so," replied Henrietta. She laid his eavesdropper on the seat between them.

Thirteen

When Arthur van Zandt and Theodore Cariatis got back to the city, it was about two thirty, and the streets, more because of the snow than the hour, were nearly deserted. Only a few taxis moved sluggishly, stopping with exaggerated care long before the intersections.

"The bars are still open, Cariatis," van Zandt said. "Are you a drinking man? Would you care to join me for one?"

Cariatis was worn out, but, on the other hand, he did not particularly relish returning to his empty apartment and to the thoughts that awaited him there for the hours before dawn, so he had his driver drop them at a bar near van Zandt's apartment. He and Arthur went inside and found there were a surprising number of people, most of them, at that late hour, quite drunk. Two places at the bar were empty, those nearest the front window, and here they sat and talked, Cariatis looking mostly down into his glass, van Zandt, so much taller, looking over his head out the window, enjoying the starnge effect of the people passing in the falling snow.

"I don't suppose there is much point in discussing what went on tonight," van Zandt said. "I sense you feel that way, too. I can't apologize for my wife, and I am no longer responsible for what Artie does. So what is there to say about it?"

Cariatis waved a hand without looking up. The diamond glittered on his little finger. "I care, actually, less than you might think. Ursula has not, it seems, had a very happy life. If this brings her any happiness, I suppose I should be thankful."

"At least Artie turns out not to be a disaster, not a downright disaster. He may not be what you would want, but he really is not a disaster—as was, for example, Henrietta."

"I pity you," Cariatis said. "I loved my wife. I have been in love with many women since, but never the same. I think that were I obliged to make a choice, I would not trade her against all the others, including the two others I also married, even though she lived only ten years, and the others have occupied twice that long. It is a long time to keep a memory, twenty years. Still, great love is great love, and one must obey its imperatives, when it happens. Which is, I believe, rare."

Van Zandt grunted. "Great loves. Imperatives. You are a romantic, I see, Cariatis. What about your current? Is that a great love?"

Cariatis smiled a little. "That, too, in its way, was different."

"These distinctions elude me, but that is probably because we are of such different temperaments. I find most of the generalizations made about love are merely so many words. No, love should be but mentioned and left behind."

"Yet it seems to be of universal interest," Cariatis replied gently, as the only defense he could make of his avocation.

"Sex is. I'm not sure that love is. But then, don't take my opinion to be worth much. After all, I married Henrietta."

"May I ask you something personal?"

"Certainly. We seem to be becoming friends, at least for the night. Perhaps that is its most unexpected turn, eh?"

Cariatis smiled again, and now he did look up at his big neighbor. "Why have you not sought love with a mistress?"

Van Zandt made a face. "I have, now and then. I've had what I'd call girl friends. But they never amounted to much, and somehow, it has never seemed worth the trouble—the subterfuges, and all that. Henrietta has always disliked me, I think, ever since on our wedding night I told her that her breath had the same odor as the incense in an Episcopal church—she's very religious, you know. Too bad. I didn't mean it unkindly. I thought it was funny. It was true, too— she'd gargled with something—and seemed to me funny, so I told her. She didn't understand me. She was terribly offended."

"You weren't, as the saying goes, made for each other."

"Hardly. And how sad that each of us was so organized that other considerations outweighed the discomforts of our marriage. And then only tonight I discover that she was unfaithful to me not long after we were married. She hasn't been since, I believe. Since she grew really to hate me, she has been faithful."

"It is quite tragic," said Cariatis.

203

"So here I am."

"And here am I. I with my endless chain of loves, you with none, yet we seem to have arrived at the same place. I am interested in my business. Yes, that still interests me. That is all."

"And I in my collection."

"And what of people?" asked Cariatis sadly. "I do not much enjoy the people I know. Nor, I think, do you."

"I have known for a long time what a desperate and terrible world I live in," van Zandt said. After a moment he added, "But in it, I think, the women are even more terrible than the men."

Cariatis thought of Angélique. "That is true, in our world," he replied. "Perhaps not in others." He ordered another round of drinks for both of them. "As you must know by now, we have both lost that Watteau. I lost it, and because of it I lost the only person I wanted."

"It was perhaps the last *thing* I shall ever want." Suddenly van Zandt jumped. "By God," he said, "I just saw that Tait fellow go by outside. I wonder what he's doing up at this hour. You know, I'll bet he knows who got the picture. I'm going to run out and collar him, and make him come in and have a drink with us."

He rushed outside. Pearson Tait scuttled sideways like a crab, but before he could get away, he was grabbed by the sleeve and dragged back through the door.

"We want you to have a drink with us," van Zandt said loudly, attracting some attention.

Pearson Tait's eyes rolled strangely in his head as he searched up and down the room for enemies. "Drink? Drink? They do not sell the potion that I need."

"Ask for it, and maybe they'll have it."

Tait seized van Zandt by the lapels. "You think it exists,

204

do you? You know about it? You know everything, then?"

Van Zandt looked down at him coldly. "I don't know what you're talking about. It seems to me you've been taking in a lot of potion of some sort already tonight."

"I have had nothing to drink," Tait answered, turning away. He massaged his eyes with his knuckles. "I am tired. I must go home."

"No you don't," van Zandt said, grabbing his arm again. "Not until you tell us who bought the Watteau off Maule."

"Aieee!"

The cry brought all heads in the bar to attention, and the bartender sauntered up from the other end. "Something wrong?" he asked van Zandt. "We don't want any trouble. No kooks allowed."

"He has a funny laugh, that's all," van Zandt said. He turned back to Tait. "Now come on, Doctor, tell us."

Tait was trembling. "I heard only today that it was sold. I had been hoping against hope. Imagine my despair."

"Why despair? I don't understand."

Tait peered suspiciously at van Zandt, then turned his head upon his neckless torso to stare at Cariatis. "Who sent you here to question me?" he asked.

"You're not making any sense. How could we have known you'd walk by here at three A.M.?"

"That's for you to explain," Tait replied.

Some people were almost at the door, ready to leave, and he jerked loose and darted in front of them, so that they blocked any immediate pursuit from behind. Van Zandt didn't try to follow him, but he did go to the window and look out. He saw Tait run across the street, then go at top speed to the end of the block and around the corner. Shaking his head, he came back to his stool, picked up his drink, and finished it.

"That's a surprise," he said. "He's just about the last person I'd ever expect to have that problem. I've never heard a whisper about it, either—but you can't get around the evidence. Nothing to drink, eh?"

Cariatis agreed. "Everyone has an evil secret," he said solemnly.

Tait, out of sight of the bar, lost his footing, slid several feet to a sitting position, and continued to slide until he hit the gutter. He sat dazed for a minute, then remembered what had happened and looked behind him, terror on his massive face. He saw nobody but an old woman hobbling along with a cane, and surely, he told himself, van Zandt could not have got himself a spy so quickly. He got up and stood in an entryway until he was certain nobody was coming after him. Then he walked swiftly back to his own apartment. He was sweating heavily, and had to rest as soon as he passed through his own door. Then he went to his laboratory and there took out the notebook labeled *Parodies*. In it he wrote the following:

"Maule telephoned me to tell me to finish up with the Watteau. It has been sold, as the gift for a museum. It will be featured at the opening of a new wing and reproduced in full color in *Life*.

"What do I do now?

"If I say nothing, then what do I become?"

He closed the notebook and returned it to its place. After wiping his forehead on his sleeve, he sat down and wrote a brief note to his wife, addressing the envelope to her hotel in New Zealand.

"Dear Martha," he wrote, "very unhappy things are happening to me. I am surrounded by enemies and sick with fear. If anything should happen, if I am not here when you return, I order you, as my last wish, to enter the laboratory here at the apartment, jimmy the strongbox on the left wall, which contains my records, and read the notebook called *Parodies*. Then go into the next room and open the steel storage chamber there—the combination is 7-7-7—and look at what is in it. Then do as you think best. Your ever respectful Pearson."

After mailing the letter out in the hallway, Dr. Tait put himself into bed, but with little hope of sleeping.

Meanwhile, far away, in another bed and another city, another doctor was tossing and turning. At length he reached out and put on his light. "No more, no more," he said, grabbing for the telephone. "*Endlich muss ich doch McCaffrey telephonieren.* I must say: the Watteau—*wissen Sie?*—there is something . . . something . . . *ach!*"—he stopped and puzzled over a word—"*beunruhigend.* So. But he will say, Ulrich, it is always thus with you. You can never say a simple yes or no. *Ob ja oder nein, dazu können Sie sich niemals entscheiden, Herr Doktor Pretorius.* But I must do it or I will not ever sleep again." He dialed a number. It rang several times, and then a voice answered. Dr. Pretorius opened his mouth to speak, but nothing came out. He tried again. Still nothing happened. Finally he replaced the receiver, put down the telephone, turned out the light, and lay in his bed, staring at the ceiling. "*Lieber Gott, lieber Gott,*" he said hoarsely. "What now?"

Matthew McCaffrey swore when the dial tone came back on. He looked at his watch and swore again. Then he glanced over to the other bed where Chickie lay sleeping so soundly. The phone could have rung half an hour without awakening her. He saw that she had knocked over a glass that was on the rug beside her bed, and he picked it up and put it on a table. More and more often. Nearly every night now. Soon he would have to start going out without her. He, too, put off his light and lay back on his bed, staring at the ceiling; but within two or three minutes he was fast asleep again, for he had nothing to speak of on his conscience.

PART FOUR

Three Weeks
Later

One

When the three men walked grimly into the reception room, Thackeray smiled pleasantly and stood up. "I'm afraid Mr. Maule is still in his apartment. He should be down soon. In the meantime . . ."

"Call him and tell him to get down right away, not just soon," said Barney Kant.

"Tell him it's urgent," said McCaffrey.

Dr. Pretorius nodded.

"Well," replied Thackeray, at a loss what to do in this unprecedented situation, but listening carefully now, "Mr. Maule doesn't like to be called at home. I . . ."

"Tell him they get a man up early in jail," said Barney.

"Careful, Barney," McCaffrey said.

Thackeray had a good instinct for what was important and what was not, and naturally his loyalties were with Maule. He guessed that a full warning was desirable, and so he gave it as well as he could. He retired to Maule's own office, called him, and repeated everything that had been said. Then he returned to the reception room. The three visitors were all standing now, legs apart, back to him, looking down into the street. Thackeray sat at his desk and watched them until he heard Maule coming. Then he watched Maule, learning what he could.

The old dealer gave no evidence whatsoever that he had heard of any unpleasant remarks. He was formal, as usual, but friendly. "Gentlemen. Gentlemen, what a pleasure to see all three of you at one time. An embarrassment of riches, eh?" He selected Dr. Pretorius as the special object of his graciousness, the only one of the three with whom he would shake hands. "It's been years, hasn't it, Dr. Pretorius?" he said. "I think the last time was at the Giorgione *mostra* in Venice. Time flies."

Dr. Pretorius was mortified to be thus picked out; nevertheless, he could not refuse Maule's hand, nor could he but confirm the accuracy of Maule's memory. "Yes, that is right," he said, nodding his head. "We encountered each other in front of the Castelfranco altarpiece."

"A Friday. In September."

Pretorius nodded again, glancing miserably at Barney and McCaffrey. "Correct. Quite correct," he said.

Barney Kant exploded, his wizened, ancient-boy's face screwing up like an angry monkey's. "See here, Maule, just how do you explain this?" He waved a piece of paper in front of the dealer.

Maule took the paper from Barney and read it, slowly and carefully, concentrating as he might have on an indictment, but at the same time quite aware of his audience. Another lesson for Thackeray: not the twitch of the smallest muscle, nothing at all, betrayed the fact that Maule was suddenly face to face with the most serious crisis of his later life. He handed the paper back to Barney, who, however, refused to accept it. It now belonged to Maule, with all its disturbing ramifications.

"Preposterous," the dealer said. He turned to McCaffrey. "A jealous colleague of yours, I should think."

"Nuts," said Barney. "Who would know?"

"Word gets around," Maule replied. He looked from one to the other of them. "But you can't be taking this seriously. No, I see you are. I am astonished, gentlemen. Perhaps we should go into my office and discuss the matter further.

Thackeray, be good enough to see that we are not disturbed." And, stiff-legged, he led them away.

Once in there, McCaffrey tried to get control of the movement of the conversation, being distrustful of Barney and Pretorius in negotiations. He put the troubled-young-man expression on his frank and open face, ran his hand over his crew-cut hair, and said, "Edward, you must consider our position. We have to take it seriously, even though there may not be a bit of truth in it. We owe responsibility to an Institution, to the People of our Community, to the Public and the Public Interest. A breath of this outside could spell something like ruin to all of us. Scandal, on a nation-wide scale—involving the dealer, too, you know." He smiled, just for a moment.

"Even Dr. Pretorius," he added, letting the slightest edge creep into his tone of voice, "who has come up with some reservations about the picture himself, a little too late for convenience."

Pretorius looked at him and worked his jaw mutely several times, like an eel.

Maule had taken his place behind his desk, a defense against so many opponents. "I quite understand all that, Matt," he said. He scrubbed a mustache. "I was surprised, outside, that you didn't simply laugh the whole thing off, but I understand." He turned to Pretorius and, taking his cue from McCaffrey, said rather sharply, "And just what are those reservations, Dr. Pretorius, and why have they not come forth until now?"

Pretorius spread his hands. "But you see, they only gradually came into my mind. Perhaps when I see the picture . . ."

"Odd," said Maule dryly. "Usually one's reservations come at once."

"Ulrich has a weakness for afterthoughts," McCaffrey said.

Then Maule observed stiffly, "I also find it odd that Dr. Pretorius was not sent to see the painting in person."

"An oversight. We should have. But he's not really a stylist, you know, and our travel budget is way down for the year already."

"What are your reservations, Dr. Pretorius?" Maule asked.

Pretorius breathed heavily. "Well, there is something I can't put my finger on. Something that surprises, which takes by surprise."

"But the painting is, after all, unknown," Maule said. "Everything about it is a surprise."

"Something about the way it is put together. Yes, that is it. It is something about the way the figures are put together."

"Are you saying there is something wrong with the composition?" Maule asked. He went to a file of photographs, took one out, and tossed it across his desk. "What about that? Quite close. And nobody has ever questioned the Dresden painting, so far as I know."

Pretorius nodded. He was beginning to sweat. "Yes, it is true. It is a good parallel. Perhaps I am being overscrupulous."

"Ulrich," said McCaffrey sharply, "if you withdraw your doubts so easily at this point, you had better begin to look for another job." He laughed, moved over to his assistant's side, and clapped him on the shoulder. "I mean, when you are convinced either way, we will want to know about it, but in the meantime, don't let Edward hypnotize you." He faced the dealer again. "If the painting is acquired under my administration, I want no reasonable doubts. What if this letter," and he pointed to the paper now lying on Maule's desk, "had gone to one of our local newspapers the day of the gala opening?"

Barney Kant interrupted angrily. "To hell with all the talk of newspapers," he said. "What about the money?"

"Of course, Barney. I mean, that's fundamental, too."

"You're damn right it's fundamental. It matters as much as the newspapers. Although speaking of them, Ed, I'm not going to be made into a fool, either."

"Fools are born, Barney, and you weren't born one," said Maule. "By the way, could this be from one of your enemies? He picked up the paper and dropped it again—merely to touch it demanded all his will power.

"Naw. They'd wait. Bigger stink later."

"Who knows about the picture?" McCaffrey asked.

"Tait. The four of us. Anybody you've told—your wives, for instance." Maule looked at each of them in turn. "On this end, several people have seen it. Theodore Cariatis, a friend of his, and Arthur van Zandt." Suddenly he stopped. "Van Zandt," he repeated softly.

"Who's that?" Barney wanted to know.

"He's the greatest collector in the field in America," McCaffrey explained. "We've been in touch with him to see if he'd lend to our opening in the fall. He won't."

Maule went on. "He can be difficult. I started to say that he had liked the painting very much and would, I believe, have taken it for his own collection—no small compliment." He turned to Pretorius. "Does that help?" he asked.

"Van Zandt's opinion I respect." Pretorius bobbed his head.

McCaffrey, a skilled diplomat and sensitive to nuance, had caught something else. "He must have been very disappointed when he didn't get it."

"So was Cariatis," Maule countered quickly.

"Either of them, however, could have written the letter."

"I hardly think so," Maule replied. "Cariatis is too wily to get involved in something like that, and van Zandt is, after all, a gentleman."

"Crap," said Barney Kant.

"Edward," McCaffrey said ominously, "haven't we come almost inevitably to the chief mystery about the picture? Aren't you going to have to unveil that?"

"The mystery?"

"Where does it come from?"

Maule could feel blood pressure mount, point by point. It was the dreaded moment. "I have told you I am not at liberty to reveal the owner's name. The former owner's name."

"Don't be so sure he's former, Ed," Barney interjected.

McCaffrey held up a hand. "Wait, Barney, wait," he said. "There is still absolutely nothing to go on except an anonymous letter and Dr. Pretorius's customary misgivings. Both are inconvenient, I admit, but neither is very conclusive. I think Ulrich would admit that himself." McCaffrey smiled. "So it's not quite time yet to ask for all your money back. Now, Edward, if the allegations are untrue, one of the important ways of establishing it, aside from judgments of style and whatever more Tait can tell us, is to fill in the gaps in the picture's history."

"Provenance," Dr. Pretorius said. "Yes. Provenance."

By now Maule's knees were shaking, but fortunately

they were out of sight. He tried to be firm and quick. "That is absolutely impossible," he said.

McCaffrey looked at him a long time. "I see," he said slowly. "We'll argue about that later. I think the next thing to do is to see Tait. Does he still have the picture?"

Maule nodded. "He wanted to observe something. He sent a rather irregular letter to ask if he could keep it. Something about the craquelure."

"We want more X rays. The letter mentions . . ."

"He has taken X rays. I sent them to you."

"Not of the whole," Dr. Pretorius corrected him. "Specifically mentioned in the anonymous letter is the lower right-hand area. There was no X ray of that."

"True," Maule agreed. He dialed Tait's offices, asked to speak to him, then put a hand over the mouthpiece. "Well, gentlemen, I don't know what to do now; Dr. Tait is not in his office and will not be there until this afternoon, after two o'clock."

"We'll be there then," said McCaffrey.

Maule went back on the line and made the arrangements. Then he said, "We will also want X rays of the Watteau, of the parts that were never taken, particularly the lower right-hand corner." He replaced the receiver. "This will give Dr. Pretorius a chance to have a look at the painting itself," he said, "and to quiet his inner voices."

"Let us hope so, for your sake, Edward," McCaffrey said.

As they were leaving Barney Kant stepped back into the inner office. "Look," he said viciously, "I don't like getting taken, Ed, and I hope that's not what you were planning. I've got my check to prove the deposit, but don't think you're going to keep the stock certificates, either." He hurried out to rejoin McCaffrey and Pretorius.

But McCaffrey, too, wanted a private word with the dealer. He, too, came back in and leaned over the desk. "Edward," he said, "you'd better do some thinking about your mysterious owner between now and two o'clock. I just happened to find out that you called the number for the weather forecast when we were here. I haven't told Barney yet, because he'd want to know why I didn't tell him before; but I'll have to soon. I thought it was part of the game, Edward, but I'm beginning to wonder. Mistakenly selling a forgery is one thing, Edward, but deliberate attempt to defraud—that's another, you know. The one can cost you some money, but the other . . ."

Maule's eyes closed. "Matt," he said weakly, "I can explain."

McCaffrey smiled frankly, openly. "That's good. Anyway, we have to think of everything, and I've always believed it was best to come out and say things, not keep them hidden. See you at two."

Maule sat for perhaps ten minutes, slumped down at his desk, his mind, now that there were no enemies nearby to force it to remain clear, clouded and turbulent. Words and images raced through it—paintings, people from past and present, sums of money, even, briefly, a jail cell and then a scaffold. The pace quickened, the symbols followed faster upon each other, until they hardly remained present long enough for him to identify them. Faster and faster and faster, until he groaned so that Thackeray heard him.

"I must *do* something," Maule said. He got to his feet and forced himself to walk back and forth, in the old way. It helped, but only for a little while. He knew that he did indeed have to do something. He had to cover up somehow. If only he could sell out from under this crew, get the bidding going again—the old auction psychology—get the wolves to wrangling among themselves, and the fox would slip away with the bone. He went to the door and called to Thackeray to get Arthur van Zandt on the telephone. Then he changed his mind. Get Theodore Cariatis.

Cariatis could not be reached.

"Get van Zandt, then." Van Zandt was home, and after a brief wait, Maule spoke to him.

"Something shocking has happened, Arthur," he said. Van Zandt was cold. "What?" he asked.

"Could you come to Tait's offices at two this afternoon? I would like your help. And it might prove . . . interesting for you."

"I hardly feel like helping you," van Zandt said. "What's the matter?"

"It's the Watteau. A doubt has been raised." Maule thought a second. "An anonymous letter. Silly, but you know what cowards people are."

This time the pause was a long one, and then van Zandt said, "Unfortunately, Edward, this is a very busy day for me. I will be at the airport at two o'clock. Moreover, although I am a curious man, I have not forgiven you. I am sorry." And he hung up.

Maule began to pace again. What would he do now? He looked up to find Thackeray watching him with great concern, a friendly face. "Thackeray," he groaned.

"Is there anything I can do, Mr. Maule?" Thackeray asked, coming into the inner office. He was afraid that Maule might stumble, even fall, and he went over to him and got him to a chair. "You just rest here," he said. "You're overwrought."

"Thackeray, write a note to that Angélique de la Couronne d'Epines creature and sign my name to it."

"And say what?"

"Tell her that the painting in which she was so interested may not be wanted by the party who was going to buy it, and that I wondered if she still might wish it for her collection. Make up a polite letter, but keep it vague."

"I see," said Thackeray. "Oh, Mr. *Maule*."

Maule's head drooped. "Yes," he said. "Trouble. Serious trouble."

"I'll do the note right away and let you read it." Thackeray hurried to his desk.

Once again by himself, Maule turned the entire situation over and over in his mind, every fact he knew, every guess he could make. Who could have written such a thing? Was it an enemy of Barney or McCaffrey? Was it his own enemy, a person who somehow knew his secret and wanted to embarrass him? Was it, could it have been, van Zandt? Then all lucid consideration of the crisis began to splinter, and sheer desperate worry took its place; so that when Thackeray came in with the letter to Angélique, Maule could not hold it and would not read it. He told Thackeray to sign it, find out where she lived, and if she was in, to deliver it to her personally. After Thackeray had left, he crept back to his desk and sat in the chair, put his head in his hands, and wallowed in the tormenting thought that he had gotten himself into his difficulties, but couldn't get himself out. He had thought he was so clever. He had thought to climax his career with such a coup. And his ethics . . . (Groan!) What of them? Everything was backfire. Blow-up. And now? Now?

"Now, Edward Maule," he accused himself, "you are nothing but an old fag in a dither."

Two

Angélique answered her own door—an indignity Theodore Cariatis had once offered to spare her—dressed in a fiercely ruffled peignoir of sea-green satin, projecting around herself a powerful effluvium of the latest perfume, *Sans Reproche*. She did not recognize Thackeray.

"I work for Edward Maule, mademoiselle," he explained. "Of Edward Maule and Company. The art dealer. You came there not long ago with Mr. Cariatis."

"Ah, yes. I remember. But of course. And I have seen you since somewhere."

"At the theater," Thackeray said.

She made a gesture with her shoulders that could have meant anything. "Perhaps. And what do you want of me?"

"I have a note for you from Mr. Maule," Thackeray replied, holding it out. "It is important. He wanted it delivered by hand."

Angélique took it; then, when the elevator brought someone else to the same floor, she remembered her dishabille and beckoned Thackeray through the door into her hallway. There she opened the envelope and read the note.

"For sale again?" she said. Then she laughed. "Poor Theodore." She reread the note. "Three weeks ago," she said to Thackeray, "this might have mattered. But now? Now it is the intelligence report that arrives after the battle is lost."

"Should I tell that to Mr. Maule?"

"If you wish. I am pressed for time right now. I would

221

prefer not to have to stop to write him. Could you remember to tell him something else I will tell you?"

Thackeray nodded. "My memory is famous," he said.

"Ah? I had not heard of it. Well, tell him, please, that I am not able to buy the painting. Tell him also that I do not see Mr. Cariatis any more, and so I am not able to have him buy it, either. Will you remember all that?"

"You cannot buy it," Thackeray said, "and Mr. Cariatis cannot buy it for you."

"That is more or less correct. Correct enough. Thank Mr. Maule." She started to dismiss Thackeray, then stopped and asked him, "And tell me something about this Edward Maule. He has a large business, does he not?"

"Oh, very. He's a *great* dealer."

"He is not married?"

"No, mademoiselle."

"*Là, là.* He could give the painting to the right person." She flashed her smile, internationally admired, upon Thackeray. "No?"

"Well, I suppose so."

"Dare I be *indiscrète?* You will not—what is that charming *enfantillage?*—you will not 'tattle' on me?"

"Oh, no, mademoiselle. I wouldn't dream of it."

"Would he give it to a woman?"

Thackeray stepped backward, astonished. It took him a moment to recover himself, then he replied, "I really don't know."

Angélique seemed to have found out what she wanted to know. She became distant, once more the busy woman of the world. "I thought you might. Well, in any case, I fear there is no more to say to your Mr. Maule. And now— *au revoir.*" As Thackeray reached the door she repeated herself. "*Au revoir*. You are a very handsome young man," she added.

When Thackeray got back to the office, he went immediately to deliver his message to his employer, but Maule was gone. There was a note on Thackeray's desk telling him that Maule was upstairs in his own apartment and didn't want to be disturbed until 1:45, when he would leave for his appointment at Pearson Tait's studio. Thackeray typed out a memo of his conversation with Angélique, omitting its end, and went in to put it on Maule's desk. There he saw the significant piece of paper that Barney Kant had waved in the reception room that morning. Maule, in his distracted state, had left it lying upon his blotter. Thackeray picked it up and read it over. He went back, and went through it sentence by sentence. He whistled.

"My goodness. My *goodness*."

There was something about it, something very strange, but something familiar. Deep in thought, he returned to his desk, opened a drawer, and took out a lip pomade, for the weather was still raw, and he was sensitive to the cold. He stopped as he was applying the camphor ice, midway through the nether lip. "That's it. I'm sure it is." He continued to apply the medication, finished, turned the stick slowly back into its sheath, and replaced it in his desk. "But why anonymous?" More thought, then, "Something funny going on," he said, "and Mr. Maule is going to want to know about it."

Aware now, however, of just how disturbed his employer must be, he decided to wait until he descended, and not to bother him while he was resting. But Maule, contrary to his habit, went straight from his apartment to the entrance of the building, before Thackeray, listening inside the office, realized what had happened. The receptionist rushed to the stairs, but Maule had found a cab just outside; when Thackeray got to the street, he saw it pull away, make the light at the corner, and turn downtown. Without access to the locked files Thackeray could not prove what he had guessed, and so he had to wait until later in the afternoon to submit his discovery. Submit it he must, that he knew, out of loyalty to Maule, even though it would involve his admitting that he had snooped into the anonymous letter left lying unguarded on Maule's desk.

Three

Theodore Cariatis shrugged his shoulders in perplexity. "But why?" he asked. "I do not think of you, Arthur, as a man much in touch with the younger generation. No more am I. Furthermore, long custom has made me mostly a stranger here. Still, in this case, you are so calm, so accepting. You seem to understand behavior I have no insight into. As between two outsiders, you are better able to see over the fence." He smiled, and made a remark he could have made only to an intimate. "Perhaps it is because you are so much taller," he said.

Van Zandt laughed. "Yes, one might have thought that they would want sympathetic parents with them, that we could help, even; but Artie said explicitly that they would like to go it alone, and do you blame them? I don't. Also, perhaps it is only Artie."

"Taxis—luggage—clerks. They are all inconveniences. They are all . . . enervating. They have no meaning. To surmount them is a difficulty, I will admit, but not an ennobling one."

"He is just starting. A year ago, six weeks ago, Henrietta would have all but carried his luggage for him. They are backward, Theodore, both of them. They do, for the first time, things most people would have done five or ten years before. Here they come now. At least they permitted us to come and wave them off."

"Ursula," said her father, still a little peevish, "by what line do you travel? I don't even know that. I would have sent something to the plane—flowers, or champagne."

Ursula looked very happy, and with a surprising pang in his heart, her father realized that she finally looked grownup, too. "We'd be conspicuous," she said. "Anyway, we aren't exactly newlyweds, Father."

Theodore continued to be puzzled. "Only a week," he murmured. "I thought of myself as a newlywed for a year."

"It is, after all, a honeymoon," said van Zandt, coming to his rescue.

"Not at all, Father," Artie replied with a laugh, high and nervous—that had not changed. "This trip is for recuperation." He blushed. "Our honeymoon was last week in Nyack."

"So that was where you went. Back to the scene of the crime."

"Back to the scene, in any case," Artie said.

"In any case," his father agreed.

They strolled slowly toward the terminal from which the two travelers would leave. All of them felt somewhat awkward, and Artie wished he had forbidden even this much; however, there it was, and eventually it was over and their flight was called out.

As he was shaking hands with his father he said, "I never could get Mother on the telephone. I finally wrote her—about us." He glanced at Ursula. "No answer. Is she all right?"

"Much better. The pneumonia cleared right up. But a picture of her mind would still show a few clouds, I believe. One proof of it is that she would want to go to Connecticut to stay. I insisted on a companion, you know. I wouldn't trust her with nobody but a servant or two around. Not with all my things there."

"Is it that bad?" Artie asked, frowning, feeling some of the old guiltiness.

"When your mother was fully herself, it was bad. Who knows now?"

"Will she be all right?"

"I assume so. When she wants to be. I think she is making a point. Yes, they say she will be."

"Come on, Artie," Ursula said. "We're the last to board."

But he lingered. "Is there anything I can do?"

The elder van Zandt now kissed his new daughter-in-law, and released Artie to Cariatis for handshaking. When all that was over, he answered the question. "I think you might telephone her when you have arrived in London. That will be quite final, and she will know it. She will have lost her last chance. And it might flatter her." He smiled at a small joke. "You see, I am now in a position to prevent her from doing anything very drastic, for reasons we won't go into, Artie; but I cannot actually control the terms of her will; for, with her death, my hold on her ends. Moreover, I shall almost certainly predecease her. So now that you have had your own way, it might be a good idea to get back into her favor. She is still, as I once told you, a rich woman."

He turned. "Sorry to talk family business at a time like this," he said.

"Her fortune, you know . . ." Cariatis shrugged. "No consequence."

"I know, I know. Still, there's no point in wasting Henrietta's money. God knows what exasperating charities she'll find for it if she doesn't leave it to Artie. Now run along. Good-by. Good luck."

Off went the junior van Zandts. Their fathers waited long enough to see the great jet climb into the March clouds, then walked back to the Cariatis limousine.

As they rode in from Long Island, Cariatis said, "You know, Arthur, I am leaving for Europe today, too. I just decided early this morning. One of my ships will sail with the tide late this afternoon, and I suddenly thought that I did not want to be in New York for a while. And so we, too, must say good-by."

Van Zandt, looking out the window, a hand hanging on one of the straps, said glumly, "That is depressing news, Theodore, and I was already depressed. I am sorry you are going. Unfortunately, I now must always wonder, whenever I say good-by to a friend, if we will ever meet again. It is not tragic, perhaps, that consideration; still, it tends to increase a certain inborn propensity toward melancholia."

"I will write," Theodore said.

" 'A strange thought strikes me, that we will receive no letters in the grave,' " van Zandt replied. "Sidney Smith."

"Come now."

"Yes, of course. The mood of the moment. And what will you do in Greece, Theodore? Nothing but business, eh?"

Cariatis smiled shyly. "To the contrary. I am going to go

into semiretirement, relinquish my hold. I have for a long time wanted to interest myself in archaeology, and particularly Byzantine archaeology. There are sites in Greece and in the islands, you know—much, much to be done. I will finance excavations, restorations. If, incidentally, classical material is unearthed, well, that is no great loss."

"But that sounds fascinating," van Zandt said enthusiastically. "What luck, that you have both the means and the interest."

Theodore smiled modestly again. "I have been studying," he said. "I have gathered a small library here, and there is more at home. I have been to see the necessary expert people here—Princeton, Michigan, Dumbarton Oaks. They contradict each other, but all are enthusiastic."

"I shouldn't wonder, Theodore. And so you will become a kind of Schliemann."

"With God's help," said the occasionally pious Cariatis.

"Granted the size of your fortune, I will be surprised if He withholds it," van Zandt observed.

"You will come and visit me in Greece, Arthur?"

"I will if there is time."

They were now in New York City, which reminded van Zandt of Maule's call. He thought about it, and decided to mention it to Theodore. "I heard from Maule this morning. You may have heard from him yourself. He said that some doubt had been raised about his Watteau. He asked for my help. Ironic."

Cariatis shrugged. "I have no more interest in that picture. But I remain offended with Maule."

"Yes. No doubt. I must admit that I would still buy it— the point for me is, after all, to get it, and my feelings about Maule are of no importance—and the price might be way down now. I wonder . . ." He looked out the window to read a street sign and find out precisely where they were. "I wonder if you would have your driver let me out at Tait's studio. They were going to be there at two o'clock. Maybe they still are. I'll just go in and nose around a little bit."

Cariatis gave the appropriate order, and the great car swung around a block or two, then stopped.

"You won't come in?" van Zandt asked.

Cariatis shook his head. "No. I have many things to do. Time and tide wait for no man, Arthur."

"Then we will have to say good-by."

Cariatis nodded. He held out a hand. "Good-by, Arthur," he said.

"Good-by, Theodore. I don't go in for gush, you know, but I'm glad at the way things have turned out. *Partager le désespoir*—it's a firm basis for a friendship."

"I, too, am glad. And come and see my excavations."

"Agreed." Van Zandt quickly turned and lumbered toward the door of the office building, whereupon Cariatis tapped against the window behind the driver and the car drew off.

At Tait's studio van Zandt was told by an assistant that everyone, including Dr. Tait, had left, except for Dr. Pretorius. Who was everyone? van Zandt wanted to know. Maule and the two other gentlemen, who came from the same town as Dr. Pretorius. So that's who bought it, van Zandt noted. It was three o'clock, and he decided it would do no harm to drop by Maule's house, just in case he had gone back there. He found himself whistling. He knew Pretorius; he could begin to fill in some blank spots. Something told him that his own chances were improving. He was an old hand, and he smelled trouble for Maule. All he himself had to do was to wait for the right moment, if that was so, and a bright new addition might well drop into its appointed place in the van Zandt collection.

Four

Pearson Tait had not yet arrived at his office when Maule, McCaffrey, and Barney Kant assembled there, along with Dr. Pretorius. There was no other place for them to wait, and so they were put in Tait's own office; and when he did arrive at a quarter after two, he pretended at first not to see them. He went to a hook on the wall where he put his overcoat. Then he put on a white duster. When he turned around, he pretended not to recognize them. "What? What?" he said, glancing back at the door through which he had just come.

His four visitors looked at each other, eyebrows raised. Barney Kant snickered. "He'll sure solve our riddle," he whispered to McCaffrey, who put a finger to his lips in reply.

"Good afternoon, Dr. Tait," Maule said. "Dr. Tait?"

The great body swiveled at the torso so that the eyes could be directed upon the dealer. "What are you here for?"

"Did you get our message?" Maule asked.

"Why should I tell you?"

"Then you know what we are here for. Perhaps you don't know Dr. Pretorius. He is an expert from Mr. McCaffrey's museum. He wants to look at the Watteau. He has seen only photographs so far."

"Oh, he does, does he? So he does, does he? Does he? He does?" Tait said rapidly. "Why?"

"Why not, Dr. Tait?" McCaffrey asked.

"I said it first," Tait replied. He attempted to hide his hands in the sleeves of his duster.

Pretorius took a step forward and bowed slightly. "I want to check one or two things. A doubt has arisen," he explained.

Tait laughed harshly. "You think I hurt it when I cleaned it?"

"No no no," Maule said impatiently. "Please. We are rather rushed, all of us. Do just take us wherever you have the picture."

Tait's face turned red. "Why should I? Why should I let you see it?"

"Because it belongs to me."

"Not exactly," McCaffrey said. "Not any longer."

"Not yet," said Barney.

A door opened at one side of the room and a woman entered. She was sunburned, and had a number of almost-healed cuts and scratches on her hands and face. Her hair was done up in a kind of pie on the top of her head, and behind her spectacles gleamed the eyes of a fanatic. She was big and beefy, and her voice, when she spoke, was hoarse.

She identified herself. "I am Martha Tait," she said, coming to her husband and putting a hand on his arm.

"Delighted," said Maule. "This is Mr. McCaffrey, Mr. Kant, and Dr. Pretorius."

"They want to see the picture," Pearson said to her. "What should I do?"

She stepped slightly ahead of her husband. "Why do you torment him?"

Maule, pushed beyond endurance, became angry. "What is going on here?" he snapped. "Who is tormenting him?

We merely want to see the Watteau. Is your husband ill, Mrs. Tait?"

Tait whispered into her ear so that they all heard, "You see?"

"Why should you see it?" she asked. She scratched an old insect bite on her left hip with the hand that did not restrain her husband. "It is safe in Pearson's care."

McCaffrey spoke soothingly. "There must be some little misunderstanding here," he said. "What we are interested in has nothing at all to do with your husband—directly, at any rate. My museum has . . . ah . . . tentatively acquired the painting, and Dr. Pretorius wishes to look at it. Also, we want X rays of those portions that were not taken originally. Mr. Maule telephoned. . . ."

Neither Tait said anything, but Mrs. Tait's hand clamped more firmly upon her husband's arm.

"In fact," McCaffrey said, varying his voice, "we insist on it."

"No!" Tait said.

"Excuse me. Yes," McCaffrey replied.

"One moment, please," Dr. Pretorius interrupted. "I would like to ask Dr. Tait a question or two."

"Ask them in front of the painting," McCaffrey said.

"If they want to see it, Pearson, they do have the right," Martha Tait said.

"Let them see it then," her husband replied sulkily. "But I won't look at it with them."

"Then I will ask my questions here," Dr Pretorius said.

"Go ahead," said McCaffrey, "and good luck."

"Do you, Dr. Tait, have any doubts about the authenticity of the Watteau? Have you any reservations, even just in the back of your mind? Has science any light to cast?"

"Doubts! Of course I have doubts. I have more than doubts."

"What?" Maule cried. "But that wasn't what you said to me the day you first saw it."

Tait became matter-of-fact. "The first day, I said I did not give opinions of that sort. Had I chosen to give such an opinion, I would have said what I have now said. Today I feel like giving such an opinion—thanks to my wife."

Everyone looked at her, wondering what she had to do with it. While suffering their stares, she scratched her scalp, making the pie that crowned her head flop backward and forward. She explained, "In my travels I encounter many a hungry creature that nips or burrows."

Dr. Pretorius returned to her husband. "May I ask you why you doubt?"

"I can't stop you."

"Very well then. Why?"

Dr. Tait looked at his wife, and she answered for him. "Because Pearson thinks the painting is modern," she replied.

"But why?"

"It is just as good as a Watteau," said Tait, for the moment more his old self. He raised a forefinger. "It is a superb imitation, if you will, an essay in the style of Watteau." The finger came down. "Not a forgery, you understand, but an exercise. The kind of thing poets do, a practice, like a poem in the style of someone else."

"You mean you think it is a kind of parody?" Maule asked.

Tait turned bright red again. "Your word, not mine."

Martha Tait tugged at her belt to relieve pressure upon welts lying beneath it. "So that settles everything," she said.

"Not quite," Maule replied angrily. "I have a few questions of my own to ask Dr. Tait."

"He has not been very well," she replied. "I will not allow you to tire him."

"I don't like the smell of any of this," Maule said. "Mr. Kant has received an anonymous letter claiming that the Watteau was not a genuine eighteenth-century painting. I will show it to you." He reached into his pocket. "Damnation. I left it behind. Anyway, he did receive it. Then Dr. Pretorius comes up with doubts. Now you do, Tait—with some very strange doubts, it seems to me. So one question I have for you is this." Maule raised his voice. "Did you send the letter?"

Pearson Tait's heavy lids quivered and then slowly dropped down over his eyes, like those of some moribund Jurassic monster, last of its species. He looked at his wife. "What should I say?" he asked her.

"Tell the truth, Pearson."

"No," he said to Maule.

"I guarantee that he did not," said Mrs. Tait.

"Where are we?" asked Barney Kant.

Maule turned to McCaffrey. "What do you think, Matt?"

"No evidence," McCaffrey answered. "I see no reason to think he did. In fact, it strikes me as unlikely."

Maule nodded. "I agree. Well, with that out of the way, we can proceed to the painting and the X rays I requested."

Tait turned to his wife. "I'm going home, Martha."

"Not without me, Pearson." She frowned. "I had hoped to prevent all this, for everybody's sake, but I see that you are determined to pursue your reckless course." She pinched the bridge of her nose between two fingers, as if the interior tissues were inflamed and itchy. "Pearson's assistant will show you what you want to see. But I have warned you. Meanwhile, I will take my husband home."

"We're not through with him," Maule said.

"He, however, is through with you." She opened the door into the rest of the offices. "Venable," she called.

A moment later a man, also in a white duster, appeared in the doorway.

"Venable, show these gentlemen whatever they want to see." She jabbed with a contorted thumb at an inaccessible spot in the small of her back. "Including the new X rays." Squinting her eyes, she looked menacingly at the visitors. "I ordered them to be taken. I knew," she said. She waved a hand. "Now go."

"This has all been most disquieting, Mrs. Tait. I am worried for the safety of the painting," Maule said. "I am going to have it brought back to my office. I can no longer entrust it to Dr. Tait, in his condition."

"Ha!" cried Tait.

"Whatever you want to do, do it," said Mrs. Tait, and they left.

Venable, the assistant, said there would be a few minutes to wait before the negatives were developed, and McCaffrey asked him, "Isn't it unusual for Dr. Tait not to take complete X rays?" He turned to Maule. "Frankly, that is one of the mysteries about all this, too, Edward. Tait has always had his limitations—I mean his refusal to paint over damage and that kind of thing—but at least he used to be thorough about the technical end of his trade."

Venable interrupted, quite offended. "Dr. Tait is the most scientific restorer in America or the world."

McCaffrey asked, "Have you noticed any changes in him recently?"

"He is tired," Venable replied. "Overworked. And now *her* again."

"Ah, yes. The itching distaff. But no more than that, no more striking changes?"

"I . . . He . . . No! No more than that."

"We are concerned, you know. If you do have any ideas —it might be better for Dr. Tait in the long run."

"Well," Venable said, looking over his shoulder, "he fired me twice last week."

Dr. Pretorius frowned and cleared his throat. "That is hardly scientific," he said.

"And it is definitely tautological," McCaffrey remarked.

"It may be important," Maule interjected, exasperated by the facetiousness of McCaffrey's remark, which, he could see, had effectively shut up the assistant.

"Say, what about those X rays? I don't have all year," said Barney.

"And the painting. I must see the painting," said Pretorius.

"Right away. You wait here." Venable disappeared, and a moment later came back wheeling a movable easel on which stood the Watteau.

Everybody looked first at it, then at Pretorius. He walked slowly forward, and stood before it for at least five minutes without speaking. Then he said, evidently deeply moved, "It is so beautiful."

"Ah," Maule breathed out.

"But—"

"But?"

Pretorius waggled a thumb, twiddled a finger, indicating areas on the surface. "Something here, something there. I don't know. Perhaps. Yes, perhaps, but on the other hand . . . Who can say? Is it, isn't it? Or even . . ." He sighed and smiled faintly. "Such a difficult decision," he muttered.

"What do you think?" McCaffrey said, turning on Venable.

"We don't give opinions."

"Tait just did. He said it was modern."

The face crumpled. "I told you he was overworked."

"Is there any scientific evidence you know of to support your employer in what he said?" McCaffrey turned to Maule. "He must have some reasons, scientific ones, to support such a statement."

"I don't know of any," Venable said. "Maybe Dr. Tait knows something I don't know."

"Aw, he was either drunk or crazy," Barney said. "Now what about the X rays, since it's so Goddamned important to see them."

Venable looked at his wrist watch. "I guess you can see them now. Just follow me." He led them into another room, where there was a machine with a frosted-glass panel in front and lights behind, and clips to hold negatives up for observation. He disappeared, but soon came back holding a large negative in each hand. "Lower right," he said, "and lower left. Small painting, as they go. That's everything missing."

Pretorius took the lower right from him and clipped it to the viewer. He looked at it methodically. Then Maule looked at it. McCaffrey, rumpling his youthful hair, looked at it. Eventually Barney Kant looked at it. For on that film, if Barney's letter did not lie, was recorded Truth.

Finally Pretorius spoke. "I see nothing but that pentimento—and it is slightly visible in the photographs."

"That what?" asked Barney.

"He means that place. The figure was painted there, first, but then moved to the left a little bit, and the original outlines covered over with flowers. And the man, who is to the left of her, was changed, too. It shows in the X ray more clearly than it does in the painting. Matter of fact, part of it, most of it, was in the X rays already taken," McCaffrey explained.

"The girl was changed when she was moved, too," Pretorius observed.

"That is the figure after the Rotterdam drawing," Maule said. "Which is closer to the drawing, Dr. Pretorius, the first or the second version of the girl?"

Pretorius thought a moment. "The one painted out."

Maule was triumphant. "Then that is conclusive proof. Watteau used his own drawing—an unquestionably authentic one—for a model. He often did that, as you all know—put this figure here on the right, then changed his mind, and to improve the general composition, moved her a little to the left, and when he did, changed her a little. That can only be the master himself at work. The painting cannot be a forgery."

Pretorius looked around, lips pursed. "But if Watteau could do that, why could not a forger?"

Maule was furious. "What forger, Pretorius? Who knows that much? Who is that careful?"

"Who?" The doctor shook his head wisely. "I cannot say who. But this I can say: the forger who knows that much, and is so careful he uses an eighteenth-century canvas and only old pigments, is precisely the forger who could do such a magnificent imitation, no? Or parody, to use your word, Mr. Maule."

"Then where are we?" demanded Barney.

"The other negative, please," said Pretorius. Venable clipped it to the board, and after he had examined it, Pretorius said, "This one shows us nothing new." He snapped off the lights and stood up. "Gentlemen," he said in an authoritative tone of voice. He paused.

They all waited eagerly.

Pretorius was sure of his ground now. "Gentlemen, I want to say that I consider all the evidence so far, both historical, stylistic, and technical, all the evidence so far I consider—"

"Yes? Yes?"

"Inconclusive."

"My God," Maule said, "after all that."

"Where *are* we?" demanded Barney.

McCaffrey glanced at Venable. "We are in Tait's studio," he said. "Which is not the place for any further discussion —and, Edward, further discussion there must be. We will leave Ulrich to continue his examination of the painting, and you, Barney, and I will return to your office. Is that agreeable to you? Or would you rather talk elsewhere?"

"Whatever you say," Maule replied. "But I don't want the painting to remain here. Perhaps Dr. Pretorius could bring it over with him when he is through."

"Yes. We will want him in on our discussion when he has made up his mind," McCaffrey said. "And make it up he must."

"It's irregular," said Venable, "to take it away like that."

"Mr. Venable," said Maule, "let me assure you that that is the least of it." With weary steps he led the way from Tait's studio. He sat in the taxi with his head lowered, eyes cast down, sorrowing. And that was why he did not notice Theodore Cariatis and Arthur van Zandt when they passed by in the former's large black limousine.

Five

"And so now you understand," Maule said, "why I *couldn't* reveal the name of an unknown owner to you, Matt, even if I had wanted to. As for the telephone call I made that day when you were here—well, that was simply an error, I suppose. I don't know why I did it. A confession of weakness? I probably did it just to bolster an idea, the idea of the mysterious owner."

Barney Kant fairly hopped back and forth across the dealer's office. He doubled up his fists and pommeled an imaginary opponent. "Thundering mud! Why did I ever let myself get mixed up in *this* game, where every time you clear up one thing, you come to a dozen others. So we know Maule's secret now, Matt—just where does that get us? As far as that's concerned, what does it answer?" He turned to the dealer. "What do you think it answers, Ed?"

"Nothing much—not for you."

"Now what about the anonymous note? I mean, does it mean that somebody else knows your secret, Edward?" McCaffrey asked.

"My secret really has very little to do with the authenticity of the painting. I don't think it affects it one way or the other. The painting was never claimed to be anything but unknown."

McCaffrey nodded. "Yes, I can see that. But . . ."

Thackeray interrupted with a light tap on the door. He had been listening there since the three men had come in, and had heard everything up to a moment before, when a

240

caller had buzzed to be let upstairs and Thackeray had to take his ear away from the keyhole. It was Arthur van Zandt, who wanted to see Maule if he was in. Thackeray slipped into the inner office and delivered the message.

Maule turned to his companions. "Would you mind if van Zandt got in on this? Not all of it, necessarily, but at least the note and the question of authenticity it raises. I think he might be of assistance."

"Why not?" McCaffrey said. "I'd like to hear his opinion on the painting from his own mouth—although frankly, Edward, I will probably advise Barney to withdraw his offer of purchase."

"I am sorry."

"Everything considered, don't I almost have to?"

Van Zandt now entered the room. When Maule introduced him to Barney Kant, he said, "Barney is the man who bought the Watteau, Arthur—to give to Matt's museum."

Van Zandt looked down on Barney with dislike. "So?" he said.

"But then," Maule continued slowly, watching van Zandt very carefully, "as I told you over the telephone, someone sent an anonymous letter, sent it to Barney. Mystery number one, as far as I am concerned, is this: who sent that letter? Mystery number two, why? You don't have any thoughts about those two mysteries, do you, Arthur?"

"Me? Why would I?" Van Zandt began to smile. "Ah, I believe I catch a little echo of suspicion in your sweet voice, Edward, just a tiny echo of it. No, Edward, it would have been a good idea, but I didn't do it. It didn't occur to me. Moreover, I didn't know until just now who did buy the painting, although I'll admit I might have been able to find that out. But hasn't it put all of you on a spot, that letter." He smiled again.

"We have been to see Tait once more. We had more X rays taken." Maule explained to van Zandt what the X rays had shown. "Dr. Pretorius, who now doubts the picture, says that the X-ray evidence could equally well show that the picture is genuine, or that the forger was very, very deft."

"True," said van Zandt, "if you admit any doubt about it in the first place."

"And you do not?" McCaffrey asked sharply.

Van Zandt grunted. "Huh. What should I say? If I say I do not, then you might well be swayed to keep the picture. If I say I do, you might well not believe me, since, as Maule has probably told you, I wanted the painting myself at one time, and you might think I was angling for it—and as a bargain, too. So why say anything?"

"I give up," said Barney. "Mr. van something, I want to tell you that since this whole blasted thing started, I haven't heard one straight answer to one question from anyone, nothing a man could sink his teeth into and chew on. And yours is just the same."

"Why, there's a difference for you, Mr. Kant," van Zandt replied, mockingly. "There, sir, is precisely the difference between the art world—an ideal world where we deal with concretions and dream of truth—and your world, a realistic world, where you deal in abstractions and dream that they are facts."

"Pooey," said Barney.

"Two plus two make four, or four million, but canvas and paint do not necessarily make a Watteau. You allege the one; we, at least, admit the other."

"Double pooey."

Van Zandt laughed. "Let us return to this letter. May I

242

look at it, Edward? I'd like to see such a letter. I have wanted to write so many of them, after visiting our country's great museums."

"Certainly," Maule said. He went around to his desk and looked through such papers as were on it. "I must have left it here." He looked again. "No. Funny. Maybe in a drawer." He searched through the top drawer, but still could not find it. Then he buzzed for Thackeray and asked him if he had seen it.

It was Thackeray's great moment. "Yes, Mr. Maule. I came in to straighten up your office while you were gone and noticed it lying there. I put it away, sir, because I thought it shouldn't be out like that." He leaned close to his employer and whispered something in his ear.

Maule looked surprised, then took out a key and went into the back office. He returned in a moment with another letter and spread it out on his desk alongside of the anonymous note that Thackeray had brought in from the front office. "Let's see, let's see," said the dealer. "So that's the story, is it? So that's it. I thought there was something funny about the way . . ." He looked up. "Of course. And this is so obvious," he said to Thackeray, indicating the comparison on his desk.

"I guess it is," Thackeray said, somewhat squelched.

"I didn't mean it that way. I meant it was obvious once it had been pointed out. You have done us all a great service today, Thackeray, a great service. You are an honor to the profession."

"Oh, I just *noticed*, that's all."

"I am getting old," Maule said. "Twenty years ago I would have noticed it myself. Young eyes, a clear young mind—no substitute for them. Thank you, Thackeray."

He turned to the mystified trio in front of his desk. "Thackeray has solved the mystery of the anonymous letter, or at least he has partly solved it."

"That figures, that 'partly,' " said Barney.

"I now know on whose typewriter it was written."

"Then speak up," said van Zandt.

In reply, Maule turned the two letters around so that the other three could read them. McCaffrey said the words of the first partly aloud. " '. . . I would, therefore, like to keep the painting until . . . craquelure may perhaps need . . .' This must be the letter you got from Tait when he wanted to keep the picture, isn't it? There's his signature. And—yes! You're right. Same machine. The ribbon thing doesn't work correctly. Half the capitals are black, half red. And probably, if we look more closely—yes, that too. The letter *t* is askew. Doubtless because he bangs down on it so hard when he's writing his own name." McCaffrey stood back to give the other two a better look. "So it's Tait," he said. "And he lied just now."

"The man's a drunken fraud anyway," said van Zandt, as he bent forward over the desk.

"Gentlemen," Maule said, "I believe there is only one thing to do. We must see Tait again and confront him with this comparison. Thackeray, get hold of Dr. Tait. I don't want to talk to him; you do so. Tell him we want to see him. Either he will come here, or we will go to him. Tell him that if he refuses to see us, I am going to the police at once. If you can't get him, talk to his wife. Try him at home first. Do you have any idea where he lives, any of you?"

"I've got a pretty good idea myself," Thackeray said.

"Well, try there first. And hurry." When Thackeray had gone out of the room, Maule talked on to himself. "What an outrage. How dare he do a thing like this to me? That neckless nobody." Then he addressed McCaffrey. "It will all be straightened out. It's some kind of a delusion that man has—drink, dope, who knows? It will all be all right. We can all forget this horrible day."

But McCaffrey had been thinking. "There remain Pretorius's doubts, Edward. And now what you just told us about the source of the picture. I can't afford to get my hands dirty."

Maule glanced swiftly at van Zandt, who turned slowly to face him.

"Dirty source, Edward?"

"Sorry, Edward," murmured McCaffrey. "It slipped out."

"Just what was its source, Edward? You are hardly in a position now to keep that secret from me, when I know so much."

"I *found* the picture," Maule admitted.

"Found it? Good God. Where?"

Maule hung his head. "In an attic," he said, almost inaudibly.

"An attic!" Van Zandt burst out laughing. "Edward. O! my poor Edward. An attic. All this," and he waved a hand at the luxurious office, "all this, and yet it is your fate to live out, at the apogee of your career, the most vulgar fantasy of every little Third Avenue antique peddler. Oh, my poor Edward." He laughed again.

Then he sobered. "Whose attic?"

Barney Kant interrupted. "That's the pay-off," he said.

"My own attic," Maule confessed.

"Your own attic? Edward, you have made all of this up. It isn't possible."

Maule nodded his head sadly. "Unfortunately, Arthur, it is all too true."

"And it doesn't help to know it, either," McCaffrey put in.

"Doesn't help what?"

"Help on the provenance. The hiatus now starts with Edward here. One person farther back, that's all."

"Yes, I can see that." Something occurred to van Zandt. "And another point, Edward. Just where do you have an attic to find it in?"

"Ah, that," replied Maule. "Right here. This house. You see, after I bought it, I was going through it by myself, clarifying my ideas about how I wanted it done over, so that the architect I was using wouldn't spend too much money; and while I was up in the part that has been turned into a study and roof garden, I found a storage area that hadn't ever been cleared out. Forgotten about. A piece of the wall had to come out to get at it, a loose piece of insulation. I just happened to poke at it, and saw it was loose, so I got a flashlight and looked in. The usual stuff—a chamber pot or two, some books, and . . . a painting. It was covered with dust, but it was clearly of good quality, and in an eighteenth-century frame. So I took it back to my then apartment with me, dusted it off, put it in storage, and six months later you saw it here."

"Simply inconceivable." Van Zandt considered implications. "If I am not mistaken, this does more damage to the solidity of its legal ownership than it does to its authenticity, Edward."

Barney Kant snorted. "So you fancy fellahs are going to get to that now, are you?"

"That was why I was reluctant to tell anyone where it came from," Maule said. "I didn't steal it; but on the other hand, was it mine? Legally and morally mine."

"What does the law say?" McCaffrey asked.

"That depends. Here, in New York, it could be mine, since it was left in the house when I took possession; but it is not as cut and dried as it might be. Yes, very probably I would, in the long run, be able to hang onto it, or the profit from the sale of it, or at least most of the profit. But profit, gentlemen, isn't everything."

"No?" said Barney.

"There would have been lawsuits, no doubt about it. Litigation, publicity, amounting, in the end, to notoriety. Arthur here will agree with me, I am sure, that in a business whose transactions are conducted with the discretion, the delicacy, yes, even the secrecy of those conducted here in this office, to draw details out for the benefit of the newspapers and their subway public would be little short of disastrous. Almost better that I should never have found the Watteau. Yes, almost better that." Maule ended with a certain fervor, which implied that very probably, at that moment, he did indeed wish he had never found the painting. "And not just one lawsuit, but several," he added.

"Several?" van Zandt asked. "You mean appeals? That sort of drawn-out thing?"

"Appeals no doubt," Maule replied. "But that wasn't exactly what I had in mind. I have looked into the former ownership of this house, and, prior to myself, there have been four owners. None of them was known to be a collector of paintings of any consequence. None of them, so far as I have been able to discover, bought important paintings from the obvious sources—Knoedler, Duveen, Agnew, Wildenstein, and so on. None of them ever lent to any exhibition that I can discover. In three cases there was an auction, and I have checked those catalogues—oh, I have been thorough, as you can well believe—and there was nothing in any of them to indicate a collection of which the

Watteau might have been a forgotten part. Expensive junk, with maybe a ruin of an antique chair or two, that's all. There was no such sale for the first owner, and, unfortunately, I think that she is the most likely of the lot to have bought this painting or inherited it. She was a great traveler; she had a French grandparent; and she did, in the early part of her life, collect something. Not pictures, but snuff bottles—those jade things—and then some miniatures."

"Doesn't sound too serious," van Zandt said.

"No. But if not she, then who? She might well have had one good painting among the lesser ones that surely hung in her house. After all, paintings she did have—no other way to cover her walls. She could have bought it from the last owner whose name I can trace—old Achille Proust, assuming that my painting is the one described in his collection—or from his son, or her parents might have bought it. Not so valuable in those days. Things often got overlooked, or their real names forgotten. Let's say she had it stored one time in her attic while she was away, and then didn't think to have it brought out—maybe she got a new picture on that particular trip, and wanted to hang it, and didn't have room for Momma's old eighteenth-century thing. Lots of ways to explain it. Anyway, she died without heirs. A few small legacies, and the balance of her fortune, along with this house, to certain causes, and one in particular. It would probably have the best claim to the painting, after myself."

"What was it?"

"It seems she had a beloved younger brother who was killed in college while drinking. And she herself died in the late twenties, when drink was such an issue. She left the bulk of her fortune to further the cause of temperance."

"Temperance?" Van Zandt laughed once more. "Good God, Edward. You mean that if word of all this gets out, that lovely painting of yours may be sold to support the W.C.T.U.?"

"Precisely. You see my dilemma now in full. Legal technicalities aside, I felt I had a moral responsibility."

"Edward, you old hypocrite, you."

Thackeray interrupted. "Mrs. Tait says she will see you at the Taits' apartment, Mr. Maule," he said. "Shall I tell her you will come over?"

"What about Tait himself?"

"She wouldn't say."

Maule turned to the other men. "Will we? Or won't we?"

"We will," McCaffrey replied.

Maule nodded to Thackeray, who returned to the telephone, then went on. "So now you understand everything, gentlemen. Or at least you understand as much as I do. I really don't know, didn't know, what to do except what I did do. I thought, after all, that it would save trouble all around. And so it would have, if it hadn't been for that anonymous letter."

"It was risky, Edward. I don't much appreciate being connected with that risk, even though I didn't know about it," McCaffrey said.

"I don't give a damn about the risk," van Zandt said. "I thought, of course, that your mysterious owner was a European, probably French, who was getting his picture out of his own country illegally, avoiding those laws prohibiting the export of great works of art."

"I don't know that I'd have liked that much better," McCaffrey added, in his most honor-system manner.

"Bullshit," van Zandt replied. "That's exactly what you

thought, too. But you thought it didn't matter, so long as the painting was unknown in the literature, hence unknown to whatever authorities would be involved, and in any case couldn't be traced back. That much risk you were willing to take."

"Willing to let me take," said Barney.

"Besides, if one wants the work of art," van Zandt said to Barney, "he doesn't ask too many questions. Especially as a private collector. When such a painting has gone into a private collection and doesn't come out, nobody is ever the wiser. You will be surprised some day to see what turns up in South America or Houston."

Thackeray came back in. "Mrs. Tait awaits," he said.

"Good. Thackeray, I think you had better come along with us, if you gentlemen don't mind. Just in case we want something taken down."

"I'm coming, too," van Zandt stated. "Most curious about all this."

"I thought you would want to," Maule said, not at all displeased.

As they were putting on their coats van Zandt asked, "Would you have any idea, from the amount of dust or litter, about how long the painting had been stored up there, Edward? That might be useful to know."

Maule shook his head. "I thought of that, too. But you see, there had already been workmen around, plaster and so on torn out, dust filling the air. Frankly, the picture might have been there anywhere between two weeks and twenty years, as far as I can see."

They went downstairs, where it was decided that they would take two taxis. Maule was careful to put Barney and McCaffrey in one, and himself in the other with Thackeray and van Zandt, for he did not want two clients to have the ride together without him.

Six

They were admitted to the Tait apartment by a Filipino manservant, who had been swabbing down the tiled entrance hall with some kind of heavily aromatic soapy solution, and were taken to the dining room, where Mrs. Tait was seated at the large table, before stacks of boxes, parcels, notebooks, folders, and even a crate or two, which spilled over onto the floor and the other chairs. She looked up, her eyes glittering.

"Sorry about the smell," she said, "but it's the only germicide I know of that isn't allergenic. Pearson developed it for me when we were newlyweds." She stared at van Zandt and Thackeray. "Who are they?" she asked Maule.

Maule introduced them and explained why they were present.

"I see." She put the dried frond of a fern into a transparent envelope, already labeled with a special pencil that lay by her hand. "You catch me setting my house in order," she said. "I am just back from a fern-collecting trip to the South Seas. Most of my new specimens will be coming by sea, but I brought a few with me."

"A few?"

"Oh, not all this. Most of this is old. I'm bringing parts of my collection back into Pearson's apartment, now that I'm staying here." She held up her newly prepared specimen. "It's only *Nephrolapsis hirsutula*," she explained. "Very common out there, but isn't it charming? I call it the . . ." She sneezed several times. ". . . the dandelion of the Antipodes." She sneezed again. "Excuse me," she said. "Dust from my specimens." She wiped her nose with a paper handkerchief, which she pulled from a box that was hidden behind other, larger ones. "I'm a martyr to my hobby."

Thereupon she had a true seizure, which prolonged itself for several minutes, at the end of which she was purple in the face, her eyes streaming. "Dust, dust, dust," she was finally able to gasp. "At least it doesn't give me asthma." The fit died down. She breathed deeply a few times and scratched her head with the dull end of her pencil, so that her hair with its crowning pie moved oddly back and forth, as if it might get pushed loose all in a hunk, like a lichen. "Did you know that the spores of ferns were once supposed to make a person invisible?" She cleared her throat. "Folk-lore."

"Mrs. Tait," Maule said, "perhaps we had best come to the point."

From over a wad of paper handkerchiefs her eyes were wary. "Yes," she agreed. "By all means come to the point. I have much to do, as you see."

"Your husband?" Maule asked.

"Will not see you," she replied.

"He should be here."

"That is for me to decide."

"Perhaps, when you have seen this, you will change your mind, Mrs. Tait." Maule took the two letters from his pocket, the anonymous note to Barney Kant, and the note that Tait had sent asking to hold the Watteau for observation. Maule spread them out on the little cleared area right in front of her. "Please look carefully at these, Mrs. Tait. They tell the whole story."

She merely glanced at the anonymous letter, but read the other one. "What story do they tell you, Mr. Maule?" she asked. She wiggled in her chair. "An import from New South Wales," she remarked. "Or so I think. A sand flea. I seem to have brought a few home with me."

"I thought it was paradise on earth down there," van Zandt said.

"Unless I miss my guess, there will be mosquitoes in heaven."

"Please, Arthur," Maule said irritably. "Now what about the letters, Mrs. Tait? As you can see, they were written on the same typewriter. And a singular typewriter. Rather obvious."

"Oh, I know that now. I ought to."

"What do you mean, you ought to?" Barney Kant asked. "Let's get down to brass tacks here."

"I wrote the anonymous note to you, Mr. Kant," she said. "That's why I ought to know about it."

"Your husband denied knowledge of it this morning," Maule accused.

"No he didn't. You asked him if he wrote it. I told him to tell the truth. He did. He didn't. I did. On his typewriter. That's what I said. How can we get down to brass tacks if you don't listen to what I say?" She massaged the inflamed lobe of one ear.

Maule rapped the table top. "Do you realize the seriousness of this? Do you realize that I can bring legal action? Enormous damages. This note may well cost me the sale of the painting. It is irresponsible and ridiculous. Why didn't your husband simply come out openly and say he doubted the painting and let it go at that—provided he was prepared to back his statement up?"

"He didn't know what to do. He was afraid to. He didn't do anything at all."

"Afraid to? Why?"

"I will explain in a moment," Mrs. Tait said. "In any case, I take responsibility for the note. I wrote it, although with Pearson's permission, and unfortunately I wrote it on his typewriter, one he keeps here at home. I didn't dream he ever used it for business correspondence, much less that anybody would notice even if he did."

Maule glanced approvingly at Thackeray. "Not just anybody would."

"And I knew the seriousness of it, but I thought it had to be done, to spare Mr. Kant later embarrassment. Perhaps it wasn't wise."

"Wise," Maule said. "Wise!"

"Excuse me," van Zandt interjected, "but I am just as confused as ever. Why is your husband so certain that the painting is a forgery? You see," he said, looking around at everyone in the room, "I happen to disagree, and I'll stand by that opinion."

"Ah," Maule said. "At last."

"You will?" said McCaffrey, thoughtfully.

Mrs. Tait lifted her head and opened her mouth several times; but she seemed beyond sneezing, for nothing happened. "I am forced to expose Pearson," she said. "I had really hoped to avoid it, but I can't. It may teach him a lesson anyway—none of this would have happened if we had not separated in the first place. He is certain the painting is a forgery for the best reason in the world that I can think of. He is certain it is a forgery because he is the forger —if that is the right word for him."

254

"Tait? Impossible," Maule said.

"It is unfortunately possible. It even makes sense. Pearson has his creative side, too, which he restrains in his scientific work, but as he says, it must find expression somehow. As for the forgery part, that was quite unintentional. One of those things. He never expected it to get on the art market." Mrs. Tait waved a hand at her herbarium. "We all have hobbies, don't we? I have my pteridophyte friends—and how simple is their world compared to the world of men! Pearson's hobby is to amuse himself, during his quiet nighttime hours, by doing his imitations—he calls them 'parodies'—in the style of the old masters whose works he treats during the day in his office. One such picture was your Watteau, Mr. Maule."

"I don't believe it," Maule said.

"Assuming it's true, Edward, how in the world did it get into your . . ."

"Wait," Maule said sharply. "There is no reason to discuss that in front of Mrs. Tait, Matt. Not yet, at least. Let me put your question a different way. If, as you say, the painting was painted by your husband, how in the world did it get out of his hands? How did it get to me?"

Mrs. Tait itched the back of a wrist. "That is a problem, isn't it," she admitted. "You see, my husband has been under a very great strain, so great that at one time he thought of suicide, all over this picture of yours—or his. That's why I came home. That's why I'm here. Somebody had to straighten things out, and I was nominated, as they say in politics."

"Straighten things out—wow!" said Barney.

"Pearson, I might add, is suffering a little nervous . . . ah . . . crisis. That is why I do not wish to let you see him today. I have him locked in his room." She shuffled under some specimens and drew out a little container. "His razor blades," she explained. "Now one result, I believe, of his great worry, and also one cause of it, is that he suffers from moments of amnesia. To answer your question, he doesn't remember how the picture left his possession. But for some time before you called him to come and look at it and then clean it, he was sure that *a* picture had got away from him. Then the second you told him about your new Watteau, he knew that that was the one. But he can't remember how it happened. He also destroyed his records about it—quite natural, I think—probably when the painting strayed. When he is feeling better, I am sure he will remember. And of course, there are his other parodies to prove that he painted it, that he could have painted it. Meantime, it seemed best to me to act before something irrevocable had been done. The essential thing was to protect everybody, including you, Mr. Maule; for I know that you would not want to sell anybody a forgery."

"Good God. Protect me," said Maule.

Mrs. Tait shook her head. "Isn't life unkind. Such an innocent, my dear Pearson is. So well equipped to do his parodies. After all, he knows everything about those old-fashioned methods. And that his harmless hobby should turn out like this."

Van Zandt now spoke. "Edward, let me ask you something. You have not distinguished yourself for candor in this whole affair. Do you swear you were telling us the truth about the provenance of the painting?"

Maule nodded. "I do."

"This whole preposterous story is quite impossible."

Mrs. Tait glared at van Zandt. "Impossible is a strong word. There are those who would say that the way a fern reproduces itself is impossible. But here they are."

Van Zandt shrugged. "I simply don't believe any of it."

"But there is proof. You have already seen it."

"What proof?" Maule asked.

"The X ray. Pearson always puts a message in the lower right-hand corner of his parodies, an initial, a date, something, then paints it over so it won't spoil the effect. But it will show on the X rays."

"Mrs. Tait, there was nothing on the X rays at all, except a slight modification of the composition we already knew about."

For the first time she seemed to waver. "No 'T. *fecit?*' No date?"

"Nothing at all."

Thackeray spoke to his employer. "Mr. Maule, is it all right if I ask Mrs. Tait a question?"

"Why not? Go ahead."

"When did you say your husband made his parodies?"

"At night. Before going to bed."

"And where does he do them?"

"In the studio he has here in our apartment."

"Northern exposure?"

"Of course."

"Painted all white? Venetian blinds, and a big easel?"

Mrs. Tait was puzzled. "How do you know all this?"

Thackeray replied, with modesty, "By accident. I was once looking out of the window of the apartment belonging to some friends of mine—theatrical people—who live across the street, and I saw Dr. Tait at work."

Mrs. Tait was skeptical. "You must have awfully good vision, young man. I could use you on my collecting expeditions."

"Field glasses," Thackeray admitted.

"Oh-ho," said van Zandt.

"Where in hell is this getting us?" Barney Kant wanted to know.

"I'll tell you, Mr. Kant. I think it would be a good idea if all of you had a look, at least, at the parodies Dr. Tait has been doing."

"Good suggestion," van Zandt agreed. "I, for one, am curious. And I think it will establish the impossibility of it all, Edward."

Martha Tait was hesitant. "I *could* do it, but I shouldn't. I promised Pearson not to, except in case of a catastrophe."

"Mrs. Tait, this entire day has been a catastrophe," said Maule. "And I think I have the right to insist," he added. "A matter of three quarters of a million dollars is at stake."

"Not quite that much after all this, I should think," said McCaffrey, looking at Barney Kant.

Van Zandt smiled. "How unjust is justice, Edward."

"I can't worry about that now," Maule said. "Madame, I insist."

She gave in. "Very well. Follow me. But come quietly. I don't want Pearson to know." As she stood up she brushed a specimen to the floor and had to lean over and pick it up. She examined it closely for damage, put it down, sneezed just once, turned, and led the way out of the dining room toward her husband's laboratory and studio. In the former she paused and pointed to his strongbox on the wall. "The notebooks," she said. She opened it and took out the notebook called *Parodies*.

Van Zandt, having the longest arm, got hold of it first. He turned a few pages near the end, allowing the others to look, too. He read, skipping. " 'What a rape it is! . . . great breasts heaving free of the gauzy draperies . . . hot and frantic blood . . . laid on a glaze under her armpit . . . touched her lips with saliva.' Mmm. Your husband's artistic impulse would seem to be only a part of the repressions he expresses in his nocturnal labors, Mrs. Tait." He gave her back the notebook.

She then led them all into the studio, where she turned on the bright lights, whereupon Thackeray looked around, clucked to indicate that it was the room he had described, caught his employer's eye, and winked at him to give him encouragement, for the dealer was looking exhausted. Meanwhile, Mrs. Tait spun the combination lock on the storage cabinet, then turned the handle and swung wide the door. Inside were revealed some racks, into which were slipped eight or nine canvases nailed to stretchers. The forward rim of each one was labeled in crayon: Rubens, *Rape*; Poussin, *Bacchanale*; Rembrandt, *Salome Before Herod*; Fragonard, *A Game of Post Office*; Raphael, *Venus and Mars*, Dürer, *Willibald Pirckheimer as Narcissus*; and several others, as yet not marked.

"Mr. Thackeray," McCaffrey said, "we are the youngest here. We'll do the manual labor. What'll it be first, gentlemen? The Rubens?"

"Anything, Matt. Just get a move on," said Barney.

"The Rubens it is," said McCaffrey. He approached the cabinet and took hold of the canvas so lettered, but then stopped. "You know, if this turns out to be true, if what she says is really true, and Tait did not only the Watteau but also all of those others, and equally well, he'll be one of the greatest geniuses in the entire history of art."

"That is undeniable," said van Zandt.

"Who has ever denied Pearson's genius?" said Mrs. Tait, who stood by the doorway so that she could hear in case her husband suspected something and began to make a racket.

"All the fuss over Van Meegeren—that'll be nothing in comparison," said McCaffrey.

"Just pull," Thackeray said.

A moment later the large canvas was out of its slot, and the two of them hoisted it up and put it on the easel.

The five men stood back and stared at it. For perhaps thirty seconds nobody could find anything to say. They could only look, first at the painting, then at each other, then at Mrs. Tait, who was moving slowly in their direction, her ear still tuned in on her husband's bedroom.

Barney Kant broke the silence. "Jesus Christ."

Van Zandt said, " 'Hot and frantic blood.' That must be over there on the right."

McCaffrey slowly shook his head. "I'll be damned."

"Let's have a look at the Poussin," van Zandt suggested.

Maule held up a finger. "Wait. Wait a moment. I want Mrs. Tait to see the Rubens. Yes, I do indeed."

The lady finally stood where she could see her husband's masterpiece. Gradually her ruddy face turned redder. "I don't understand," she whispered. "Is it . . . is it upside down?" She bent over and twisted her head around to get an idea of what it would look like if reversed, then straightened up. "No."

"Quite right. No."

She turned to the dealer. "Mr. Maule, what have I done?"

"What indeed, madame? Now Matt, Thackeray, let us look at the Poussin."

The Rubens was replaced and the Poussin put out.

"Oh." It was a little cry from Mrs. Tait. "Oh, if only . . ."

"A consistent stylist, in any case," van Zandt remarked.

"Oh, if only I had disobeyed poor Pearson. If only I

had come in and looked before I leaped. I . . . I don't know what to say."

"I know what to say," Barney snarled. "I want to say that I'm sick and tired of nuts, that's what I want to say."

"The Frago, gentlemen," van Zandt requested. "My field, you know. Not too far in style from Watteau, either. Proof, eh?"

Out came the Fragonard, and after glancing at it, van Zandt gave a contemptuous look at all those around him. "Precisely as I said—preposterous. This is getting quite boring, Mrs. Tait and gentlemen. If you care to waste more of your time, it is your business. It is all saved from banality only by virtue of the fact that it is not taking place in an insane asylum. Out here, on this side, it is a bit fresher."

There was another little cry from Mrs. Tait, which elicited a merciful suggestion from Maule. "Arthur, I don't believe any further comments are necessary right now."

Thackeray, the producer of the entertainment, now dared to speak an opinion. He cocked his head and looked at the so-called Fragonard. "What you said, Mr. McCaffrey, about Dr. Tait's genius—it has set me to thinking. It's not true as you said it, but on the other hand, just look at that painting for its own sake. Look at the juxtapositions."

McCaffrey was surprised, but then, catching the spirit of Thackeray's criticism, he took a serious look. "You know, you're quite right. There, where that dazzling red is put against a real warrior green, and the two of them umpired by magenta."

Thackeray nodded. "A real instinct for plastic orchestration."

"I'm glad you made me have another look. Something of Pollock, I'd say, and perhaps a little—do you think Arshile Gorky?"

Thackeray arched his eyebrows. "Perhaps just a whisper, in the ancestry. Or, better put, just a ricochet—a part of the same *Weltanschauung*, you know. Yes, a *flavor* of Pollock, but more Apollonian, more tooled, parallel to, not a development out of. Definitely."

"So much for that," McCaffrey concluded. "Let's put it away."

They did so.

Maule now addressed Mrs. Tait, who had seated herself on a metal chair with stilted legs, high enough so that it could be used to paint from. She was sniffling, tears of sorrow.

"I am sure, Mrs. Tait, that you now understand the necessity of keeping your husband under strict observation and control."

She nodded.

"I do not want any more talk about forgeries or anything of the kind. Not a word. What action I take against both of you, for the allegations contained in that unfortunate anonymous note, will depend on how securely you are able to keep your husband secluded. Perhaps a trip—"

"I just got back from one," she objected, slowly rubbing her left elbow.

"However you choose to do it, keep him from further indiscretions. If not, there will be consequences unpleasant to both of you. And now, gentlemen, I believe we have no further business here. Let us return to my office—Dr. Pretorius should be coming back with the painting. I am sure Mrs. Tait would like to be alone—with her ferns."

"And with her thoughts," added van Zandt.

"And don't forget her husband," said Barney.

Maule softened. "I am sorry, Mrs. Tait, about him. But he has done me great harm, and so have you."

Suddenly she rose and, like a sleepwalker, passed by all her visitors without looking at them, went out of the room, through the laboratory, and off toward the dining room. "We will withdraw," she called back. "Pearson into his dreams, and I into my own, my better world." The men found their way to the front door, where the Filipino gave them their coats. Just before the door was closed behind them they heard from within the apartment one rousing sneeze.

"*Gesundheit*," said Thackeray.

Seven

"You go on into my office. I want to speak to Thackeray for a moment," Edward Maule said. He stood in the doorway and partially closed the door after them, for he did not want anybody to overhear him. "What did that Frenchwoman say?" he asked him.

"I left you a memo, Mr. Maule."

"I missed it. One more thing gone wrong this afternoon. Anyway, is she still interested—meaning, is Cariatis interested?" Thackeray said that she was not, and that Cariatis was eliminated, too, as far as she was concerned. "She didn't nibble at all?" Maule asked, disappointed.

"Not at the picture," Thackeray said.

"Too bad." Maule walked over and looked out the front windows. "It's not too promising, Thackeray, not too promising." He glanced back at his office door. "You did very good work today, my boy, very good; but you will understand the ironies of our profession the better when I tell you that in spite of it, in spite of the clearing of the good name of my Watteau, the day has probably cost me several hundred thousand dollars."

"You ought to sue," said Thackeray.

"It would only make matters worse, and I'd probably not collect very much from those Taits. My reputation. Loss of dignity. A good art dealer is like a prince of the blood, Thackeray. He simply doesn't sue if he expects to remain in business."

"It's just that Dr. Tait's interference was so *unfair*."

Maule put a hand on his shoulder. "Thank you for your sympathy," he said. "And now, I must go in to face them."

Barney Kant was just saying, "Well, Matt, now where in hell are we? Do you know?"

McCaffrey didn't quite have his answer yet. "Not exactly, Barney. It's a tough one."

Van Zandt, who was examining the photograph Maule had brought out earlier to show to Dr. Pretorius, glanced at them. He smiled slightly.

Maule sat down at his desk and cleared his throat. "Gentlemen, we have now reached the end of the day and the end of our investigations, as far as I can see. All the facts are in. There was never any real reason to doubt the painting, except that its provenance is . . . irregular. Nobody would have anything to gain by making that fact known— I, I will admit, least of all." He pursed his lips. "It will remain the Watteau that Edward Maule sold for Mr. X; that is all. Now then, Matt, your problem hasn't changed. You still need a great masterpiece, if not this one, then another. Barney, your reasons for buying in the first place are your own business, but I do not see how today can have affected them." Maule was rather pleased by the firm ring to his summary so far, and he permitted himself to scrub a mustache. "As for you, Arthur, you have indicated that you stand by your original evaluation of the painting, for which I am grateful."

"I also stand by my evaluation of what I thought of you for selling it out from under me," van Zandt replied, but he was clearly more amiable now—a danger signal, Maule wondered? "I do have to thank you, Edward, for an amusing afternoon, one that has quite confirmed what I have always thought about honest art dealers, scientific restorers, and scrupulous scholars. To say nothing," he added, "of ambitious museum directors, and, of course, those who buy works of art for reasons other than love of them. New money, flexing its muscles where it doesn't belong."

"Say, wait a minute," Barney said.

But van Zandt could hardly be intimidated by Barney. "No offense, Mr. Kant. Facts, that's all. And I have misjudged you if, upon thinking it over, you won't see exactly what I mean—in all the categories I just mentioned."

Barney thought it over. "I sure can't claim I inherited my dough," he admitted.

McCaffrey chose to ignore van Zandt's remark about directors. He spoke instead to Maule. "You see, Edward, there is still Dr. Pretorius. He's mine, and I'm stuck with him; and although I think he is often inclined to be an old woman, I hesitate to go against his judgment. Also, there is . . ." He grimaced. "There is somehow a bad taste to me now connected with your picture. Yes, I've got to have my masterpiece, and I even admit that your Watteau is probably just that. But it's like a painting over which there already has been litigation. Do you know what I mean?"

"The feeling will pass, and the taste."

"And of course, the price must come down. I don't pay three quarters of a million for a picture dragged out of an attic, Edward." McCaffrey's boyishness rang sour.

"Why is it you have to have a great masterpiece?" van Zandt asked.

McCaffrey explained about the new wing to his museum, its size and technical refinements, and its empty walls and corridors. "We'll open it in September. We asked you to lend, but you turned us down. You wouldn't like to reconsider?"

Van Zandt shrugged noncommittally. He turned to Maule. "I'll give you three hundred thousand for the painting, no matter what Pretorius says. There. You have an offer, Edward."

Maule winced.

Barney smelled a bargain. "Hey, wait a minute," he said. "I still have my option on the picture, you know. It hasn't quite been said here just yet that I'm going to give it up, although I may. But if the value of the picture has come down that much, I'm sure as hell interested to know about it. Your old money might just happen to have some competition from some new money, van Zandt. I'll meet that offer, Maule."

Maule smiled.

"Why then, in that case," van Zandt replied, giving the dealer a long look, "it becomes a question for Edward to decide. How rare it is, Edward, for such a decision to be offered for our choice twice in a lifetime."

Maule frowned.

McCaffrey said, "Barney, it's not a question of how little we can get the picture for. If we're going to put it all over the newspapers and art magazines, to say nothing of *Life*, *Time*, and *Fortune*, the risk of a backfire is the same, whether we pay a quarter of a million for it or three times that much."

"We? Who said anything about we? Maybe I'll just buy it and keep it for myself."

"Now, Barney. Be reasonable. What would you do with it?"

"Let it go up in value. Maybe donate it—when my tenure as president was decided, Matt."

Maule thought of the stock certificates that he now held. He preferred, if he had to sell his Watteau off as a bargain, that it go to van Zandt, who had, after all, stood by him. On the other hand, what about those certificates. Could he keep them if Barney bought now? And there was the future. Both van Zandt and Barney were old, but the former was, *soi-disant*, a dying man. And so what should he say? To whom sell? One of them, or perhaps a third party? He decided upon the wisest thing to do and the wisest thing to say: nothing. He allowed the soup, as he later told Thackeray (for he told Thackeray everything later), to simmer a while longer, to bring out more flavor.

And then Dr. Pretorius provided an interruption by arriving with the painting. He and McCaffrey carried it upstairs to the exhibition room and set it out on the easel there, Maule, Barney, and van Zandt following along.

"Well, Ulrich?" McCaffrey asked.

"I have made up my mind," Dr. Pretorius said. "I think, now, that it has a good chance. A very, very good chance. I do not think it can be a forgery. I think that the person who wrote the letter may have been mistaken."

"We know who wrote it. Tait's wife. You can forget it."

"Forget it?"

"Forget it. I'll explain later."

Pretorius shook his head in sorrow. "Without the letter this would never have come up. I would have held my tongue."

McCaffrey groaned. "Why didn't I go into business?" he said.

"But you did," van Zandt remarked.

Everyone again looked at the Watteau, indifferent cause of so many complications.

"Now what happens?" Barney asked.

Van Zandt sat down in one of the chairs. "This time, Mr. Kant, I will tell you what happens. You will take another chair and sit down. So will the rest of you. Gather round me, for I have an interesting little speech to make to you, one that may resolve the puzzle if we can all agree. Edward, you must have more chairs somewhere."

Maule went into the workroom, found two more chairs, and with the help of McCaffrey brought them into the exhibition room. When all were seated, van Zandt spoke up once more.

"First of all, I have some questions to ask." He asked them. Then he said, satisfied with the answers, "And now it is my turn." He then spoke for perhaps five minutes before he was interrupted by a question or two from Barney. Then Maule telephoned downstairs and got Thackeray to bring drinks for everybody, including even Dr. Pretorius, who on this exciting occasion broke with his usual temperate habits. There was much more talk, many more questions, a trading of opinions and information.

Perhaps half an hour later it was all over. Hands were shaken and the hulking figure of the great collector disappeared into the elevator, for he had an engagement for cocktails. Maule accompanied him, then returned to the exhibition room, where he interrupted conversation between the three men still remaining there.

"Well," he said, rubbing his hands. "*Well*."

"What a collector," said Dr. Pretorius.

"What a deal," Barney said.

"What an end for such a day," McCaffrey said.

"What a day!" said Maule.

And then they all went downstairs.

Eight

Edward Maule was the first to go to bed. It was only 7:55, but he could not possibly have stayed up later, and there was no reason to do so. As he lay waiting for sleep to come or not to come, as the case might be—it made little difference, since he would be able to remain resting for fourteen hours if he so wanted—he turned the events of the preceding ten hours over in his mind, and, in general, he was not too displeased. It could have been worse, his own loss much greater. At the end, he *had* managed to balk, unless he got the securities. It hadn't all been their show. And the air had been cleared; everything was aboveboard, everybody knew what was what. The solution, van Zandt's genial inspiration—he smiled secretly. It could hardly have been better timed or more suitable, or more pleasing. Arthur would have made quite a dealer himself. He, Maule, would write him in the morning saying just that, striking a note of urbane irony. And, finally, there was Thackeray.

It was hardly an impulse. He had really been waiting for the courage to do it ever since he had come back to his apartment. He reached over, took the telephone and the directory, found the number of the theater where *Green Leaf, Yellow Leaf* was playing, telephoned there for Philip Dane, and got him in his dressing room.

"Good evening, Philip," he said. "Sorry to bother you at this moment—I expect you're busy fixing yourself up for Wanda Sickert, eh? I wouldn't have done it, except that I thought it might be well for you to hear about it from me first—sort of more official, don't you know?"

"I *am* busy, Edward. Hear about what?"

"Well, it seems that there is going to be a new gallery opening up in the basement of my house, dedicated to the most up-to-date kind of thing. These old walls will have quite a case of aesthetic schizophrenia, don't you think?"

"Really?"

"Yes. You know your friend Thackeray has made most extraordinary progress these last several weeks. Leaps and bounds. He was invaluable to me just today."

"Really."

"Yes. We plan a fall opening. I shall guide him at first, of course, although I intend to let him have a pretty free hand. Know nothing about the stuff myself, naturally."

"Naturally."

"So . . ."

"So?"

"So, it seems I'll probably be vacationing in Portugal this summer. I'll sandwich in a couple of weeks there between Rome and Paris."

"It seems a bit out of your way, Edward."

"Not at all. Thackeray and I have a great deal to talk about."

"I dare say."

Maule's voice grew firm. "A bargain, my boy, is a bargain."

There was a pause. "I suppose so. But you are to be on good behavior, Edward. You know what I mean."

"I hardly think that will be a problem."

"And not be underfoot all the time."

"I repeat, Philip: a bargain is a bargain. *Quid pro quo*. And not subject to subsequent qualifications." Maule laughed.

Philip did not. "We'll see. Now I've got to go. Good-by, Edward."

"Good-by, Philip. I hope it's a good performance."

"It always is."

After he had replaced the receiver, Dane sat looking into his mirror and soliloquized. "What a bore. Why did I ever agree to it? I should have known Edward would come cringing around." He thought about it. "Well, I can't keep him from being there, but we won't have to see much of him." He snapped his fingers. "That's it. I'll put him on one meal a day with us, and if it's the evening, then he leaves by eleven. He can take his choice, lunch or dinner, and that's that." He reached for his cosmetics. "Yes indeedy, it's going to be *demi-pension* for Uncle Edward this summer."

Maule himself, after he had finished a prolonged yawn, could not help but smile. How very disagreeable Philip could be, had been just now. He, Maule, could well imagine that there might have to be a little fuss or two before their vacation got organized. Philip wouldn't take to the whole thing, not at all. Maule smiled again. He recalled the remark Thackeray had made to him after he had said to the colored youth that, were he to join up with the Portugal party, he was afraid Philip would be too nasty to be borne: "Don't you worry about that, Mr. Maule. I know how Philip can act, but don't worry. Together we can take care of him. You see, I'm on your side. It's two against one, the odds are in our favor."

*   *

271

Out at sea, Theodore Cariatis nodded over a book on the iconoclastic controversy in his own corner of the little passengers' saloon of the *Lysippus*, where the other passengers, deferential to the owner, had left him alone—there were only eight of them besides himself aboard the freighter. Quite automatically he had looked the women over, but none would provide material even for a shipboard affair; moreover, as he reminded himself, he was planning to change avocations, was leaving gallantry for scholarship.

His mind wandered from the edicts of Leo the Isaurian to his own past and future life. He should have been feeling quite melancholy, but he did not. For the first time, really, in several years, he felt contented. He actually looked forward to the long voyage to the Aegean. His stateroom was stocked with books; he would be left alone; he could speak his preferred language; and the food would be a nice change from New York. Thinking of food, he found himself hungry.

The steward had disappeared somewhere, very possibly to nap behind a lifeboat, since nobody was ordering anything. Cariatis frowned. He would mention it tomorrow. But tonight? Why not help himself? He was, so to speak, at home. He went into the small pantry off the lounge to see what kind of tidbit he could find. There was a refrigerator there, which had been left unlocked, and which was mostly filled with soda water and beer, but there were a few things to eat. He looked them over and found a small jar of pickled mushrooms, already opened on the former voyage from the looks of it. He sniffed them—nothing seemed to be wrong. He spooned a pile of them on a cracker and tasted them. They were strong of spices and had a slightly odd taste he could not identify, but it was neither very strong nor certainly ominous, and he was hungry. He ate more. Finally he ate the entire jarful, put it into the sink, returned to the saloon to retrieve his book, and went off to his cabin. A cockroach scampered from a crack in the joint between the linoleum and cabinets of the pantry and found a fragment of cracker and mushroom that Cariatis had dropped. It explored them both, disdained the mushroom, and, after carrying the bit of cracker back to safety, began to devour it.

Meanwhile, Cariatis had put on his pajamas and got into his berth, but found he was too sleepy to read any more, shrugged—what did it matter, he had the rest of his life to read—and turned out the light. He began, as a soporific, and also a useful exercise, to run through the names of the emperors, starting with Justinian, on through the image breakers to the Macedonian dynasty, and onward still further; but long before he reached 1453 he had dropped into oblivion.

A tired-looking woman, dressed in gray, who exuded an air of downtrodden gentility, entered the drawing room of Arthur van Zandt's country house and directed her discreet steps toward the fireside place that, amidst all the splendors of the famous collection of French seventeenth- and eighteenth-century art, was impoverished by the presence of Henrietta. She, the downtrodden one—Henrietta, even now, was anything but that—had many instructions from the doctors and from the master of the house regarding the activities of the lady she had been hired to companion, but none governing long-distance telephone calls; although this one, being so startling, she had very nearly turned down on her own infirm authority.

"Mrs. van Zandt. There is a long-distance telephone call for you, Mrs. van Zandt."

Henrietta raised her eyes from her book:—*The Pith of the Theban Anchorites*. She was slightly annoyed, for Mrs. Ward-Wilcox's voice contained something unusual—excitement. "I do not like them," Henrietta said. "I probably do not want to receive this one, Mrs. Ward-Wilcox. It is not, by any chance, from my husband?"

"No. At least I don't think so. I think it must be from your son. It is from an Arthur van Zandt, but in London. The call is from London."

"London?" Henrietta said. "London? But why would he have gone there to call me?"

"Perhaps he was there anyway."

"Unlikely."

"In any case, what shall I tell the operator?"

"Tell her that Mrs. van Zandt does not choose—no, wait a moment, wait a moment. London . . . London . . . Perhaps I ought, after all, to talk to him. Who knows what exigency has driven him to London, and what additional one has caused him, once there, to call upon his mother's aid. I will take the call."

The two ladies went for the telephone together, or rather, according to rank, Henrietta in the lead. Mrs. Ward-Wilcox would have to hover in the shadows while her mistress spoke, her instructions being under no circumstances to leave Henrietta alone.

"Hello, Mother. Mother, how are you?"

"Well, thank you, Arthur. Connecticut is at least a state in which one can mend. And read."

"Mother, did you get all my letters? I mean, you know why I'm here in London?"

"Your letters? Yes, I think so." Henrietta turned to one

side. "Mrs. Ward-Wilcox, did we get letters from Arthur? Yes? Yes, Arthur, I got your letters."

"I had to write, Mother. I mean, since you weren't seeing people and refused to answer the telephone."

"There is no cause to apologize for writing, Arthur. It remains by far the most civilized method of communication."

"And the slowest," Artie said. There was a pause, and some muffled rumblings from Great Britain, while Artie talked to Ursula, his hand over the mouthpiece. Then he came back to his mother. "Anyway, now that we've landed, I wanted to telephone you first of all."

"Are you in distress, Artie?" Henrietta asked, wanly eager.

"No. It was a very smooth flight. Neither of us had a twinge of *that*, thank God."

Henrietta now looked slightly bewildered, as the first-person plural pronoun came across the Atlantic to her. "Us? We? Surely your father didn't go with you, not to London."

"But Mother, you said you got my letters. I explained . . ."

"I received them, Artie. I did not read them."

A deep sigh. "Oh." Another. "God."

"I hope you call upon His name with full realization, Artie."

"Don't I, though. Listen, Mother, I'm married. That's it in a nutshell. I married Ursula Cariatis, and we're on our honeymoon, sort of."

Smoothly, without faltering, Henrietta asked, "Were you married in civil or religious ceremony, Artie?"

"Religious. Greek Orthodox."

"Greek Orthodox? No."

"They're in communion with the See of Canterbury, Mother."

"Ah, yes. I recall that."

"By an archbishop, Mother, also sort of. And we received the congratulations of the Patriarch of Constantinople. Now known as Istanbul. I hope you're not too upset, Mother. You'll love Ursula when you get to know her. Better."

"My head is spinning with all this, Arthur. I think it would be better, for the time being, if I forgot your call. Perhaps later we can try again."

"Mother, just believe me. It's all for the best."

"Arthur, I hope you have an umbrella. If not, go at once and buy one."

"I have one, Mother. I took one of Father's."

"A final point, Arthur. Since you are in London, let me urge you to go and call upon Lord Coyne—if he is still alive. Tell him that you come from Henrietta."

"Yes, Mother."

"And Artie, if you took your Father's umbrella, do compare it to the ones you see around you. Make sure it is acceptable."

"Yes, Mother. Mother, before we hang up, I just want to be sure. You have understood about me and Ursula, haven't you? I mean, I'm not going to have to start at the beginning, not really, am I, the next time I talk to you? Mother? Mother?"

But Henrietta, a sweet smile on her face at the thought of all the nice umbrellas in London, had quietly put down the receiver.

She stood up, and Mrs. Ward-Wilcox came forward from her dark corner. "It is late, Mrs. van Zandt. Time to go to bed. Shall I read to you for a while?"

Henrietta walked to the stairs. "Please do, Mrs. Ward-Wilcox. Let us have some of my favorite passages from the Bible."

The downtrodden one sighed, but so gently it was inaudible to Henrietta. "A pleasure, Mrs. van Zandt," she said. "My favorite book."

A half hour later Henrietta was lying in bed, having already taken the sedatives that, in a short while, would put her out for the night. Mrs. Ward-Wilcox, who slept in the adjoining dressing room, was in the bedside chair with a large, limp-leather-covered Bible on her lap. She put on her chaste spectacles and turned the pages.

"Where does our preference lie tonight?" she asked. "Genesis? Chronicles? St. Matthew?"

Henrietta considered the momentous choice. "Tonight, Mrs. Ward-Wilcox, let it be Chronicles," she decided.

Mrs. Ward-Wilcox turned to the correct place, for it was marked with a slip of paper. " 'First Book of the Chronicles. Chapter One, verse two,' " she read. " 'Adam, Sheth, Enosh; verse two, Kenan, Mahalaleel, Jered; verse three, Henoch, Methuselah, Lamech; four, Noah, Shem, Ham, and Japheth. Five, The sons of Japheth; Gomer, and Magog, and Madai, and Javan, and Tubal, and Meshech, and Tiras. Six, And the sons of Gomer; Ashchenaz, and Riphath, and Togarmah. Seven, And the sons of Javan; Elishah, and Tarshish, Kittim, and Dodanim. . . .' "

Henrietta nodded with pleasure. "It is so soothing," she said. "And particularly now that good practice has taught you how to say all the names without a stumble."

"Thank you, Mrs. van Zandt. Shall I go on?"

"Please do."

" 'Verse eight, The sons of Ham; Cush, and Mizraim, Put, and Canaan. Nine, And the sons of Cush; Seba, and Havilah, and Sabta, and Raamah, and Sabtecha. And the sons of Raamah; Sheba, and Dedan. . . .' Mrs. van Zandt?"

"I still hear you. 'Sheba and Dedan.' How suitable a sense of genealogy the Jews had in those days, Mrs. Ward-Wilcox. Go on."

" 'Verse ten, And Cush begat Nimrod: he began to be mighty upon the earth. Eleven, And Mizraim begat Ludim, and Anamin, and Lehabim, and Naphtuhim; twelve, And Pathrusim, and Casluhim (of whom came the Philistines), and Caphthorim. . . .' Mrs. van Zandt?"

There was no answer.

Mrs. Ward-Wilcox closed the Bible and went to her little cubicle, where she undressed and then took out her own book, which was in a drawer beside her bed. She looked once guiltily toward the slumbering Henrietta out in the bedroom, then began to read. It was a volume she had got through a remainder house, a cheap edition of *Pamela*.

Dr. Pearson Tait, who had also been given a strong sedative, had yet enough consciousness left to continue to complain.

"I don't think I can go to sleep with this on," he said to his wife, who lay reading in the bed next to his.

She did not look over at him. "Nonsense, Pearson, dear," she replied. "It's light as a feather."

"But won't it get all wrapped around me if I turn over?"

"If it gets too tight, I'll feel the tug and I'll wake up and revolve you until you're untangled," she promised.

"What's the good of it anyway? I'm a strong man, Martha. I could break it just like that."

"I've explained over and over to you, Pearson, that I just want to know what you're doing. You can do what you want to, but I just want to know about it." Her tone of voice sharpened. "After what happened today," she added.

"I don't want to hear about that again."

"I don't want to go through anything like that again. I will take good care of you, Pearson, forever and forever; but I insist on knowing what I'm taking care of. I need the facts, Pearson. As a scientist you must understand that. I need the facts if I'm going to do the job. I have to know whether I'm dealing, just for example, with a forger, a restorer—or whatever."

"I don't know myself."

"I do. And now go to sleep. I'm trying to read."

Pearson Tait raised his hairy left wrist, to which was attached one end of the tiny silver chain, the other end of which was attached to the right wrist of his wife. "I feel like a dog," he said.

"Bow-wow. And nighty-night," said Martha Tait. Deliberately, she put her free hand under the covers and scratched out her evening salute to the South Seas. Then she withdrew the hand and turned a page. She read on, turned another. Time passed. "I think I will take you on my next collecting expedition, Pearson," she said. "I truly believe that if you could only grow to love the pterido-phytes, it would solve all your problems."

But he had, in the interim, fallen fast asleep.

Before he went to bed, Thackeray telephoned his mother, and to her recounted most of the events of the day, withholding only those he thought might be indiscreet or incomprehensible. "And so, Momma, it's all settled. After I get back from Portugal, I'll start getting this gallery ready to open. And I've got an idea for the first show, too. Mr. Maule is going to help me—in fact, we're going to start seeing about getting it fixed up tomorrow, Momma.

What? No, of course not, Momma. It'll all be done by people hired for the job. You don't understand, Momma. This
will all be very professional. Just imagine it, Momma—a
beautiful gallery for contemporary art, and me running
it. We're going to have thick-pile nylon carpeting, and
hand-rubbed Danish furniture, and of course lots of philo-
dendrons. I'm not going to call it by my name, because nobody's ever heard of me and they'd probably think I
sold books or prints—you know, the literary associations.
But I've got an idea for that, too. I'll tell you when I've
finally made up my mind. And, oh! Momma, I'm so excited. I'm really on my way at last, really going somewhere. It's a dream come true. My own gallery, Momma
—isn't that something? And Momma, I don't need to tell
you this, do I Momma? I don't need to tell you what makes
me proudest of all. What means the most to me, Momma,
is: it's a first."

PART FIVE

An Epilogue:
The Last Saturday
in September

Matthew McCaffrey, tall, handsome, youthful, and trim, still tanned from the summer's swimming and from a last-minute vacation spent fishing in Canada, was ending his speech.

"And that, in brief, is how the vision of so many dedicated men and women has at last been realized, brought into being; and it is this realization that you are here to see for the first time tonight. How much we owe to all of those who have helped can scarcely be said, to those who planned and hoped and labored." He looked to the darkness at his left where, he knew, was seated a special delegation from the labor unions. "Those who built with their hands." He looked to the right, where the chief architects were seated. "Those who built with their minds.

"Two individuals should, I feel, be specifically mentioned once more as I conclude. The first, our former president, Benjamin Gloag, whose devotion has reached even across the valley of the shadow, and whose legacy provided a major share of the funds that have been used. Ben cannot be present to speak to us tonight . . ." He allowed a moment's silence to pass. ". . . but the second individual can be, and is. I have already mentioned his name, too. Yet, since such a large share of those works of art that ornament the new wing belong to him, since he is providing us with such a wonderful experience, I think it is only proper that you should all meet him, should all see him, all hear him. I have, therefore, much against his will, prevailed upon him to address us tonight, to close these ceremonies, after which the galleries will be opened to you. No, let me correct myself. After which *your* galleries will be opened to *you*, the people of this city, for the first time. Let him speak for all the others whose generosity in lending works they cherish has helped fill still others of our new rooms.

"Ladies and gentlemen, it is with the deepest appreciation and the greatest pleasure that I present to you Mr. Arthur van Zandt, owner, and donor, of the magnificent collection of French art that you will soon see. Mr. van Zandt."

McCaffrey stepped back from the lectern, and his place was taken by the massive figure of a man, gray-haired, black-browed, a little thin now, a little tired, and more than just a little drunk. He stared out into the darkened auditorium, whose very exit lights were so subtly shielded that he could not see them, looked down and blinked at the light that fell upon the sheet or two of paper that he placed beneath his hand. He looked up, then down, then up once more, and turned his head to and fro, like some kind of blinded creature, as he tried to see the hundreds of fortunates with invitations giving them the privilege of seats, and thought of the many hundreds more who stood outside in the lobby and corridors, listening through the public-address system.

He cleared his throat gruffly. "It is a fortunate thing, ladies and gentlemen, that I wrote down the speech I am supposed to make this evening, because otherwise, so filled am I with sorrow, I doubt if I would be able to say anything at all."

There was a titter. He was, the audience assumed, about to make a joke, since it was impossible that he could mean what he said.

But he did not smile. He did not seem to notice their response. "With a great sorrow," he said, not following his notes now, "and, I must confess, with a great disgust."

Another titter. The anticipation of the punch line.

Angrily, van Zandt leaned forward and stared at the panel of dials and switches that faced him from the back rim of the lectern, as complicated as part of the console of an organ. He fiddled with one of them, but succeeded only in producing a hum, which McCaffrey, jumping up from his nearby seat, immediately rectified. Van Zandt turned to the director and whispered, "How do I turn the f——g lights up, McCaffrey? I agreed to speak, but I'll be damned if I'll submit to the indignity of being watched and laughed at by people I can't even see." His words could not be heard by the immediate audience, which therefore missed what was, indeed, a punch line; but they were duly carried outside by the more sensitive long-distance microphone, and there either appreciated or deplored, as the case might be.

McCaffrey turned another knob, and the lights within the new auditorium brightened slowly, until the audience was almost as visible to van Zandt as he was to it.

"That's better. Now then . . ." He looked down at his notes.

"You have already heard enough platitudes—yes, I promise you I wrote this speech in advance; but I am an old hand, and I knew the kind of thing that would be said before I got my turn—you have heard enough platitudes about educational values and life enhancement, about the heritage from past generations and the responsibility to future ones. You have heard about elevating aesthetic levels, cultural levels, moral levels, about elevating just about every level anybody could imagine elevating—all this elevating to be done, somehow, by a new wing to an art museum. Well, I am not going to talk about things like that. I am not going to talk long about anything; but there is one subject I am qualified to talk about, and which some of you are qualified to understand—that eliminates any meaningful discussion of the objects in my collection—and that is the very process of collecting.

"Why did I collect? And why have I now given my collection to this museum? Those two questions some of you can understand, and I can answer. I should answer them, if anybody is going to. I, and I alone.

"First of all, I didn't collect so that one day I could leave my collection for the pleasure or instruction, much less elevation, of the public of this or any other city. I don't think it will do that. I don't think more than one per cent— a very outside figure—of the visitors to this museum will ever understand in the slightest what my paintings and sculpture and tapestries and porcelains and so on are about. Various ways will be devised, by those whose jobs and self-respect depend upon it, to delude them into thinking that they do—the substitution of the written word, blurbs, for the visual experience of looking, for instance, so essential if one is to flatter the perceptually retarded. But however adroitly deluded and deceived, they will not understand. Believe me they won't. It has taken me a long lifetime to understand what, let us say an inkwell, done for a forgotten banker in the eighteenth century, is about. The subtlety of the hand of Fragonard I am only beginning to grasp. Watteau is at least as mysterious to me as is the Holy Ghost." He glanced over to the side of the platform to where his wife sat, for Henrietta was present. He smiled with some of the old malice.

Seeing his smile, the audience tittered once more.

"I do know, have learned, that all the critical and historical clichés are wrong and idiotic, but I long ago concluded that such things don't matter. Just remember—this would be my only advice to an earnest beginner—that all the clichés are wrong. The second you have noticed the same thing said twice in the same way, doubt it. They tell you that the art of the Old Regime was aristocratic—that is meaningless, because the kind of person who says it doesn't even know what aristocratic means. They tell you it is frivolous. That's nonsense. Boucher was not as talented as Rembrandt, I admit, but he was at least as profound; for the hierarchy of values that puts the kind of murky spirituality typical of much of Rembrandt above more fleeting joys—of life and love—is a hierarchy devised by Sunday-school teachers, and no more valid than any other of the things they say.

"Now, back to my collecting and my collection.

"I collected because I was, in the most profound sense, a lover. I have loved everything that you will see here. I am not an eccentric, a human squirrel, pack rat, or magpie; I repeat, I am a lover. My collection is an extension of me, chosen by me, has been formed and shaped by me. Perhaps it doesn't make sense to say this, either psychologically or metaphysically, but it is, in my feelings, an extension of me. My collection *is me*.

"How many of you have ever managed to love anything that much? Except your children. How many have ever been able, in the realms where emotion and intellect merge, to pass beyond the limitations of the female rat?

"I take great exception to many of the commands of Jesus Christ, but to none more than this: lay not up for yourselves treasures upon the earth. There speaks the carpenter's apprentice, not the *maître-ébéniste*.

"That is why I have been a collector, because I was in love.

"And now for the reason why my collection is here. The reason is vanity.

"My collection is truly a collection. It is not a miscellany. It does not express my fortune; it expresses me. I am a physical thing, and so is it, my extension. Like any other physical entity, like myself for example, it can be endangered by time and events—if you prefer, moths, rust, and thieves. Collections get dispersed, destroyed, chipped away. I am very glad that I have sufficient vanity and sufficient pride to want to keep my collection in one place and keep it safe. It is, after all, me. It is, I hope, as safe here, in this new wing, as law and science can make it. That much I can say for this new building—and for the deed of gift.

"And, too, it will shine forth here, to that outside one per cent. I have looked at the other stuff on permanent display here, and I have this to say: it will be a long time before the rest of your museum will shine forth as brightly as my collection. For that I am glad.

"As for you other ninety-nine one-hundredths of humanity, don't ever call me a benefactor or a philanthropist. I have made this speech tonight solely to prevent that, by contradicting the whole idea in public statement. *I am a collector*, and I want to provide, as well as I can, that *my* collection will endure. I dislike the thought that other people will be looking at it when I am dead. I dislike you, as I look out at you now, because most of you will be looking at it when I am dead. I tell you, ladies and gentlemen, I am anything but a philanthropist."

Now he raised his head. "I said I was filled with disgust and with sorrow. Sorrow because I must give my collection away. My disgust is at the thought that my collection must endure, as the price of its survival, your profanation. "Good evening."

He started to back away from the lectern, but then stopped and suddenly burst into laughter. "One more thing I was supposed to say and almost forgot. Another reason my collection is here is this: your president, Mr. Kant, a great benefactor and philanthropist, has made possible the complicated and expensive installation, not yet completed, which I exacted as part of the bargain. His name will have a prominent place on all signs and labels. I agreed to that. He has also given enough endowment to pay for a special curator. I demanded that. Without him, the van Zandt collection would never come here. So if you want to thank anybody, thank him. He'll be delighted." He gathered his notes together. "That's all I have to say."

McCaffrey leaned over to Will Nesbitt. "Thank heavens," he whispered, rising to the sound of Barney Kant's snickering and some unenthusiastic applause from the audience of notables. He praised the departing speaker most warmly, his forthrightness, his rugged individualism, his honesty, and his taste. "Now, led by His Honor, Mayor Howard, who will cut the ribbon, we will all go into the new galleries."

And then, at a signal, an orchestra in one of the courts outside began to play the first of the musical selections (a Mozart medley), whose program had been arranged by Barney Kant.

A short while later a group of reporters covering the opening prevailed upon van Zandt to grant them an interview. It was arranged through McCaffrey, who was almost evenly balanced in his feelings between pro and con; but the pro—that is, the desire for as much publicity as possible (and Arthur van Zandt was clearly a natural for that) —won out over the con, that is, apprehension of what van Zandt might say. Will Nesbitt volunteered to stand by during the session so that he could, if necessary, break it off.

"I don't like reporters," van Zandt said, glowering at them when they were brought up to him, "or newspapers, and I won't talk to you more than a few minutes; so come right to the point, if you have any."

For a rich man not to like reporters was hardly news; however, it gave one of them an idea. "What do you think about our art criticism, Mr. van Zandt? Who are our best critics?"

"There is no such thing as good art criticism, not in the journalistic sense. And I see no distinctions between critics, saving one: there are those who are on the top of the heap, and there are those who are scrambling to get there. I never read any of the stuff in the newspapers or the current magazines myself."

The group was gathered in one of the period rooms that had been assembled from van Zandt's collection, everything in it dating from 1770 to 1790. "You seem to own more furniture and bowls and things like that than anything else, Mr. van Zandt. Why?"

"It is quite natural that I should have more decorative arts than paintings. More that is good, in these media, has survived, because of simple durability, toughness. Therefore we can be selective of quality and know what we are about—there is more comparative material. Let any Florentine painting survive, say, from the fourteenth century, and you'll find a fool to buy it and call it Giotto. The collector exclusively interested in paintings swallows examples gladly that, in comparable quality in his own line, the collector of majolica would send off to his kitchen."

"But you do have paintings, too."

"Naturally. And when I am going to buy an eighteenth-century painting I always say to myself: is this really as good, in its own way, as my Riesener desk? That is why I have so few paintings." He laughed. "That is why other collectors have so many."

"What do you think of other museums?"

"Which ones? They're sprouting like motels over the countryside."

"Well, the Metropolitan, for instance?"

"A mammoth *omnium gatherum*."

"And the National Gallery of Art?"

"That place!"

There was some laughter. Then, "Would you say there are other collections comparable to your own, Mr. van Zandt?"

"Two of them. For quality, there is the Frick Collection, in New York." He looked around the room, so magnificently furnished. "Mine, too, is very fine from that point of view. But neither of them is the Wallace Collection. On the other hand, I came along too late. Hertford and Sir Richard had already bought so many of the things I would have liked."

"Where is that?"

"In London," van Zandt replied, staring down at the reporter. "That's in England."

"How much is your collection worth?"

"How the hell should I know?"

"Is everything you have going to stay here from now on?"

"Certainly not. I'll keep a certain number of things near me, and change them from time to time. That's all written into the agreement."

"That's right," Nesbitt said, stepping smoothly into the circle. "I am the museum's counsel, and I can testify to it."

He was ignored. "Do you have any anecdotes, funny stories, connected with your collection that you could give us? Like, what's the most unusual way you ever got hold of one of your important things?"

Van Zandt grinned. He looked around at the reporters, then at Nesbitt. Then he laughed. "I'm saving all those for my memoirs," he said. "Now go away and leave me alone. Go out and look at the Watteau in the middle of the main hall. My newest acquisition. Probably the most important picture I own."

"Where did it come from?"

"Originally France. Now I want to go and speak to my wife a minute. There's somebody here I want her to be sure to meet."

"Well. Are you enjoying yourself, Henrietta? It's not too much for you?"

"No, not too much, Arthur. Most of the people do not seem to be my kind; nevertheless, I am content that I decided to come. It is more suitable. You have a wife and she should be here."

"Quite. I agree. Actually, I am grateful. But as for the people—you may be missing something, or someone. There are lots of dignitaries of one sort or another, invited—all expenses paid—to act as international witnesses to this great triumph of the arts in America. Have you met many of them? Let me see. . . . Over there, near the door, is old Damien. Curator of something important at the Louvre. And there is Signora Belpezzo from the Brera. Ah, yes, and right over there is someone I specifically asked be invited, one of the trustees of the National Gallery in

London, Henrietta. An earl, he is, or some such thing. A man you should meet. A great traveler in his day. May I?"

He took her to an elderly man, red-faced, heavy of chin and belly, and said, "I would like to introduce you to my wife. Or I should rather say, I would like to reintroduce you to my wife, since it is my understanding that you knew each other long ago. Henrietta, this is Lord Coyne." He watched them a moment, then said as he left them, "I know you have a lot to talk over."

Henrietta was at first mute, struck dumb. Then, "Oswald. You!" she cried.

"Eh? Eh?"

"You don't remember? You don't remember me? You don't remember Philadelphia? Twenty-five years ago? The waltz at the Bellevue-Stratford?"

Lord Coyne frowned nearsightedly. "Were you a . . . a Miss Penn?"

"Alas, no. I was already a Mistress—Mrs. van Zandt. I was your Henrietta."

Light dawned. "Egad. Of course. Henrietta. The name had slipped my mind—almost everything does these days, don't you know. Henrietta. I remember well. Did you ever get your letters back? Seems to me I had my secretary send them on to you, after the usual wait."

"Would that you had burned them, Oswald. Arthur got hold of them several months ago, after all these years."

Lord Coyne looked around uneasily. "Was he angry? He didn't seem angry."

"Not Arthur, for he doesn't love me, nor ever did. Not as you did. Your passion drenched those precious pages. I mean, your half of the exchange."

Lord Coyne blushed. "Now, Henrietta, my dear, you flatter my epistolary style, I'm sure. But your letters—I remember them now. You had a charming little love call."

Henrietta pressed her fingertips together and leaned toward him. "I had a son, Oswald, only eight months after you left Philadelphia," she whispered dramatically.

"Did you now."

"I have always believed he was our son, Oswald, yours and mine, not mine and Arthur's."

"What good would that do him? The bar sinister, and all that."

Henrietta tried a slightly different tack. "He is married, Oswald. Recently. Not well, perhaps, but magnificently. To the sole heiress of Theodore Cariatis."

"Cariatis? Cariatis? The restaurant fellow?"

"No. The billionaire. He died at sea just a few months ago. Botulism. While crossing on one of his own ships."

"I dare say." Lord Coyne coughed damply. "Too bad."

She tried still again. "I understand the king and queen attended the memorial service."

"King? King? He's not a king, my dear, he's a prince."

"I meant the king and queen of Greece, Oswald."

"Of Greece? Hmmm. Oh. I dare say."

Van Zandt was distracted by a voice at his elbow. "That is Mrs. van Zandt with Lord Coyne, is it not? I'm so glad she could come."

He turned to find Edward Maule beside him. "Didn't want her to, Edward, but she insisted, for appearances. Rightly, I suppose. That is her strength."

"She seems to be going off toward the door. Is she leaving so early?"

"Probably. She'll be all right—we brought her driver out with us. She hasn't been well. And it isn't every night we meet our fantasies turned to flesh. Besides, she'll be up

294

and to church tomorrow."

"What devotion."

"Not really. It's an attitude, or a habit, I would say. As is so often the case, you know. Under the miasma of piety lies a deadly bog of worldliness."

"What church does she go to?"

"That depends. Usually Episcopal. Sometimes, just to be irritating, she flirts with the Friends. And to prove she comes from Pennsylvania. Her maiden name was Ford, and she doesn't want to be taken for one of those people from Detroit."

Edward Maule, amused, said, "And your son? How is he, Arthur?"

"All right. He's in Athens now. I guess you know Cariatis died. It was a great shock to me. I grew fond of him toward the end—something I owe to you, I suppose, Edward, and to Henrietta. A significant re-evaluation. It doesn't often happen. Fine man. Very tragic. One thing, it seems Artie has started to collect art, Edward. That ought to make your ears prick up. He bought a fine little sketchbook by van Goyen, I understand. I find myself, well, touched by it. Proud of him, you know. Of course, van Goyen isn't in my line, but the Dutch were respectable artists. He might have bought a Renoir."

"And how is his wife?"

"Ursula? Getting along. Both of them getting along. They seem to be making it so far. She's going to see to it that some projects her father wanted to start will be carried out."

"Speaking of Cariatis, Arthur, there is his ex-lady friend over in the corner, talking to Barney Kant. I think I'll go say hello to her. Excuse me, Arthur."

* *

"Mademoiselle de la Couronne d'Epines! What happy chance brings you out here to this opening tonight?" Maule said gaily, wondering from whom she had her emeralds, assuming they were real.

"Monsieur Maule." Angélique was delighted to find someone she knew, lest Barney think she was a nobody. "It was an accident. I have been making a little voyage from one to another of the important cities of the United States, to correct my ignorance of your geography and to enlarge my acquaintance; and today, I found myself here. Naturally friends arranged for me to come."

"And have you seen the Watteau?"

She nodded. "Charming," she said. "I wish it had become mine." Her beautiful face clouded over. "Poor little Theodore."

"They say it was some bad pickled mushrooms."

She shook her head. "I know better," she replied. "A man like Theodore does not eat bad mushrooms. They have kept the secret, of course, to avoid scandal. Also, perhaps, the insurance. But what happened is clear, and will be on my conscience until the day I die, although I have talked of nothing else in the *confessionnal* for weeks and weeks." She put a hand to each temple. "How ironic it is, Monsieur Maule, that, after all, he should have proven himself worthy to stand beside my most heroic lovers, if not in physical, at least in moral stature." She glanced at Barney. "It has given me new ideas."

"Irony, indeed," said Maule. Then, to change the subject, he asked, "And where did you go on your tour?"

"Everywhere, everywhere, everywhere. But everywhere. Sewickley, Shaker Heights, Indian Hill, Guilford, Grosse Pointe, Lake Forest, Belair, Burlingame. Everywhere. Such a delightful country, after all. One had the feeling that one might never have left Neuilly."

Just then Barney, whose attention had been diverted for a moment by one of the ubiquitous newspaper reporters, turned back to Angélique. "Talking to Maule, eh? Now see here, Ed, don't think you can take this charming mam'-selle away from me, because you can't."

"If I can't," Maule replied, "then I had better not try." He took Angélique's hand and bent over it. "Surely," he said, "you will one day have some small need that will bring you back to my offices."

Angélique smiled. "Perhaps. I do have that blank space on my wall that cries out for a nice painting."

"Blank space? Do you? It does?" Barney said.

"I shall look forward to seeing you then," Maule said, moving away.

"Say, mam'selle, where are you staying?"

"With friends. But we are so crowded. They have other guests."

Barney grinned. "My house isn't crowded. Why don't you just move in there? I'll send for your baggage. I've got about fifteen empty bedrooms, and you might as well fill one of them. And you'll really fill it, too," he added.

"And what about Mrs. Kant?"

"She's been away for months. Confidentially, she found herself a boy friend out west. Younger'n you, even."

"I suppose I could speak to my friends. It would be a favor to them if I left. It might look strange, but then . . . Let us go and look for them, Mr. Kant."

As they started off Barney said, "Say, is it true that you're one of those noble people?"

Angélique nodded. "*Et comment!*" she said.

"First one I ever knew. I'm real proud."

"But after all, *chéri*," Angélique answered, tapping him

on one skinny upper arm, "a robber baron is yet a baron, for all that."

When Edward Maule left Angélique and Barney, he encountered Thackeray, who was slowly walking toward the place of honor in the museum, the crossroads, accented by banks of flowers, spotlights, and, of course, Arthur van Zandt's new Watteau.

"Thackeray. Are you enjoying yourself?" the old dealer asked.

"Ever so much," said Thackeray.

"You are getting a good general view of the world you wish to inhabit, Thackeray. I don't see why you want to. What is more, I don't think it is worth doing. But then, I speak as an old party. I no longer care, because everything is so familiar to me."

"And yet, you are going to stay in business for a while, Mr. Maule."

"That is habit, Thackeray. As you will learn, habit makes us do things long after the substance has left them. Which accounts for why anybody ever has more than three children."

"I guess that's right," Thackeray agreed. Then, more seriously, he said, "But don't forget, Mr. Maule, that the important thing is that a person should have a chance to inhabit the world you're tired of, whether it's worth doing or not."

"Of course," Maule said kindly. "I quite understand." Suddenly he started. "Oh-oh. Look over there. That has the appearance of a newspaper reporter. And asking Dr. Tait questions. I don't like it, Thackeray. We'd better go over and chaperon him."

Maule's concern was so far unnecessary, for Mrs. Tait

was on the job. "No," she was saying with firmness to the reporter, "Dr. Tait does not want to make any statement to the press about cleaning this or any other picture."

"He did clean it, though?"

"He did clean it. Yes."

"What's it like to clean a painting worth hundreds of thousands? Aren't you afraid you'll do something wrong, Dr. Tait?"

"Science does not make errors, young man," Mrs. Tait said.

"Can't he answer for himself?"

"Answer the question, Pearson."

Tait, a sluggish lizard prepared to snap, looked balefully at his wife. "Science makes no errors," he said. Suddenly he laughed.

"Pearson," she said between her teeth.

The reporter scribbled with his pencil, then paused a moment to think of some other question. "Here's my last one, Dr. Tait. You work on all these great paintings by important artists. You must know a lot about how they do things. Do you ever paint yourself?"

Mrs. Tait gripped her husband's arm, but it was to no avail. The dangerous question had been posed. Slowly the great head rotated on the neckless torso until it faced the Watteau, glittering amidst all the pink and white flowers.

"That question I will answer," he said. "Listen to me, there."

"Pearson. *Pearson!*"

But he gave his wife a push that sent her stumbling out of range. "Yes, I paint. Yes, I do paint. You see that Watteau over there, the one all the fuss is over? Well, let me tell you something. . . ."

At that moment Thackeray entered the conversation.

He stepped in front of Dr. Tait and said loudly, "Since I am your agent, why don't you let me tell him about your painting, Dr. Tait?"

Tait looked confused. "What? What?"

"His agent?" the reporter said.

Thackeray nodded. "So to speak. His dealer. You see, Dr. Tait does indeed paint. In fact, I might say that he is going to be as well known as Watteau one day—that's what he was about to say, weren't you, Dr. Tait? Artists aren't famous for their modesty, you know."

"His dealer?"

"His dealer. He's not only a restorer, he is also a *very distinguished* contemporary painter. I'm opening my own gallery in New York City in a few weeks, and the inaugural exhibition will be Dr. Tait's first one-man show. It's called the Galerie Lendemain—you know, 'day after tomorrow.' "

The reporter scribbled. "What kind of paintings does he do?"

Thackeray knitted his brows. "Hard to describe. I think you might call them what he calls them—parodies. He does abstract expressionism, action painting, of course, but each one is done as a parody of an old master, an homage to an old master. For instance, there will be one, geometrical shapes of blue and red and yellow and green and orange and violet, called *A Bacchanale by Poussin*. Then, there's a *Rape of the Sabine Women by Rubens*. That's wilder, naturally. He's trying to show the links that join the old masters with modern art. He is in a unique position to do that."

"Interesting idea."

"It's going to be a major exhibition. Keep your eye on Tait. He'll be hanging in the Whitney one day."

Meanwhile, Mrs. Tait had returned to her husband's

side. She was pulling him backward, away from the reporter's questions, and this time her grip was too strong to be broken.

"But. But," he said. Then, "Ouch."

She had pinched him, hard and sharp, the tweak she used to pluck a tough frond from the mother plant if there were no shearers handy. "Silence, Pearson. Not another word. One more word and I'll do it. I mean it. Remember, they won't let you have paints and brushes once you're in there. Not another word."

He looked at her sullenly, reached up with one hand to rub the place she had pinched, then with the same hand went to his shoulder, where he had a mosquito bite received through shirt and undershirt that afternoon out in a bog by the river where she had taken him. He permitted her to lead him away toward the coatracks.

"Maybe I'd be better off there," he said.

"Try it. I'll certify you any time you ask me to."

He didn't answer.

"I've had enough, Pearson, and I think you've had enough for the night, too. And we've got things to do early tomorrow before we fly back. My kinds of things. We didn't half exhaust the bog today."

Maule and Thackeray trailed behind them to be sure they really did leave, then Maule turned back toward the midst of the crowd. "Beautifully handled, Thackeray," he said. "Quick thinking. Done with real suavity, real elegance. No one could have guessed how near we came to catastrophe." He frowned. "I was all against having Tait here, you know, but they thought it would look funny. All the other important restorers are here. There's McCaffrey. I'm going to tell him about this."

Thackeray started to hang behind.

"Coming along?"

"No, sir. I see a pay telephone, and I promised my mother I'd call her right in the middle and tell her all about it."

"Now, there's a thoughtful lad." Maule smiled benignly as he walked over to the director, to whom he repeated what had just happened with Tait and the press.

But McCaffrey refused to worry. "Too big a night to think of things that almost happened but didn't quite. He's gone, so that's that. Quite an affair, isn't it, Edward?" He passed a tanned hand over his short hair. "And that speech of Arthur's. Nobody's going to forget that in some time."

Maule was surprised. "I would have thought you might be just a bit . . . offended by it. Pretty strong talk."

"I was taken off guard for a second. But offended? Not me. I don't give a damn what they say, just so long as they keep talking about us," McCaffrey replied. He saw a random millionaire and edged toward him.

"I haven't seen Mrs. McCaffrey, Matt," Maule said. It was one of his principles to be attentive to the wives of directors.

"Chickie? Poor old Chickie. She's brokenhearted, but she just couldn't make it tonight."

"Nothing serious I hope."

"I don't think so," said McCaffrey. "See you, Edward." He approached his quarry, leaving the dealer behind.

"Mr. Evans—what do you think of it all? I'm so glad you could come. It's not often we get a trustee of the Boston Museum out in these parts." The white-haired old gentleman, who wanted only to sit down or to leave, murmured polite comment. "By the way, have you looked into the other part of the building at our three American primitive portraits? Nothing like your own collection, of course, but it's a start. I have always believed it was an obligation of any

302

museum to have something in that field. After all, it is the beginning of our own national school of painting. They're right down here and to the left. Let me come along and make sure you find them."

Maule continued to stroll back toward the new wing, and on his way almost collided with Dr. Pretorius, who was hurrying down the corridor.

"Dr. Pretorius. Nice to see you. Everything looks splendid. Wherever are you going in such a hurry?"

Pretorius shook his head. "A reporter. A reporter. They are everywhere, Mr. Maule. Like hornets. One of them asked me a question just now that I was unable to answer, and I am going to the library to look it up. I must hurry." He cantered off, saying to himself, *"Ach! welch' eine ungeheu're Gesellschaft."*

Stopping now and then to speak to an acquaintance or a customer or, as was often the case, a combination of the two, Maule progressed through the new wing—the great, glittering steel, glass, and terrazzo galleries, variously trimmed and finished, some of them filled with objects loaned by private collectors, several displaying an exhibition of things chosen by the directors of rival museums as among their own favorite possessions and lent to this congratulatory grouping, and, of course, the galleries, partly permanently arranged, partly only temporarily so, of the collection of Arthur van Zandt. It began to grow late, and the crowd was thinning out—among other reasons, there were many parties following the opening, which, in the protocol of things, took precedence over the actual opening itself. At length he came into a room whose other doorway was blocked by a screen. The screen was pushed slightly aside, and with professional curiosity, Maule peered into the darkened gallery whose access it was supposed to block. Someone was there with a flashlight, and Maule was about to back away, thinking it must be a watchman, when the familiar, harsh voice of Arthur van Zandt called to him.

"Come on in, Edward. But pull the screen to behind you. I don't want anybody else coming in here now."

Maule did so and, when his eyes grew accustomed to the darkness, saw that he was in a room hung with tapestries. Under them, not yet arranged, were some cabinets, and there was a carpet partially unrolled in the middle of the floor.

"One of the places they couldn't get done in time," van Zandt explained. "My stuff." He flashed his light at the floor. "Best Savonnerie carpet in the country." At the walls. "My tapestries. The hunting series, after cartoons by Desportes. They once hung in the apartment of Louis XV at Fontainebleau—he loved to go there and kill animals, you know." Van Zandt looked around the room and slowly shook his head. "Well, Edward . . ." It was not a question.

"I liked your talk, Arthur. You have good reason to be proud."

"I suppose so. Yes, of course I have. I meant what I said. But I wasn't thinking just now about how fine everything looks, how it all holds up, how well I've done. I wasn't thinking of all that, you know."

"What were you thinking about?"

"Oh, various things. How I got these. Where. What they have meant to me. And, oddly, I have just seen a little rabbit in that one over there that I had never noticed before, or at least never really looked at. Incredible, isn't it? That's part of what I was doing, Edward. I was simply *looking* at them, my beautiful tapestries. I'm incorrigible, you know. I'll

304

never stop. And then, just when I saw you poke your head in, I was thinking about . . ." He stopped.

"Yes?"

"Well, you remember, I told you one time." Van Zandt looked Maule full in the eyes, a half smile on his own face, almost apologetic. "That little story of Brienne. That's what I was thinking about, Edward. I was thinking about old Mazarin."

Maule felt a sudden tightening in his throat. He turned away. "So. Yes," he said, just to fill in. He went to the blocked-off doorway. "I suppose I'd better be off. Are you coming to Barney's party?"

"Later. I want to stay here a while."

"Don't get locked in, Arthur."

"I won't."

"All right, Arthur. I'll see you at Barney's."

Maule gave the screen a shove so that it rolled away enough for him to edge through, then pushed it back until it was flush with the moldings of the doorway. Then he turned and walked back to the entrance of the museum, where the last of the guests were finding their coats and going out to their automobiles.